James Patterson is one of the best-known and biggest-selling writers of all time. He is the author of some of the most popular series of the past decade: the Women's Murder Club, the Alex Cross novels and Maximum Ride, and he has written many other number one bestsellers including romance novels and stand-alone thrillers. He has won an Edgar Award, the mystery world's highest honour. He lives in Florida with his wife and son.

Praise for James Patterson:

'The man is a master of this ge   fans will have one wish for him: write even faster'   *USA Today*

'Unputdownable. It will sell mil   *The Times*

'Packed with white-knuckled tw   *Daily Mail*

'A novel which makes for sleeples   '   *Daily Express*

'Breakneck pacing and loop-the-   tting'
                                      Publishers Weekly

'Reads like a dream'   *Kirkus Reviews*

'A fast-paced, electric story that is utterly believable'
                                                Booklist

'Ticks like a time bomb – full of threat and terror'
                                      Los Angeles Times

'Absolutely terrific'   *Bookseller*

'Patterson's action-packed story keeps the pages flicking by'   *The Sunday Times*

'A fine writer with a good ear for dialogue and pacing. His books are always page-turners'   *Washington Times*

'Patterson is a phenomenon'   *Observer*

'Keeps the adrenaline level high'   *Publishing News*

By James Patterson and available from Headline

When the Wind Blows
Cradle and All
Miracle on the 17th Green *(and Peter de Jonge)*
Suzanne's Diary for Nicholas
The Beach House *(and Peter de Jonge)*
The Jester *(and Andrew Gross)*
The Lake House
Sam's Letters to Jennifer
SantaKid
Honeymoon *(and Howard Roughan)*
Lifeguard *(and Andrew Gross)*
Beach Road *(and Peter de Jonge)*
Judge and Jury *(and Andrew Gross)*
Step on a Crack *(and Michael Ledwidge)*
The Quickie *(and Michael Ledwidge)*
You've Been Warned *(and Howard Roughan)*

Alex Cross novels
Cat and Mouse
Pop Goes the Weasel
Roses are Red
Violets are Blue
Four Blind Mice
The Big Bad Wolf
London Bridges
Mary, Mary
Cross
Double Cross

The Women's Murder Club series
1st to Die
2nd Chance *(and Andrew Gross)*
3rd Degree *(and Andrew Gross)*
4th of July *(and Maxine Paetro)*
The 5th Horseman *(and Maxine Paetro)*
The 6th Target *(and Maxine Paetro)*

Maximum Ride series
Maximum Ride: The Angel Experiment
Maximum Ride: School's Out Forever
Maximum Ride: Saving the World and Other Extreme Sports

JAMES PATTERSON

THE BIG BAD WOLF

headline

First published in Great Britain in 2003
by HEADLINE BOOK PUBLISHING

This edition published in 2014
by HEADLINE PUBLISHING GROUP

1

Cataloguing in Publication Data is available from the British Library

ISBN 978 0 7553 4937 1

Typeset in Palatino Light by Palimpsest Book Production Limited,
Falkirk, Stirlingshire

Printed and bound in Great Britain by
Clays Ltd, St Ives plc

Headline's policy is to use papers that are natural, renewable
and recyclable products and made from wood grown in
sustainable forests. The logging and manufacturing processes
are expected to conform to the environmental regulations of
the country of origin.

HEADLINE PUBLISHING GROUP
An Hachette UK Company
338 Euston Road
London NW1 3BH

www.headline.co.uk
www.hachette.co.uk

THE BIG BAD WOLF

THE GODFATHERS

Chapter One

There was an improbable murder story told about the Wolf that had made its way into police lore, and then spread quickly from Washington to New York to London and to Moscow. No one knew if it was true, but it was never officially disproved, and it was consistent with other outrageous incidents in the Russian gangster's life.

According to the story, the Wolf had gone to the high-security supermax prison in Florence, Colorado, on a Sunday night in early summer. He had bought his way inside to meet with the Italian mobster and don, Augustino 'Little Gus' Palumbo. Prior to this visit, the Wolf had a reputation for being impulsive and sometimes lacking patience. Even so, he had been steadily planning this meeting with 'Little Gus' Palumbo for nearly two years.

He and Palumbo met in the Security Housing Unit of the prison where the New York gangster had been incarcerated for seven years. The purpose of the meeting was to reach an arrangement to unite the East Coast's Palumbo family with the Red Mafiya, thereby forming one of the most powerful and ruthless crime syndicates in the world. Nothing like it had ever been attempted. Palumbo was said to be skeptical, but agreed to the meeting just to see if the Russian could get inside Florence Prison – and then manage to get out again.

From the moment that they met, the Russian was respectful of the sixty-six-year-old don. He bowed his head slightly as they shook hands and appeared almost shy, contrary to his reputation.

'There's to be no physical contact,' the captain of the guards spoke from the intercom into the room. His name was Larry Ladove and he was the one who had been paid $75,000 to arrange the meeting. The Wolf ignored Captain Ladove's order. 'Under the circumstances, you look well,' he said to Little Gus. 'Very well indeed.'

The Italian smiled thinly. He had a small body, but it was tight and hard. 'I exercise three times a day, every day. I almost never have liquor, though not by choice. I eat well, and not by choice, either.'

The Wolf smiled, then said, 'It sounds like you don't expect to be here for your full sentence.'

Palumbo coughed out a laugh. 'That's a good bet. Three life sentences served concurrently? The discipline's in my nature, though. The future? Who can know for sure about these things?'

'Who can know? One time I escaped from a gulag on the Arctic Circle. I told a cop in Moscow, "I spent time in a gulag, you think *you* can scare me?" What else do you do in here? Besides exercise and eat Healthy Choice?'

'I try to take care of my business back in New York. Sometimes, I play chess with a sick madman down the hall. He used to be in the FBI.'

'Kyle Craig,' said the Wolf. 'You think he's crazy like they say?'

'Yeah, totally. So tell me, boss, *pakhan*, how can this alliance you suggest work? I am a man of discipline and careful planning, in spite of these humbling circumstances. From what I'm told, you're reckless. Hands-on. You involve yourself with even the smallest operations. Extortion, prostitution, stolen cars. How can this work between us?'

The Wolf finally smiled, then shook his head. 'I am hands-on, as you say. But I'm not reckless, not at all. It's all about the money, no? The bling-bling? Let me tell you a secret that no one else knows. This will surprise you, and maybe prove my point.'

The Wolf leaned forward. He whispered his secret, and the Italian's eyes suddenly widened with fear. With stunning quickness, the Wolf grabbed Little Gus's head. He twisted it powerfully, and the gangster's neck broke with a loud, clear snap.

'Maybe I am a little reckless,' said the Wolf. Then he turned to the camera in the room. He spoke to Captain Ladove of the guards. 'Oh, I forgot, no touching. Now let me out of here.'

The next morning, Augustino Palumbo was found dead in his cell. Nearly every bone in his body had been broken. In the Moscow underworld, this symbolic kind of murder was known as *zamochit*. It signified complete and total dominance by the attacker. The Wolf was boldly stating that he was now the Godfather.

PART ONE

THE 'WHITE GIRL' CASE

Chapter Two

The Phipps Plaza shopping mall in Atlanta was a showy montage of pink granite floors, sweeping bronze staircases, gilded Napoleonic design and lighting that sparkled like halogen spotlights. A man and a woman watched the target – 'Mom' – as she left Nike Town with sneakers and whatnot, for her three daughters, packed under one arm.

'She *is* very pretty. I see why the Wolf likes her. She reminds me of Claudia Schiffer,' said the male observer. 'You see the resemblance?'

'Everybody reminds you of Claudia Schiffer, Slava. Don't lose her. Don't lose your pretty little Claudia, or the Wolf will have you for breakfast.'

The abduction team, 'the Couple', was dressed expensively, and that made it easy for them to blend in at Phipps Plaza, in the Buckhead section of Atlanta. At eleven in the morning, Phipps wasn't very crowded, and that could be a problem.

It helped that their target was rushing about in a world of her own, a tight little cocoon of mindless activity, buzzing in and out of Gucci, Caswell-Massey, Nike Town, then Gapkids and Parisian (to see her personal shopper, Gina), without paying the slightest attention to who was around her in any of the stores. She worked from an at-a-glance leather diary and made her appointed rounds in a quick, efficient, practiced manner, buying faded jeans for Gwynne, a leather dop-kit for Brendan, Nike diving watches for Meredith and Brigid, a Halloween wreath at Williams-Sonoma. She even made an appointment at Carter-Barnes to get her hair done.

The target had style, and also a pleasant smile for the salespeople who waited on her in the toney stores. She held doors for those coming up behind her, even men, who bent over backward to thank the attractive blonde. 'Mom' was sexy in the wholesome, clean-cut way of many upscale American suburban women. And she did resemble the supermodel Claudia Schiffer. That was her undoing.

According to the job's specs, Mrs Elizabeth Connelly was the mother of three girls; she was a graduate of Vassar, class of '87, with what she called, 'a degree in art history that is practically worthless in the real world – whatever that is – but invaluable to me'. She'd been a reporter for the *Washington Post* and the *Atlanta-Constitution* before she was married. She was thirty-seven, though she didn't look much more than thirty. She had her hair in a velvet barrette that morning, wore a short-sleeved turtleneck crocheted top, slim-fitting slacks. She was bright, religious – but sane about it – tough when she needed to be, at least according to the specs.

Well, she would need to be tough soon. Mrs Elizabeth Connelly was about to be abducted. She had been 'purchased', and she was probably the most expensive item for sale that morning at Phipps Plaza.

The price – $150,000.

Chapter Three

Lizzie Connelly felt light-headed and she wondered if her quirky blood sugar was acting up again.

She made a mental note to pick up Trudie Styler's cookbook – she kind of admired Trudie, who was co-founder of the Rainforest Foundation as well as Sting's wife. She *seriously* doubted she would get through this day with her head still screwed on straight, not twisted around like the poor little girl in the *Exorcist*, which she'd just seen again with her girlfriends. *Linda Blair . . . wasn't that the actress's name? Lizzie was pretty sure it was. Oh, who cared. What difference did trivia make?*

What a merry-go-round today was going to be. First, it was Gwynnie's birthday, and the party for twenty-one of her *closest* school buddies, eleven girls, ten boys, was scheduled for one o'clock at the house. Lizzie had rented a bouncy-house, and she had already prepared lunch for the children, not to mention for their moms or nannies. Lizzie had even rented a Mr Softee ice cream truck for three hours. But you never knew what to expect at these birthday gigs – other than laughter, tears, thrills and spills.

After the birthday bash, Brigid had swimming lessons, and Merry had a trip to the dentist scheduled. Brendan, her husband of fourteen years, had left her a 'shortlist' of his current needs. Of course everything was needed *a.s.a.p.s,* which meant *as soon as possible, sweetheart.*

After she picked up a T-shirt with rhinestones on it for Gwynnie at Gapkids, all she had left to buy was Brendan's replacement dop-kit. Oh yeah, and her hair appointment. *And* ten minutes with her savior at Parisian, Gina Sabellico.

She kept her cool through the final stages – *never let them see you sweat* – then she hurried to her new Mercedes 320 station wagon, which was safely tucked in a corner on the P3 Level of the underground garage at Phipps. No time for her favorite Rooibos tea at Teavana.

Hardly anybody was in the garage on a Monday morning, but she nearly bumped into a man in a BMW logo sweatshirt. Lizzie smiled automatically at him, revealing perfect, recently whitened and brightened teeth, warmth, sexiness – even when she didn't want to show it.

She wasn't really paying attention to anyone – thinking ahead to the fast-approaching birthday party – when a woman she passed suddenly grabbed her around the chest as if Lizzie were a running back for the Atlanta Falcons football team trying to pass through the 'line of spinach', as her daughter Gwynne had once called the maneuver. The woman's grip was like a vise – she was *strong* as hell.

'What are you doing? Are you crazy?' Lizzie finally screamed her loudest, squirmed her hardest, dropped her shopping bags, heard something *break*. 'Hey! Somebody, help! *Get off of me!*'

Then a second assailant, *the BMW sweatshirt guy*, grabbed her legs and held on tight, hurt her, actually, as he brought her down on to the filthy, greasy parking-lot concrete along with the woman. 'Don't kick me, bitch!' he yelled in her face. 'Don't you fucking dare kick me.'

But Lizzie didn't stop kicking – or squealing either. 'Help me. Somebody, help! Somebody, please!'

Then both of them lifted her up in the air as if she weighed next to nothing. The man mumbled something to the woman. Not English. Middle-European, maybe. Lizzie had a housekeeper from Slovakia. Was there a connection?

The woman attacker still gripped her around the chest with one arm and used her free hand to push aside tennis and golf stuff, hurriedly clearing a space in the back of the station wagon.

Then Lizzie was roughly shoved inside her own car. A gauzy, foul-smelling cloth was pushed hard against her nose and face, and held there so tightly it hurt her teeth. She tasted blood. *First blood*, she thought. *My blood*. Adrenaline surged through her body and she began fighting back again with all her strength. Punching and kicking. She felt like a captured animal striking out for its freedom.

'Easy,' the male said. 'Easy-peasy-Japanesee . . . Elizabeth Connelly.'

Elizabeth Connelly? They know me? How? Why? What is going on here?

'You're a very sexy mom,' said the man. 'I see why the Wolf likes you.'

Wolf? Who's the Wolf? What was happening to her? Who did she know named Wolf?

Then the thick, acrid fumes in the cloth overpowered Lizzie and she went lights out. She was driven away in the back of her own station wagon.

But only across the street to the Lenox Square Mall – where Lizzie Connelly was transferred into a blue Dodge van that then sped away.

Purchase complete.

Chapter Four

E arly on the morning of 16 September, I was oblivious to the rest of the world and its problems. This was the way life was supposed to be, only it rarely seemed to turn out so well. At least not in my experience, which was limited when it came to anything that might be considered the 'good life'.

I was walking Jannie and Damon to the Sojourner Truth School that morning. Little Alex was merrily toddling along at my side. 'Puppy', I called him.

The skies over D.C. were partly cloudy, but, now and then, the sun peeked through the clouds and warmed our heads and the backs of our necks. I'd already played the piano – Gershwin – for forty-five minutes. And eaten breakfast with Nana Mama. I had to be at Quantico by nine that morning for my orientation classes, but it left time for the walk to school at around seven-thirty. And *that* was what I'd been in search of lately, or so I believed. Time to be with my kids.

Time to read a poet I'd discovered recently, Billy Collins. First I'd read his *Nine Horses*, and now it was *Sailing Alone*

Around the Room. Billy Collins made the impossible seem so effortless, and so possible.

Time to talk to Jamilla Hughes every day, often for hours at a time. And when I couldn't, to correspond by e-mail, and, occasionally, by long, flowing letters. She was still working homicide in San Francisco, but I felt the distance between us was shrinking. I wanted it to and hoped she did too.

Meanwhile, the kids were changing faster than I could keep up with them, especially little Alex, who was morphing before my eyes. I needed to be around him more and now I could be. That was my deal. It was why I had joined the FBI, at least that was part of it.

Little Alex was already over forty inches and thirty-five pounds. That morning he had on a pinstriped overall suit with an Orioles cap. He moved along the street as if a leeward wind were propelling him. His ever-present stuffed toy, a cow named 'Moo', created ballast so that he listed slightly to the left at all times.

Damon was lurching ahead to a different drummer, a faster, more insistent beat. Man, I really loved this boy. Except for his fashion sense. That morning he was wearing long jean shorts, 'Uptowns', and a gray tee with an Alan Iverson 'The Answer' jersey over it. His lean legs were sprouting peach fuzz, and it looked as if his whole body was developing from the feet up. Large feet, long legs, a youthful torso.

I was noticing everything that morning. I had time to do it.

Jannie was typically put together in a gray tee with 'Aero Athletics 1987' printed in bright red letters, sweatpant capris with a red stripe down each leg, and white Adidas sneakers with red stripes.

As for me, I was feeling good. Every now and again someone would still stop me and say I looked like the young Muhammad Ali. I knew how to shake off the compliment, but I liked to hear it more than I let on.

'You're awfully quiet this morning, Poppa.' Jannie laced her arms around my free arm and added, 'You having trouble at school? Your orientation? Do you like being an FBI agent so far?'

'I like it fine,' I said. 'There's a probationary period for the next two years. Orientation is good, but a lot of it is repetitive for me, especially what they call "practicals". Firing range, gun cleaning, exercises in apprehending criminals. That's why I get to go in late some days.'

'So you're the teacher's pet already,' she said and winked.

I laughed. 'I don't think the teachers are too impressed with me, or any other street cops. How're you and Damon doing so far this year? Aren't you about due for a report card or something?'

Damon shrugged. 'We're acing everything. Why do you want to change the subject all the time when it's on you?'

I nodded and laughed. 'You're right. Well, *my* schooling is going fine. Eighty is considered a failing grade at Quantico. I expect to ace most of my tests.'

'*Most?*' Jannie arched an eyebrow and gave me one of Nana Mama's 'perturbed' looks. 'What's this *most* stuff? We expect you to ace *all* your tests.'

'I've been out of school for a while.'

'No excuses.'

I fed her one of her own lines. 'I'm doing the best I can, and that's all you can ask from somebody.'

She smiled. 'Well all right then, Poppa. Just as long as the best you can do puts all *As* on *your* next report.'

About a block from the school I gave Jannie and Damon their hugs – so as not to embarrass them, God forbid, in front of all their cool-ass friends. They hugged me back, and kissed their little brother, and then off they ran. 'Ba-bye,' said little Alex, and then so did Jannie and Damon, calling back to their brother, 'Ba-bye, ba-bye!'

I picked up little Alex and we headed home, then it was off to work for soon-to-be Agent Cross of the FBI.

'Dada,' said little Alex as I carried him in my arms. That was right – *Dada*. Things were falling into place for the Cross family. After all these years, my life was finally close to being in balance. I wondered how long it would last. Hopefully, at least for the rest of the day.

Chapter Five

New agent training at the FBI Academy in Quantico, sometimes called 'Club Fed', was turning out to be a challenging, arduous, and tense program, if a little repetitive. For the most part, I liked it, and I was making an effort to keep any skepticism down. But I had entered the Bureau with a reputation for catching pattern killers, and already I had the nickname 'Dragonslayer'. So irony and skepticism might soon be a problem.

Training had begun six weeks before, on a Monday morning, with a crew-cut broad-shouldered SSA, or Supervisory Special Agent, Dr Kenneth Horowitz, standing in front of our class trying to tell a joke: 'The three biggest lies in the world are: "All I want is a kiss", "The check is in the mail", and "I'm with the FBI and I'm only here to help you." ' Everybody in the class laughed, maybe because the joke was so ordinary, but at least Horowitz had tried his best, and maybe that was the point.

FBI Director Ron Burns had set it up so that my training period would last for only eight weeks. He'd made other allowances for me as well. The maximum age for entrance into the FBI had been thirty-seven years old. I was over forty. Burns had the age requirement waived, and also voiced his opinion that it was discriminatory, and needed to be changed. The more I saw of Ron Burns, the more I sensed that he was something of a rebel, maybe because he was an ex-Philadelphia street cop himself. He had brought me into the FBI as a GS13, the highest I could go as a street agent. I'd also been promised assignments as a consultant, which meant a better salary. Burns had wanted me in the Bureau, and he'd got me. He said that I could have any reasonable resources I needed to get the job done. I hadn't discussed it with him yet, but I thought I might want two detectives from the Washington P.D. – John Sampson and Jerome Thurman.

The only thing Burns had been quiet about was my Class Supervisor at Quantico, a Senior Agent named Gordon Nooney. Nooney ran 'Agent Training'. He had been a pro-filer before that and, previous to becoming an FBI agent, had been a prison psychologist in New Hampshire. I was finding him to be a bean counter at best.

That morning, Nooney was standing there waiting when I arrived for my class in Abnormal Psyche, an hour and fifty minutes on understanding psychopathic behavior, some-thing I *hadn't* been able to do in nearly fifteen years with the D.C. police force.

There was gunfire in the air, probably from the nearby marine base. 'How was traffic from D.C.?' Nooney asked. I didn't miss the barb behind the question: I was permitted to go home nights, while the other agents-in-training slept at Quantico.

'No problem,' I said. 'Forty-five minutes in moving traffic on 95. I left plenty of extra time.'

'The Bureau isn't known for breaking rules for individuals,' Nooney said. Then he offered a tight, thin smile that was awfully close to a frown. 'Of course, you're Alex Cross.'

'I appreciate it,' I said. I left it at that.

'I just hope it's worth the trouble,' Nooney mumbled as he walked off in the direction of Admin. I shook my head and went into class, which was held in a tiered symposium-style room.

Dr Horowitz's lesson this day was interesting to me. It concentrated on the work of Professor Robert Hare who'd done original research on psychopaths by using brain scans. According to Hare's studies, when healthy people are shown 'neutral' and 'emotional' words, they respond acutely to emotional words, such as *cancer* or *death*. Psychopaths register the words equally. A sentence like 'I love you' means nothing more to a psychopath than 'I'll have some coffee.' Maybe less. According to Hare's analysis of data, attempts to reform psychopaths made them only more manipulative. It certainly was a point of view.

Even though I was familiar with some of the material, I found myself jotting down Hare's 'characteristics' of psychopathic personality and behavior. There were forty of them. As I wrote them down, I found myself agreeing that most rang true:

glibness and superficial charm
need for constant stimulation/prone to boredom
lack of any remorse or guilt
shallow emotional response
complete lack of empathy . . .

I was remembering two psychopaths in particular: Gary Soneji and Kyle Craig. I wondered how many of the forty 'characteristics' the two of them shared, and started putting G.S. and K.C. next to the appropriate ones.

Then I felt a tap on my shoulder. I turned away from Dr Horowitz.

'Senior Agent Nooney needs to see you right now in his office,' said an executive assistant, who then walked away with the full confidence that I would be right on his heels.

I was.

I was in the FBI now.

Chapter Six

S enior Agent Gordon Nooney was waiting in his small, cramped office in the Administration building. He was obviously upset, which had the desired effect: *I wondered what I could have done wrong in the time since we'd talked before class.*

It didn't take him long to let me know why he was so angry. 'Don't bother to sit down. You'll be out of here in a minute. I just received a highly unusual call from Tony Woods in the Director's office. There's a "situation" going down in Baltimore. Apparently, the Director wants *you* there. It will take precedence over your training classes.'

Nooney shrugged his broad shoulders. Out the window behind him I could see thick woods, and also Hoover Road where a couple of agents jogged. 'What the hell, why would you need any training here, Dr Cross? You caught Casanova in North Carolina. You're the man who brought down Kyle Craig. You're like Clarice Starling in the movies. You're already a star.'

I took a deep breath before responding. 'I had nothing to

do with this. I won't apologize for catching Casanova, or Kyle Craig.'

Nooney waved a hand my way. 'Why should you apologize? You're dismissed from the day's classes. There's a helicopter waiting for you over at HRT. You *do* know where Hostage Reserve Team is?'

'I know where it is.'

Class dismissed, I was thinking as I ran to the helipad. I could hear the CRACK, CRACK of weapons being fired at the shooting range. Then I was on board the helicopter and strapping in. Less than twenty minutes later, the Bell helicopter touched down in Baltimore. I still hadn't gotten over my meeting with SSA Nooney. Did he understand that I hadn't asked for this assignment? I didn't even know *why* I was in Baltimore.

Two agents in a dark blue sedan were waiting for me. One of them, Jim Heekin, took charge immediately, and also put me in my place. 'You must be the FNG,' he said as we shook hands.

I wasn't familiar with what the letters stood for, so I asked Heekin what they meant as we got into the car.

He smiled, and so did his partner. 'The Fucking New Guy,' he said.

'What we have so far is a bad deal. And it's hot,' Heekin continued. 'City of Baltimore homicide detective is involved. Probably why they wanted you here. He's holed up in his own house. Most of his immediate family's in there with him. We don't know if he's suicidal, homicidal, or both, but he's apparently taken the family hostage. Seems familiar with a situation created by a police officer last year in south Jersey. This officer's family was gathered together for his father's birthday party. Some birthday party.'

'Do we know how many are in the house with him?' I asked.

Heekin shook his head. 'Best guess, at least a dozen, including a couple of children. Detective won't let us talk to any of the family members, and he won't answer our questions. Most of the people in the neighborhood don't want us here either.'

'What's his name?' I asked as I jotted down a few notes to myself. I couldn't believe I was about to get involved in a hostage negotiation. It still didn't make any sense to me – and then *it did*.

'His name is Dennis Coulter.'

I looked up in surprise. 'I know Dennis Coulter. I worked a murder case with him. Shared a bushel of crabs at Obrychi's once upon a time.'

'We know,' said Agent Heekin. 'He asked for you.'

Chapter Seven

D*etective Coulter had asked for me. What the hell was that all about?* I hadn't known we were so close. Because we weren't! I'd met him only a couple of times. We were friendly, but not exactly friends. So why did Dennis Coulter want me here?

A while back, I had worked with Dennis Coulter on an investigation of drug dealers who were trying to connect, and control, the trade in D.C. and Baltimore and everything in between. I'd found Coulter to be tough, very egotistical, but good at his job. I remembered he was a big Eubie Blake fan, and that Blake was from Baltimore.

Coulter and his hostages were huddled somewhere inside the house, a gray wood shingle colonial, on Ailsa Avenue in Lauraville, in the northeast part of Baltimore. The Venetian blinds were tightly closed, and what was going on behind the front door was anybody's guess. Three stone steps climbed to the porch where a rocking chair and a wooden glider sat. The house had been painted recently, which suggested to me that Coulter probably hadn't been expecting trouble in his life. So what happened?

Several dozen Baltimore P.D., including SWAT team members, had surrounded the house. Weapons were drawn and, in some cases, aimed at the windows and the front door. The Baltimore police helicopter unit Foxtrot had responded.

Not good.

I already had one idea. 'What do you think about every-body lowering their guns for starters?' I asked the field commander from the Baltimore P.D. 'He hasn't fired on anybody, has he?'

The field commander and SWAT team leader conferred briefly, and then weapons around the perimeter were lowered, at least the ones I could see. Meanwhile, one of the Foxtrot helicopters continued to hover close to the house.

I turned to the commander again. I needed him on my side. 'Thank you, Lieutenant. Have you been talking to him?'

He pointed to a man crouched behind a cruiser. 'Detective Fescoe has the honor. He's been on the horn with Coulter for about an hour.'

I made a point of walking over to Detective Fescoe and introducing myself. 'Mick Fescoe,' he said, but didn't seem overjoyed to meet me. 'Heard you were coming. We're fine here.'

'This intrusion isn't my idea,' I told him. 'I just left the force in D.C. I don't want to get in anybody's way.'

'So, don't,' Fescoe said. He was a slender, wiry man who

looked as if he might have played some ball at one time. He moved like it.

I rubbed my hand over my chin. 'Any idea *why* he asked for me? I don't know him that well.'

Fescoe's eyes drifted toward the house. 'Says he's being set up by Internal Affairs. Doesn't trust anybody connected to the Baltimore P.D. He knew you'd gone over to the FBI recently.'

'Would you tell him I'm here. But also tell him I'm being briefed now. I want to hear how he sounds, before I talk to him.'

Fescoe nodded, then he called into the house. It rang several times before it was picked up.

'Agent Cross has just arrived, Dennis. He's being briefed now,' said Fescoe.

'Like hell he is. Get him on the hook. Don't make me shoot in here. I'm getting close to creating a real problem. Get him *now!*'

Fescoe handed me the phone and I spoke into it. 'Dennis, this is Alex Cross. I'm here. I did want to be briefed first.'

'This really Alex Cross?' Coulter asked and sounded surprised.

'Yeah, it's me. I don't know too many of the details. Except you say you're being set up by Internal Affairs.'

'I don't just say it, I *am* being set up. I can tell you why, too. *I'll* brief you. That way you'll hear it straight.'

'All right,' I told him. 'I'm on your side so far. I know you, Dennis. I don't know Baltimore Internal Affairs.'

Coulter cut me off. 'I want you to *listen to me*. Don't talk. Just hear me out.'

'All right,' I said. 'I'm listening.'

I sat down on the ground behind a Baltimore P.D. cruiser, and I got ready to listen to the armed man who was supposedly holding a dozen of his family members hostage. *Jesus*, I was back on The Job again.

'They want to kill me,' Dennis Coulter began. 'The Baltimore P.D. has me in its crosshairs.'

Chapter Eight

P *op!*

I jumped. Someone had pulled open a can of soda and tapped me on the shoulder with it.

I looked up to see none other than Ned Mahoney, from the Hostage Rescue Team at Quantico, handing me a caffeine-free Diet Coke. I had taken a couple of classes from him during orientation. He knew his stuff – in the classroom anyway.

'Welcome to my private hell,' I said. 'What am I doing here, by the way?'

Mahoney winked at me, and dropped down beside me.

'You're a rising star, or maybe a risen star. You know the drill. Get him talking. Keep him talking,' said Mahoney. 'We hear you're real good at this.'

'So what are *you* doing here?' I asked.

'What do you think? Watching, studying your technique. You're the Director's boy, right? He thinks you're gifted.'

I took a sip of soda, then pressed the cold can to my forehead. Hell of an introduction to the FBI for the FNG.

'Dennis, who wants to kill you?' I spoke into the cell phone again. 'Tell me all you can about what's going on here. I also need to ask about your family. Is everybody all right in there?'

Coulter bristled. 'Hey! Let's not waste time on a lot of bullshit negotiation crap. I'm about to be executed. *That's* what this is. Make no mistake. Look around you, man. It's an execution.'

I couldn't see Coulter, but I remembered him. No more than five eight, goatee, hip, always cracking a wise-ass joke, very tough. All in all, a small man's complex. He began to tell his story, his side of things, and unfortunately, I had no idea what to make of what he was spilling out. According to Coulter, several detectives in the Baltimore P.D. had been involved in large drug pay-offs. Even he didn't know how many, but the number was high. He'd blown the whistle! The next thing he knew, his house was surrounded by cops.

Then Coulter dropped the bomb. 'I was getting kickbacks too. Somebody turned me in to Internal Affairs. One of my partners.'

'Why would a partner do that?'

He laughed. 'Because I got greedy. I went for a bigger piece of the pie. Thought I had my partners by the short hairs. They didn't see it that way.'

'How did you have them by the short hairs?'

'I told my partners that I had copies of records – *who* had been paid *what*. A couple of years' worth of records.'

Now we were getting somewhere. 'Do you?' I asked.

Coulter hesitated. Why was that? Either he did, or he didn't.

'I *might*,' he finally said. 'They sure think I do. So now they're going to put me down. They were coming for me today . . . I'm not supposed to leave this house alive.'

I was trying to listen for other voices or sounds in the house while he kept talking. I didn't hear any. *Was anybody else still alive in there? What had Coulter done to his family? How desperate was he?*

I looked at Ned Mahoney and shrugged my shoulders. I really wasn't sure whether Coulter was telling the truth, or if he was just a street cop who'd gone loco. Mahoney looked skeptical too. He had a *don't ask me* look on his face. I had to go somewhere else for guidance.

'So what do we do now?' I asked Coulter.

He sniffed out a laugh. 'I was hoping you'd have an idea. You're supposed to be the hotshot, right?'

That's what everybody keeps saying.

Chapter Nine

The situation in Baltimore didn't get any better during the next couple of hours. If anything, it got worse. It was impossible to keep the neighbors from wandering out on their porches to watch the stand-off in progress. Then the Baltimore P.D. began to evacuate the Coulters' neighbors, many of whom were also the Coulters' friends. A temporary shelter had been set up at the nearby Garrett Heights elementary school. It reminded everyone that there were probably children trapped inside Detective Coulter's house. *His family. Jesus!*

I looked around and shook my head in dismay as I saw an awful lot of Baltimore police, including SWAT, and also the Hostage Rescue Team from Quantico. A swarm of crazy-eyed spectators was pushing and shoving outside the barricades, some of them rooting for cops to be shot – any cop would do.

I stood up and cautiously made my way over to a group of officers waiting behind an Emergency Rescue van. I didn't need to be told that they didn't appreciate interference from the Feds. I hadn't either, when I was on the D.C. police force. I addressed Captain Stockton James Sheehan, whom I'd spoken to briefly when I arrived. 'What do you think? Where do we go with this?'

'Has he agreed to let anybody out?' Sheehan asked. 'That's the first question.'

I shook my head. 'He won't even talk about his family. Won't confirm or deny that they're in the house.'

Sheehan asked, 'Well, what *is* he talking about?'

I shared some of what I'd been told by Coulter, but not everything. How could I? I left out that he'd sworn Baltimore cops were involved in a large-scale drug scheme – and, more devastating, that he had records that would incriminate them.

Stockton Sheehan listened, and then he offered, 'Either he lets go of some of the hostages, or we have to go in and get him. He's not going to gun down his own family.'

'He says he will. That's the threat.'

Sheehan shook his head. 'I'm willing to take the risk. We go in when it gets dark. You know this should be our call.'

I shrugged, without agreeing or disagreeing, then I walked away from the others. It looked like we might have another half-hour of light. I didn't like to think about what would happen once darkness came.

I got back on the phone with Coulter. He picked up right away.

'I have an idea,' I told him. 'I think it's your best shot.' I didn't tell Coulter, but I also thought it was his only shot.

'So tell me what you're thinking,' he said.

I told Dennis Coulter my plan . . .

Ten minutes later, Captain Sheehan was shouting in my face that I was 'worse than any motherfucking FBI asshole' he had ever dealt with. I guess I was a fast learner. Maybe I didn't even need the orientation classes I was missing at Quantico. Not if I was already the 'king of the FBI assholes'. Which was one way of saying that the Baltimore police didn't approve of my plan to defuse the situation with Detective Coulter.

Even Mahoney had doubts. 'I guess you're not real big on social and political correctness,' he sniffed when I told him Captain Sheehan's reaction.

'Thought I was, guess I'm not. Hope this works. It better work. I think they want to kill him, Ned.'

'Yeah. So do I. I think we're making the right call.'

'*We?*' I asked.

Mahoney nodded. 'I'm in this with you, buddy – *podjo*. No guts, no glory. It's a Bureau thing.'

Minutes later, Mahoney and I watched the Baltimore police very reluctantly pull back from the house. I had told Sheehan I didn't want to see a single blue uniform or SWAT coverall anywhere around the Coulters'. The captain had his idea of what constituted acceptable risks, and I had mine. If they rushed the house, somebody would die for sure. If my idea failed, at least nobody would get hurt. Or, at least, nobody but me.

I got back on the phone with Coulter. 'The Baltimore police are out of sight,' I told him. '*I want you to come out,*

Dennis. Do it now. Before they get a chance to think about what just happened.'

He didn't answer at first, then said, 'I'm looking around. All it takes is one sniper with a nightscope.'

I knew he was right. Didn't matter. We had one chance.

'Come on out with your hostages,' I told him. 'I'll meet you on the front steps myself.'

He didn't say anything more and I was pretty sure I'd lost him. I focused on the front door of the house and tried not to think about people dying here. *C'mon, Coulter. Use your head. This is the best deal you're going to get.*

He finally spoke again. 'You sure about this? Because I'm not. I think you might be crazy.'

'I'm sure.'

'All right, I'm coming out,' he said. Then he added, 'This is on you.'

I turned to Mahoney. 'Let's get a protective vest on him as soon as he hits the porch. Surround him with our guys. No Baltimore P.D. anywhere near him no matter what they say. Can we do that?'

'Brass balls.' Mahoney grinned. 'Let's do it, try anyway.'

'*Let me bring you out, Dennis*. It's safer that way,' I said into the cell phone. 'I'm coming to you now.'

But Coulter had his own plan. *Jesus, he was already on his front porch*. He had both hands raised high over his head. Clearly unarmed. Vulnerable as hell.

I was afraid I'd hear shots and he'd go down in a heap. I started to run forward.

Then half a dozen HRT guys were all over him, shielding

Coulter from harm. They rushed him to a waiting van.

'We got him inside the truck. Subject is safe,' I heard the report from HRT. 'We're getting him the hell out of here.'

I turned back toward the house. *What about the family? Where were they?* Had he made up his story? *Oh Christ, what had Dennis Coulter done?*

Then I saw the family walking single file out of the house. It was an incredible scene. The hair on my neck stood up.

An old man in a white shirt, black trousers and braces. An elderly woman in a blowing pink dress and high heels. Tears were streaming down her cheeks. Two small girls in white party dresses. A couple of middle-aged women holding hands. Three males in their twenties, each of them with their hands up. A woman with two little babies.

Several of the adults were carrying cardboard boxes.

I figured I knew what was in them. Yeah, I knew. *The records, the proof, the evidence.*

Detective Dennis Coulter had been telling the truth, after all. His family had believed him. They had just saved his life.

I felt Ned Mahoney pat my back hard. 'Nice job. Really good job.'

I laughed and said, 'For an FNG. That *was* a test, wasn't it?'

'I really couldn't say. But if it was, you aced it.'

Chapter Ten

A test? Jesus. Is that why I was sent to Baltimore? I hoped to hell not.

I got home late that night, too late. I was glad that no one would be up to see me, especially Nana. I couldn't handle one of her soul-piercing, disapproving looks right now. I needed a beer and then I wanted to go to bed. Sleep if I could.

I slipped quietly inside the house, not wanting to wake anyone. Not a sound except for the tiniest electric hum that came from somewhere. I was planning to call Jamilla as soon as I got upstairs. I was missing her like crazy. Rosie the cat slid by and rubbed against my leg. 'Hello, Red,' I whispered. 'I did good today.'

Then I heard a cry.

I hurried up the front stairs to little Alex's room. Looked in on him. He was up and working himself into a good wail. I didn't want Nana or the kids to have to get up and tend to him. Besides, I hadn't seen my boy since early that morning, and I wanted to give him a snuggle. I missed his little face.

When I peeked into his room he was sitting up, and he seemed surprised to see it was me. Then he smiled and clapped his hands. *Oh boy! Daddy's on the case. Daddy's the biggest sucker in the house.*

'What are you doing up, Pup? It's late,' I said.

Alex's bed is a low-riser which I made myself. There are protective bars on either side, to keep him from slipping out.

I slid in beside him. 'Move over and give your daddy some room,' I whispered and kissed the top of his head. I don't ever remember my own father kissing me, so I kiss Alex every chance that I get. The same goes for Damon and Jannie, no matter how much they complain as they get older and less wise.

'I'm tired, little man,' I said as I stretched out. 'How about you? Tough day, Puppy?'

I retrieved his bottle from a space between the mattress and the guard bars. He started to drink, and then he moved in close to me. He grabbed his stuffed cow 'Moo', and he fell right back to sleep in minutes.

So nice. Magical. That sweet baby smell I love. His soft breathing – child's breath.

The two of us had a nice sleepover that night.

Chapter Eleven

The Couple was hiding out for a few days in New York City. Lower Manhattan. It was so easy to get lost there, to disappear off the face of the map. And New York was one city where they could get whatever they wanted, whenever they wanted it. The Couple wanted rough sex. For starters anyway.

They had stayed out of reach of their employer for more than thirty-six hours. Their contact man, Sterling, finally got through to them on the phone in a room at the Chelsea Hotel on West Twenty-third Street. Outside the window was a sign: *Hotel Chelsea* in an L shape. The vertical *Hotel* was in white, the horizontal *Chelsea* in red. It was a famous New York City icon.

'I've been trying to reach you for a day and a half,' Sterling said. '*Don't* ever turn off your cell on me. Consider this a last warning.'

The female, Zoya, yawned and gave the phone receiver the finger. With her free hand, she popped a DVD, *East Eats West*, into the player. Rock music kicked in hard and loud.

'We were busy, darling. We're *still* busy. What the hell do you want? You have more money for us? Money talks.'

'Turn down the music, please. *Please*. Somebody has an itch. He's very rich. There's a *lot* of money involved.'

'Like I said, darling, we're busy right now. Otherwise occupied. Out to lunch. How big an itch is it?'

'Same as last time. A very big itch. He's a personal friend of the Wolf.'

Zoya flinched at the mention of the Wolf. 'Give me details, specifics. Don't waste our time.'

'We'll do it like we always do, *darling*. A piece of the puzzle at a time. How soon can you be on the road? How about thirty minutes?'

'We have something to wrap up here. Let's say four hours. This *need* that somebody has, this itch – what kind of itch is it?'

'One unit, female. And not too far from New York. Let's say, four hours from where you are now. I'll send you directions first. Then specifics on the unit.'

Zoya looked at her partner, who was lounging in an armchair. Slava was idly fingering a pecker leash as he listened on the second phone in the eclectically furnished hotel room. He was gazing out the window at the Candyman sweet shop, a tailor shop, a one-hour photo shop. Typical N.Y.C. view.

'We'll do the job,' said Zoya. 'Tell the Wolf, we'll get his friend what he needs. No problem whatsoever.' Then she hung up on Sterling. Because she could.

She shrugged at her partner. Then Zoya looked across the

hotel room to a queen-size bed with a steel decorative headboard. A young blond male was lying there. He was naked and gagged, handcuffed to vertical rods spaced about a foot apart on the bed.

'You're in luck,' Zoya said to the blond. 'Only four more hours to play, baby. Only four more hours.'

Then Slava spoke. 'You'll wish it was less. You ever heard of a Russian word – *zamochit*? No. I'll show you *zamochit*. Four hours worth. I learned it from the Wolf. Now you learn from me. *Zamochit*. It means to break all the bones in your body.'

Zoya winked at the boy. 'Four hours. *Zamochit*. You'll take the next few hours with you through eternity. Never forget it, darling.'

Chapter Twelve

When I woke in the morning, little Alex was sleeping peacefully beside me, his head on my chest. I couldn't resist sneaking another kiss. And another. Then, as I lay there next to my boy, I found myself thinking about Detective Dennis Coulter and his family. I had been moved emotionally when they came out of that house together. The family had saved Coulter's life, and I was a sucker for family stuff.

I had been asked to stop at the Hoover Building, always referred to as 'the Bureau', before I drove down to Quantico. The Director wanted to see me about what had happened in Baltimore. I had no idea what to expect, but I was anxious about the visit. Maybe I should have skipped Nana's coffee that morning.

Almost anybody who has seen it would agree that the Hoover Building is a strange and supernaturally ugly structure. It takes up an entire block between Pennsylvania Avenue, Ninth, Tenth, and E Streets. The nicest thing I could say about it is that it's 'fortress-like'. Inside, it's even worse.

'The Bureau' is library quiet and warehouse ugly. The long halls glow in medicinal white.

As soon as I stepped on to the Director's floor, I was met by his executive assistant, a very efficient man named Tony Woods, whom I liked quite a bit already.

'How is he this morning, Tony?' I asked.

'He likes what happened down in Baltimore,' Tony answered. 'His Highness is in a pretty good mood. For a change.'

'Was Baltimore a test?' I asked, not sure how far I could go with the assistant.

'Oh, it was your final exam. But remember, *everything*'s a test.'

I was led into the Director's relatively small conference room. Burns was already sitting and waiting for me. He raised a glass of orange juice in mock salute. 'Here he is!' he smiled. 'I'm making sure that everybody knows you did a bang-up job in Bal'more. Just the way I wanted to see you start out.'

'Nobody got shot,' I said.

'You got the job done, Alex. HRT was very impressed. So was I.'

I sat down and poured myself coffee. I knew it was 'help yourself' and no formalities with Burns. 'You're spreading the word . . . because you have such big plans for me?' I asked.

Burns laughed in his usual, conspiratorial way. 'Absolutely, Alex. I want you to take my job.'

Now it was my turn to laugh. 'No, thank you.' I sipped the

coffee, which was dark brown, a little bitter, but delicious – almost as good as Nana Mama's. Well, maybe half as good as the best in Washington. 'You care to share any of your more immediate plans with me?' I asked.

Burns laughed again. He *was* in a good mood this morning. 'I just want the Bureau to operate simply and effectively, that's all. It's the way it was when I ran the New York office. I'll tell you what I don't believe in: bureaucrats and cowboys. There are too many of both in the Bureau. Especially the former. I want street smarts on the street, Alex. Or maybe I just want *smarts*. You took a chance last night, only you probably didn't see it that way. There were no politics for you – just the right way to get the job done.'

'What if it hadn't worked?' I asked as I set my coffee down on a coaster emblazoned with the Bureau's emblem.

'Well, hell, then you wouldn't be here now and we wouldn't be talking like this. Seriously, though, there's one thing I want to caution you about. It may seem obvious to you, but it's a lot worse than you imagine. You can't always tell the good guys from the bad ones in the Bureau. No one can. I've tried, and it's almost impossible.'

I thought about what he was implying – part of which was that Burns already knew that one of my weaknesses was to look for the good in people. I understood it was a weakness sometimes, but I wouldn't change, or maybe I couldn't change.

'Are you a good guy?' I asked him.

'Of course I am,' Burns said with a wholesome grin that could have landed him a starring role in the *West Wing*. 'You can trust me, Alex. Always. Absolutely. Just like you trusted Kyle Craig a few years back.'

Jesus, he was giving me the shivers. Or maybe the Director was just trying to get me to see the world his way: *Trust no one. Go to the head of the class.*

Chapter Thirteen

At a little past eleven, I was on my way down to Quantico. Even after my 'final' in Baltimore, I still had a class on 'Stress Management and Law Enforcement'. I already *knew* the operative statistic: *FBI agents were five times more likely to kill themselves than to be killed in the line of duty.*

A Billy Collins poem was floating through my brain as I drove: 'Another Reason Why I Don't Keep a Gun in the House'. Nice concept, good poem, bad omen.

The cell rang and I heard the voice of Tony Woods from the Director's office. There had been a change of plans. Woods gave me orders from the Director to go straight to Ronald Reagan Washington National Airport. A plane was waiting for me.

Jesus! I was on another case already; I'd been ordered to skip school again. Things were happening faster than even I had expected and I wasn't sure if that was a good or a bad thing.

'Does ACAS Nooney know that I'm the Director's

one-man flying squad?' I asked Woods. *Tell me that he does. I don't need more trouble down at Quantico.*

'We'll let him know post-haste where you're going,' Woods promised. 'I'll take care of it personally. Go to Atlanta, and keep us posted on what you find down there. You'll be briefed on the plane. It's a kidnapping case.' But that was all Tony Woods would tell me on the phone.

For the most part, the Bureau flies out of Reagan Washington National. I boarded a Cessna Citation Ultra, tan, with no identifying mark-ups. The Cessna sat eight, but I was the *only* passenger.

'You must be important,' the pilot said before we took off.

'I'm not important. Believe me, I'm nobody.'

The pilot just laughed. 'Buckle up then, nobody.'

It was perfectly clear that a call from the Director's office had preceded me. Here I was, being treated like a Senior Agent. *The Director's troubleshooter?*

Another agent jumped aboard just before we took off. He sat down across the aisle from me and introduced himself as Wyatt Walsh from D.C. Was he part of the Director's 'flying team' too? Maybe my partner?

'What happened in Atlanta?' I asked. 'What's so important, or unimportant, that it requires our services?'

'Nobody told you?' He seemed surprised that I didn't know the details.

'I got a call from the Director's office less than half an hour ago. I was told to come here. They said I'd be briefed on the plane.'

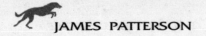

Walsh slapped two volumes of case notes on my lap. 'There's been a kidnapping in the Buckhead section of Atlanta. Woman in her thirties. White woman, well-to-do. She's the wife of a judge, which makes it federal. More important, *she isn't the first.*'

Chapter Fourteen

Everything was suddenly in a hurry-up mode. After we landed I was driven in a van to the Phipps Plaza Shopping Center in Buckhead.

As we pulled into the lot off Peachtree, it was obvious to me that something was very wrong there. We passed the anchor stores: Saks Fifth Avenue and Lord & Taylor. They were nearly empty. Agent Walsh told me that the victim, Mrs Elizabeth Connelly, had been abducted in the underground parking lot near another large store called Parisian.

The entire parking area was a crime scene, but particularly Level 3 where Mrs Connelly had been grabbed. Each level of the garage was marked with a purple-and-gold scroll design, but now crime-scene tape was draped over the scrolls. The Bureau's Evidence Response Team was there already. The incredible amount of activity indicated that the local police agencies were taking this extremely seriously. Walsh's words were floating in my head: *She isn't the first*.

It struck me as a little ironic, but I was more comfortable talking to the local police than to agents from the Bureau's field office. I walked over and I spoke to two detectives, Pedi and Ciaccio, from the Atlanta P.D.

'I'll try to stay out of your way,' I said to them, then added: 'I used to be Washington P.D.'

'Sold out, huh?' Ciaccio said, and she sniffed out a laugh. It was supposed to be a joke, but it had enough truth in it meant to sting. Her eyes had a light frost in them.

Pedi spoke up. He looked about ten years older than his partner. Both were attractive. 'Why's the FBI interested in this case?'

I told them only as much as I thought I should, not everything. 'There have been abductions, or at least disappearances that resemble this one. White women, suburban locales. We're here checking into possible connections. And of course this is a judge's wife.'

Pedi asked, 'Are we talking about past disappearances in the *Atlanta* metro area?'

I shook my head. 'No, not to my knowledge. The other disappearances are in Texas, Massachusetts, Florida, Arkansas.'

'Ransoms involved?' Pedi followed up.

'In one Texas case, yes. Otherwise no money has been asked for. None of the women has been found so far.'

'Only white women?' Detective Ciaccio asked as she took a few notes.

'As far as we know, yes. And all of them fairly well-to-do. But no ransoms. And none of what I'm telling you gets to the press.' I looked around the parking garage. 'What do we have so far? Help me out a little.'

Ciaccio looked at Pedi. 'Joshua?' she asked.

Pedi shrugged. 'All right, Irene.'

'We do have something. There were a couple of kids in one of the parked cars when the abduction went down. Apparently, they didn't witness the first part of the crime.'

'They were otherwise occupied,' said Joshua Pedi.

'But they looked up when they heard a scream and saw Elizabeth Connelly. *Two* kidnappers, apparently pretty good at it. Man and a woman. They didn't see our young lovers because they were in the back of a van.'

'And they had their heads down?' I asked. 'Otherwise occupied?'

'That too. But when they did come up for air, they saw the man and woman, described as being in their thirties, well dressed. They were already holding Mrs Connelly. Took her down very fast. Threw her into the back of her own station wagon. Then they drove off in her car.'

'Why didn't the kids get out of the van to help?'

Ciaccio shook her head. 'Say that it happened very fast, and that they were scared. Seemed "unreal" to them. I think they were also nervous about having it known they were playing around in the back of a van during school hours. They both attend a local prep school in Buckhead. They were skipping classes.'

A team took her, I thought, and knew it was a big break for us. According to what I'd read on the ride down, no team had been spotted at any of the other abductions. *A male and a female team? That was interesting. Strange and unexpected.*

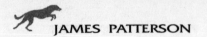

'You want to answer a question for us now?' Detective Pedi asked.

'If I can. Shoot.'

He looked at his partner. I had a feeling that somewhere along the way Joshua and Irene might have spent some time in the backseat of a car, something about the way they looked at each other. 'We've been hearing that this might have something to do with the Sandra Friedlander case? Is that right? That one's gone unsolved, for what . . . two years in D.C.?'

I looked at the detective and shook my head. 'Not to my knowledge,' I said. 'You're the first to bring up Sandra Friedlander.'

Which wasn't exactly the truth. Her name had been in confidential FBI reports I'd read on the ride down from D.C. *Sandra Friedlander – and seven others*.

Chapter Fifteen

My head was buzzing. In a bad way. I knew from my hurried reading of the case notes that there were more than 220 women currently listed as missing in the United States, and that at least seven of the disappearances had been linked by the Bureau to 'white slave rings'. That was the nasty twist. White women in their twenties and thirties were in high demand in certain circles. The prices could get exorbitant – if the sales were to the Middle East, or to Japan.

Ironically, Atlanta had been the hub of another kind of sex-slave scandal just a few years back. It involved Asian and Mexican women smuggled into the US, then forced into prostitution in Georgia and the Carolinas. This case had another possible connection to Juanita, Mexico, where hundreds of women had disappeared in the past couple of years.

My mind was flashing through these unfortunate unpleasantries when I arrived at Judge Brendan Connelly's home in the Tuxedo Park section of Buckhead, near the governor's mansion. The Connelly place replicated an 1840s Up-Country Georgia Plantation Home and sat on about two acres. A Porsche Boxster was parked in a circular driveway. Everything looked perfect – in its place.

The front door was opened by a young girl who was still in her school clothes. The patch on her jumper told me she attended *Pace Academy*. She introduced herself as Brigid Connelly, and I could see braces on her teeth. I had read about Brigid in the Bureau's notes on the family. The foyer of the house was elegant, and had an elaborate chandelier and highly polished ash hardwood floor.

I spotted two younger girls – just their heads – peeking out from a doorway off the main entryway, just past a couple of British watercolors. All three of the Connelly daughters were pretty. Brigid was twelve, Meredith was eleven, and Gwynne was six. According to my crib notes, the younger girls attended the Lovett School.

'I'm Alex Cross with the FBI,' I said to Brigid, who seemed tremendously self-assured for her age, especially during this crisis. 'I think that your father is expecting me.'

'My dad will be right down, sir,' she told me. Then she turned to her younger sisters and scolded, 'You heard Daddy. Behave. Both of you.'

'I won't bite anybody,' I said to the girls, who were still peeking at me from down the hallway.

Meredith turned the brightest red. 'Oh, we're sorry. This isn't about you.'

'I understand,' I said. Finally they smiled, and I saw that they had braces too. Very cute girls, sweet.

I heard a voice from above. 'Agent Cross?' *Agent?* I wasn't used to the sound of that yet.

I looked up the front staircase as Judge Brendan Connelly made his way down. He had on a striped blue dress shirt, dark blue slacks, black driving loafers. He looked trim and in-shape, but tired, as if he hadn't slept in days. I knew from the FBI work-up sheets that he was forty-four, and had attended Georgia Tech and Vanderbilt Law School.

'So which is it,' he asked, then forced a smile, 'do you bite, or not?'

I shook his hand. 'I only bite people who deserve it,' I said. 'Alex Cross.'

Brendan Connelly nodded toward a large library-den that I could see was crammed from floor to ceiling with books. There was also room for a baby grand piano. I noticed sheet music for some Billy Joel songs. In the corner of the room was a daybed – unmade.

'After Agent Cross and I are done, I'll make dinner,' he said to the girls. 'I'll try not to poison anybody tonight, but I'll need your help, ladies.'

'Yes, Daddy,' they chorused. They seemed to adore their father. He pulled the sliding oak doors, and the two of us were sealed inside.

'This is so damn *bad*. So hard,' he sighed and let out a deep breath. 'Trying to keep up a front for them. They're the best girls in the world.' Judge Connelly gestured around the book-lined room. 'This is Lizzie's favorite place in the house. She plays the piano very well. So do the girls. We're both bookaholics, but she, especially, loved reading in this room.'

He sat in a club chair covered in rust tone leather. 'I appreciate that you came to Atlanta. I've heard you're very good at difficult cases. How can I help you?' he asked.

I sat across from him on a matching rust tone leather couch. On the wall behind him were photographs of the Parthenon, Chartres, the Pyramids, and an honorary plaque from Chastain Horse Park. 'There are a lot of people working to find Mrs Connelly and they'll go down a lot of avenues. I'm not going to get into too many details about your family. The local detectives can go there.'

'Thank you,' the judge said. 'Those questions are devastating to answer right now. To go over and over. You can't imagine.'

I nodded. 'Are you aware of any local men, or even women, who might have taken an inappropriate interest in your wife? A longstanding crush, a potential obsession? That's the one private area I'd like to go into. Then, any little things that strike you as out of the ordinary. Did you notice anyone watching your wife? Are there any faces you've seen around more than normal lately? Delivery men? Federal Express or other services? Neighbors who are suspicious in any way? Work associates? Even friends who might have fantasized about Mrs Connelly?'

Brendan Connelly nodded. 'I see what you're getting at.'

I looked him in the eye. 'Have you and your wife had any fights lately?' I asked. 'I need to know if you have. Then we can move on.'

The corners of Brendan Connelly's eyes suddenly moistened. 'I met Lizzie in Washington when she was with the

Post and I was an associate at Tate Schilling, a law firm there. It *was* love at first sight. We almost never fought, hardly ever raised our voices. That's still true. Agent Cross, I love my wife. So do her daughters. Please help us bring her home. You have to find Lizzie.'

Chapter Sixteen

The modern-day godfather. A forty-seven-year-old Russian now living in America, and known as the Wolf. Rumored to be fearless, hands-on, into everything from weapon sales, extortion and drugs to legitimate businesses such as banking and venture capital. No one seemed to know his true identity, or his American name, or where he lived. *Clever. Invisible.* Safe from the FBI. And anybody else who might be looking for him.

He had gotten the nickname Wolf in his twenties, when he made the switch from the KGB to become one of the most ruthless cell leaders in Russian organized crime, the Red Mafiya. His namesake, the Siberian wolf, was a skillful hunter, but also relentlessly hunted. The Siberian was a fast runner and could overpower much heavier animals – but it was also *hunted* for its blood and bones. The human Wolf was also a hunter who was hunted – except that the police had no idea where to hunt.

Invisible. By design. Actually, he was hiding in plain sight. On a balmy night in late September, the man called Wolf was throwing a huge party at his 20,000-square-foot house on the waterfront in Fort Lauderdale, Florida. The non-occasion was the opening of the Monday Night Football season. The party was a three-year-old tradition among his friends and business associates. Tonight was also special because he was launching a new men's magazine called *Instinct*, which would compete with *Maxim* and *Stun*.

In Lauderdale, the Wolf was known as Ari Manning, a wealthy businessman originally from Tel Aviv. He had other names in other cities. Many names, many cities.

He was passing through the den now, where about twenty of his guests were watching the game on several TVs, including a sixty-one-inch Rumco. A couple of football fanatics were bent over a computer with a statistics database. On a nearby table was a bottle of Stolichnaya encased in a block of ice. The vodka in ice was the only real Russian touch that he allowed.

At six foot two, this Wolf could carry 240 pounds and still move like a big and very powerful animal. He circulated among his guests, always smiling and joking, knowing that no one in the room knew why he smiled, not one of these so-called friends or business partners or social acquaintances had any idea who he was.

They knew him as Ari, not as Pasha Sorokin, and definitely not as the *Wolf*. They had no clue about the pounds of illegal diamonds he bought from Sierra Leone, the tons of heroin from Asia, and weapons and even jets sold to the Colombians, or white women purchased by the Saudis and Japanese. In south Florida, he had a reputation for being a maverick both socially and in business. There were more than 150 guests tonight, but he'd ordered food and drink for twice that number. He had imported the chef from Le Cirque 2000 in New York, and also a sushi cook from San Francisco. His servers were dressed as cheerleaders and were topless, which he thought a cheeky joke, guaranteed to offend. The famous surprise dessert for the party was Sacher tortes flown in from Vienna. No wonder everybody loved Ari. Or hated him.

He gave a playful hug to a former pro running back for the Miami Dolphins, talked to a lawyer who'd made tens of millions from the Florida tobacco settlement – exchanged a story about Governor Jeb Bush. Then he moved on through the crowd. There were so many ass-kissing social climbers and opportunists who came to his house to be seen among the right – and wrong – people: self-important, spoiled, selfish, and, worst of all, boring as tepid dishwater.

He walked along the edge of an indoor swimming pool that led to an outdoor pool more than twice the size. He chatted with his guests, and made a generous pledge to a private-school charity. Not surprisingly, he was hit on by somebody's wife. He had serious conversations with the owner of the most important hotel in the state, a Mercedes-dealing mogul, and the head of a conglomerate, who was a hunting 'buddy' of his.

He despised all of these pretenders, especially the older used-to-bes. None of them had ever taken a real risk in their lives. Still, they had made millions, even billions, and they thought they were such hot shit.

And then – he thought about Elizabeth Connelly for the first time in an hour or so. His sweet, very sexy Lizzie. She looked like Claudia Schiffer and he fondly remembered the days when the image of the German supermodel was on hundreds of billboards all over Moscow. He had lusted for Claudia – all Russian men did – and now he had her likeness in his possession.

Why? *Because he could*. It was the philosophy that drove him and everything else in his life.

For that very reason, he was keeping her right here in his big house in Fort Lauderdale.

Chapter Seventeen

Lizzie Connelly couldn't believe any of this awfulness was happening to her. It still didn't seem possible. It *wasn't* possible. And yet, here she was. A hostage!

The house where she was being kept was full of people. Full! It sounded like a party was going on. A party? How dare he?

Was her insane captor that sure of himself? Was he so arrogant? So brazen? Was it possible? Of course it was. He'd boasted to her that he was a gangster, the king of gangsters, perhaps the greatest who ever lived. He had repulsive tattoos – on the back of his right hand, his shoulders, his back, around his right index finger, and also on his private parts, on his testicles and penis.

Lizzie could definitely hear a party going on in the house. She could even make out conversations: small talk about an upcoming trip to Aspen; a rumored affair between a nanny and a local mother; the death of a child in a pool, a poor six-year-old, like her Gwynnie; football stories; a joke about two altar boys and a Siamese cat that she had already heard in Atlanta.

Who the hell were these people? Where was she being held? Where am I, damn it?

Lizzie was trying so hard not to go crazy, but it was almost impossible. All of these people, their inane talk.

They were so close to where she was bound and tied and gagged and being held hostage by a madman, probably a killer.

As Lizzie listened, tears finally began to run down her cheeks. Their voices, their closeness, their laughing, all just a few feet away from her.

I'm here! I'm right here! Damn it, help me. Please help me. I'm right here!

She was in darkness. Couldn't see a thing.

The people, the party, were on the other side of a thick, wooden door. She was locked in a small room that was part closet; she'd been kept in here for days. Permitted bathroom breaks, but not much else.

Bound tightly by rope.

Gagged with tape.

So she couldn't call out for help. Lizzie couldn't scream – except *inside* her head.

Please help me.

Somebody, please!

I'm here! I'm right here!

I don't want to die.

Because that was the one thing he'd told her that was certain – *he was going to kill her.*

Chapter Eighteen

But no one could hear Lizzie Connelly. The party went on, and got larger, noisier, more extravagant, vulgar. Eleven times during the night, stretch limousines dropped off well-heeled guests at the large, waterfront house in Fort Lauderdale. Then the limos left. They would not be waiting for their passengers. No one noticed, at least no one let on.

And no one paid any attention when these same guests left that night – *in cars they hadn't arrived in.* Very expensive cars, the finest in the world, all of them stolen.

An NFL running back departed in a deep maroon Rolls-Royce Corniche convertible worth $363,000, 'made to order', from the paint to the wood, hide, trim, even the position of the intercrossed Rs in the cockpit.

A white rap star drove off in an aqua blue Aston Martin Vanquish priced at $228,000, capable of zero to a hundred in under ten seconds.

The most expensive of the cars was the American-made Saleen S7 with its gull-wing doors, the look of a shark, and 550 horsepower.

All in all, eleven very expensive, very *stolen* automobiles were delivered to buyers at the house.

A silver Pagani Zonda priced at $370,000. The engine of the Italian-made racer barked, howled, roared.

A silver-and-orange-trimmed Spyker C8 Double IV with 620 horsepower.

A bronze Bentley Azure Convertible Mulliner – yours for $376,000.

A Ferrari 575 Maranello – $215,000.

A Porsche GT2.

Two Lamborghini Murcielagos – yellow-gold – $270,000 apiece, named, like all Lamborghinis, after a famous bull.

A Hummer H1 – not as hot as the other cars maybe, but *nothing* got in its way.

The total value of the stolen cars was over three million dollars; the sales came to a little under two.

Which more than paid for the Sacher tortes flown all the way from Vienna.

And besides, the Wolf was a fan of fast, beautiful cars . . . of fast, beautiful *everything*.

Chapter Nineteen

I flew back to D.C. the next day and was home at six that night, finished work for the day. At times like this, I almost felt that maybe I had my life back. Maybe I'd done the right thing by joining the Bureau. Maybe... As I climbed out of the ancient black Porsche, I saw Jannie on the front porch. She was practicing her violin, her 'long bows'. She wanted to be the next Midori. The playing was impressive, to me anyway. When Jannie wanted something she went after it.

'Who's the beautiful young lady holding that *Juzeh* so perfectly?' I called as I trudged up the lawn.

Jannie glanced my way, said nothing, smiled knowingly, as if only she knew the secret. Nana and I were involved in her practices, which featured the Suzuki method of instruction. We modified the method slightly to include both of us. Parents were a part of practice, and it seemed to pay dividends. In the Suzuki way, great care was taken to avoid competition and its negative effects. Parents were told to listen to countless tapes and attend lessons. I had gone to many of the lessons myself. Nana covered the others. In that way, we assumed the dual role of 'home-teacher'.

'That's so beautiful. What a wonderful sound to come home to,' I told Jannie. Her smile was worth everything I'd gone through at work that day.

She finally spoke. 'To soothe the savage beast,' she said. Violin under one arm, bow held down, Jannie bowed and then began to play again.

I sat on the porch steps and listened. Just the two of us, the setting sun, and the music. *The beast was soothed.*

After she finished practice, we ate a light dinner, then hurried over to the Kennedy Center for one of the free programs in the Grand Foyer. Tonight it was 'Liszt and Virtuosity'. But wait – there was more. Tomorrow night we planned to attack the new climbing wall at the Capital Y. Then, with Damon, it was a videogame extravaganza featuring *Eternal Darkness: Sanity's Requiem* and *Warcraft III: Reign of Chaos*.

I hoped we could keep it up like this. Even the videogames. I was on the right track now and I liked it. So did Nana and the kids.

Around ten-thirty, to complete the day just right, I got hold of Jamilla on the phone. She was home at a decent hour for a change. 'Hey,' she said at the sound of my voice.

'Hey back at you. Can you talk? This a good time?'

'Might be able to squeeze in a couple of minutes for you. I hope you're calling from home. Are you?'

'Been here since around six. We had a family night at the

Kennedy Center. Big success.'

'I'm jealous.'

We talked about what she was up to, then my big night with the kids, and finally my life and times with the Bureau. But I had the sense that Jamilla needed to get off after about fifteen minutes. I didn't ask if she had anything going for tonight. She'd tell me if she wanted to.

'I miss you way out there in San Francisco,' I said and left it at that. I hoped it didn't come off as not caring. Because I did care about Jam. She was in my thoughts all the time.

'I have to run, Alex. Bye,' she said.

'Bye.'

Jamilla had to run. And I was finally trying to stop.

Chapter Twenty

The next morning I was told to attend a key-person meeting about the Connelly kidnapping, and the possibility that the abduction was connected to others in the past twelve months. The case had been upgraded to 'major', and it had the code name 'White Girl'.

An FBI Rapid Start team had already been dispatched to Atlanta. Satellite photos of the Phipps Plaza Shopping Center had been ordered in the hope that we could identify the motor vehicle the unidentified suspects (known as UNSUBS) had used to get there before driving away in the Connelly station wagon.

There were about two dozen agents in a windowless 'major case' room at the Bureau in Washington. When I arrived, I learned that Washington would be the 'office of origin' for the case, which meant the case was important to Director Burns. The Criminal Investigative Division had already prepared a briefing book for him. The important entry point for the FBI was that a *federal* judge's wife had disappeared.

Ned Mahoney from HRT sat down next to me and seemed not just outgoing, but friendly. He greeted me with a winking, 'Hey, star.' A tiny, dark-haired woman in a black jumpsuit plopped down on the other side of me. She introduced herself as Monnie Donnelley and told me she was the Violent Crimes research specialist attached to the case. She talked extraordinarily fast, lots of energy, almost too much.

'Guess we'll be working together,' she said and shook my hand. 'I've already heard good things about you. I know your résumé. I attended Hopkins too. How about that?'

'Monnie's our best and our brightest,' Mahoney interjected. 'And that's a gross understatement.'

'He's so right,' Monnie Donnelley agreed. 'Spread the word. Please, I'm tired of being a secret weapon.'

I noticed that my boss, Gordon Nooney, wasn't in the room of at least fifty agents. Then the meeting on White Girl began.

A senior agent named Walter Zelras stood in the front and started to show slides. He was professional, but very dry. I almost felt as if I'd joined IBM or Chase Manhattan Bank instead of the Bureau. Monnie whispered, 'Don't worry, it'll get worse. He's just warming up.'

Zelras had a droning speaking voice that reminded me of a professor I'd had a long time ago at Hopkins. Both Zelras and my former professor gave everything equal weight, never seemed excited or disturbed about the material they were presenting. Zelras's subject was the connection the Connelly abduction might have to several others in the past months, so it ought to have been spellbinding.

'Gerrold Gottlieb,' Monnie Donnelley whispered again. I smiled, almost laughed out loud. Gottlieb was a biology professor who used to drone on at Hopkins. Smart, nice man, but Jesus.

'Upscale, attractive, white women', Zelras was saying, 'have been disappearing at a little over three times the statistical norm over the past year. This is true both here in the States, and in Eastern Europe. I'm going to pass around an actual catalogue showing women who were up for sale about three months ago. Unfortunately, we never traced the catalogue back to whoever manufactured it. There was a Miami link, but it never went anywhere.'

When the catalogue got to me I saw that it was black and white, the pages probably printed off the Internet. I quickly leafed through it. There were seventeen women shown, nude shots, along with details such as breast and waist sizes; 'true' color of hair, color of eyes. The women had unlikely nicknames like: Candy, Sable, Foxy, Madonna, Ripe. The prices ranged from $3,500 to $150,000. There was no further biographical information on any of the women, and nothing at all about their personalities.

'We've been working closely with Interpol on what we suspect could be "white slave" trading. FYI, "white slave" refers to women specifically bought and sold for the purpose of prostitution. These days, the women are usually Asian, Mexican, South American, not white, except in Eastern Europe. You should also note that, at this time, slavery is more globalized and technologized than ever in history. Some countries in Asia look the other way as women, and children, are sold – especially into Japan and India.

'In the past couple of years, a market has opened up for white women, particularly blondes. These women are sold for prices ranging from a few hundred up into the mid-five figures and possibly higher. As I said, a significant market is Japan. Another is the Middle East of course. The Saudis are the biggest buyers. Believe it or not, there's even a market in Iraq and Iran. Questions at this point?'

There were several, mostly good ones, which showed me this was a savvy group that had been brought together.

I finally asked a question, though I was reluctant to as the FNG. 'Why do we think Elizabeth Connelly is connected to the others?' I gestured around the room. 'I mean, *this* connected?'

Zelras answered quickly. 'A team took her. Kidnapping gangs are very common in the slave trade, especially in Eastern Europe. They're experienced and very efficient at the abductions, and they're connected into a pipeline. There's usually a buyer before they take a woman like Mrs Connelly. She would be high risk, but *very* high reward. What makes this kind of abduction attractive is that there's no ransom exchange. The Connelly abduction fits our profile.'

Someone asked, 'Could a buyer request a specific woman? Is that a possibility?'

Zelras nodded. 'If the money is right, yes, absolutely. The price might go into the six figures. We're working that angle.'

Most of the remainder of the long meeting was taken up with discussion about Mrs Connelly and whether we could find her quickly. The consensus was *no*. One detail was particularly perplexing: Why would the UNSUBS kidnap the victim in such a public place? Profit/ransom seemed the logical possibility, but there had been no ransom note. Or had somebody specifically asked for Mrs Elizabeth Connelly? If so – who? What was special about her? And why the mall? Surely, there were easier abduction locations.

As we talked about her, a photograph of Mrs Connelly and her three daughters remained on the screen at the front of the conference room. The four of them looked so close-knit and happy. It was scary, sad. I found myself thinking about being with Jannie on our front porch the night before.

Someone asked, 'These women who've been abducted, have any of them been found?'

'Not one,' said Agent Zelras. 'Our fear is that they're dead. That the kidnappers – or whomever the kidnappers deliver them to – consider them disposable.'

Chapter Twenty-One

I returned to my orientation classes that day after the lunch break, and just in time for another of SSA Horowitz's awful jokes. He held up a clipboard for us to see his material. 'The official list of David Koresh's theme songs. "You Light Up My Life", "I'm Burning Up", "Great Balls of Fire". My personal favorite, "Burning Down the House". Love the Talking Heads.' Dr Horowitz seemed to know that his jokes were bad, but black humor works with police officers and his deadpan delivery was decent. Plus, he knew who had recorded 'Burning Down the House'.

We had an hour-long session on 'Management of Integrated Cases', followed by 'Law Enforcement Communication', then 'Dynamics of the Pattern Killer'. In the last course we were told that serial killers 'change', that they are 'dynamic'. In other words, they get smarter and better at killing. Only the 'ritual characteristics' remain the same. I didn't bother to take notes.

The next class was outdoors. We were all dressed in sportjackets, but with black padded throat and face protectors for a 'practical' at Hogans Alley. The exercise involved three cars in hot pursuit of a fourth. Sirens blared and echoed. Loudspeakers barked commands: 'Stop! Pull over! Come out of the car with your hands up.' Our ammo, 'simunition', consisted of bullets with pink-paint-infused tips.

It was five o'clock by the time we finished the practice. I showered and dressed, and as I was leaving the training building to go over to the Jefferson dorm where I had a cubicle, I saw SSA Nooney. He motioned for me to come over. *What if I don't want to?*

'You headed back to D.C.?' he asked.

I nodded and bit down on my tongue. 'In a while. I have some reports to read first. The abduction in Atlanta.'

'Big stuff. I'm impressed. The rest of your classmates spend their nights here. Some of them think it helps build camaraderie. I think so too. Are you an agent of change?'

I shook my head, but then I tried a smile on Nooney. Didn't work.

'I was told from the start that I could go home nights. That isn't possible for most of the others.'

Then Nooney began to push hard, tried to stir up old anger.

'I heard you had some problems with your Chief of Detectives too,' Nooney said then.

'Everybody had problems with Chief of Detectives Pittman,' I said.

Nooney's eyes appeared glazed. It was obvious he didn't see it that way. 'Just about everybody has problems with me too. Doesn't mean I'm wrong about the importance of

building a team here. I'm *not* wrong, Cross.'

I resisted saying anything more. Nooney was coming down on me again. Why? I had attended the classes I could make; I still had work to do on White Girl. Like it or not, I was a part of the case. And this wasn't another practical – it was real. It was important.

'I have to get my work done,' I finally said. Then I walked away from Nooney. I was pretty sure I'd made my first enemy in the FBI. An important one, too. No sense starting small.

Chapter Twenty-Two

Maybe it was guilt churned up by my confrontation with Gordon Nooney that made me work late in my cube on the lower level of the Dining Hall building where Behavioral Science has its offices. The low ceilings, bad fluorescent lighting and cinder-block walls kind of made me feel as if I were back at my precinct. But the depth of the back files and research available to FBI agents was astonishing. The Bureau's resources were better than anything I'd ever seen in the D.C. police department.

It took me a couple of hours to go through less than a quarter of the white-slave-trade files, and those were just cases in the US. One abduction in particular caught my attention. It involved a female D.C. attorney named Ruth Morgenstern. She had last been seen at approximately 9.30 p.m on Saturday, 20 August. A friend had dropped her off near her apartment in Foggy Bottom.

Ms Morgenstern was twenty-six years old, 111 pounds, with blue eyes and shoulder-length blond hair. On 28 August, one of her identification cards was found near the north gate of the Anacostia Naval Station. Two days later, her government access card was found on a city street.

But Ruth Morgenstern was still missing. Her file included the notation: *Most likely dead*.

I wondered: *Was Ruth Morgenstern dead?*

How about Mrs Elizabeth Connelly?

Around ten, just as I was starting to do some serious yawning, I came across a second murder case that snapped my mind to attention. I read the report once, then a second time.

It involved the abduction eleven months earlier of a woman named Jilly Lopez in Houston. The kidnapping had occurred at the Houstonian Hotel. *A team – two males*, had been seen loitering near the victim's SUV in the parking garage. Mrs Lopez was described as very attractive.

Minutes later, I was speaking to the officer in Houston who had handled the case. Detective Steve Bowen was curious about my interest in the abduction, but he was cooperative. He said that Mrs Lopez hadn't been found or heard from since she disappeared. No ransom was ever requested. 'She was a real good lady. Just about everybody I talked to loved her.' I'd heard the same thing about Elizabeth Connelly when I was in Atlanta.

I already hated this case, but I couldn't get it out of my skull. *White Girl!* The women who'd been taken were all *lovable*, weren't they? It was the thing they had in common. Maybe it was the killer's pattern.

Lovable victims.

How awful was that?

Chapter Twenty-Three

When I got home that night it was a quarter past eleven, but there was a surprise waiting for me. A good one. John Sampson was sitting on the front steps. All six foot nine, two hundred and fifty pounds of him. He looked like the Grim Reaper at first – but then he grinned and looked like the Joyful Reaper.

'Look who it is. Detective Sampson.' I smiled back.

'How's it going, man?' John asked as I walked across the lawn. 'You're working kind of late again. Same old, same old. You never change, man.'

'This is the *first* late night I've had at Quantico,' I responded a little defensively. 'Don't start.'

'Did I say anything bad? Did I even cut you with "*the first of many*" line that's right there on the tip of my tongue? No, I didn't. I'm being good – for me. But since we're talking, you *can't* help yourself, can you?'

'Want a cold beer?' I asked and unlocked the front door of the house. 'Where's your bride tonight?'

Sampson followed me inside and we got a couple of

Heinekens each; we took them out to the sun porch. I sat on the piano bench and John plopped down in the rocker, which strained under his weight. John is my best friend in the world, and has been since I was ten years old. We were homicide detectives, and partners, until I went over to the FBI. He's still a little pissed at me for that.

'Billie's just fine. She's working the late shift at St Anthony's tonight and tomorrow. We're doing good.' He drained about half of his beer in a gulp. 'No complaints, partner. Far from it. You're looking at a happy camper.'

I had to laugh. 'You seem surprised.'

Sampson laughed too. 'Guess I didn't think I was the marrying kind. Now all I want to do is hang with Billie most of the time. She makes me laugh, and she even gets my jokes. How about you and Jamilla? She good? And how *is* the new job? How's it feel to be a Feebie down at Club Fed?'

'I was just going to call Jam,' I told him. Sampson had met Jamilla, liked her, and knew our situation. Jam was a homicide detective too, so she understood what the life was like. I really liked to be with her. Unfortunately, she lived in San Francisco – and she loved it out there.

'She's on another murder case. They kill people in San Francisco too. Life in the Bureau is good so far.' I popped open the second of my beers. 'I need to get used to the Bureau-crats, though.'

'Uh-oh,' Sampson said. Then he grinned wickedly. 'Crack in the walls already? The Bureau-crats. Authority problems? So why you working so late? Aren't you still in orientation, or whatever they call it?'

I told Sampson about the kidnapping of Elizabeth Connelly – the condensed version – but then we moved back to more pleasant subjects. Billie and Jamilla, the allure of romance, the latest George Pelecanos novel, a detective friend of ours who was dating his partner and didn't think anybody was on to them. But we all *knew*! It was like it always is when Sampson and I get together. I missed working with him. Which led to the next thought: I needed to figure out some way to get him down to Quantico.

The big man cleared his throat. 'Something else I wanted to tell you, talk to you about. Real reason I came over tonight,' he said.

I raised an eyebrow. 'Oh. What's that?'

His eyes avoided mine. 'Kind of difficult for me, Alex.'

I leaned forward. He had me hooked.

Then Sampson grinned, and I knew it was good, whatever he was about to share.

'Billie's got herself pregnant,' he said and laughed his deepest, richest laugh. Then Sampson jumped up and bear-hugged me half to death. *'I'm going to be a father!'*

Chapter Twenty-Four

'Here we go again, my darling Zoya,' said Slava in a conspiratorial whisper. 'You look very prosperous, by the way. Just perfect for today.'

The Couple looked like all the other suburban types wandering around the crowded King of Prussia Mall, the 'second largest in America', according to promotional signs at all the entrances. There was good reason for the mall's popularity. Greedy shoppers traveled here from the surrounding states because Pennsylvania had no tax on clothing.

'These people all look so wealthy. They have their *shit* together,' said Slava. 'Don't you think? You know the expression I'm using – "having your shit together"? It's American. Slang.'

Zoya snorted out a nasty laugh. 'We'll see how together their shit is in an hour or so. After we've done our business here. Their fear lies about a quarter of an inch below the surface. Just like everybody else in this spoiled rotten country. They're afraid of their own shadows. But especially pain, or even a little discomfort. Can't you see that on their faces, Slava? They're afraid of us. They just don't know it yet.'

Slava looked around the main plaza, which was dominated by Nordstrom and Neiman Marcus. There were signs up everywhere for *Teen People* magazine's 'Rock and Shop Tour.' Meanwhile, their target had just bought a *fifty-dollar box of cookies* at Neiman's. Amazing! Then she bought something equally absurd called a 'Red, White, and Blue Dog Journal', which was prohibitively expensive as well.

Stupid, stupid people. Keeping notebooks for a dog, Slava thought. Then he spotted the target again. She was coming out of *Skechers* with her small children in tow.

Actually, the target looked a little apprehensive to them at the moment. Why was that? Maybe she was afraid that she would be recognized, and have to sign an autograph, or make small talk with her fans. *Price of fame, eh?* She moved quickly now, guiding the precious little ones into Dick Clark's American Bandstand Grill, presumably for lunch, but maybe just to escape the crowds.

'Dick Clark came from Philadelphia near here,' Slava said. 'Did you know that?'

'Who the hell cares about Dick Clark, Dick Tracy, or dickless,' said Zoya, and hammered Slava's bicep with her fist. 'Stop this stupid trivia game. It gives me a headache. Excedrin headache number one trillion since I met you.'

The target certainly fit the description they had been given by their controller: *tall, blond, ice queen, full of herself. But also tasty down to the last detail,* thought Slava. It made sense, he supposed. She had been purchased by a client

who called himself the Art Director.

The Couple waited about fifty minutes. A middle school choir from Broomall, Pennsylvania, was performing in the atrium. Then the target and her two kids emerged from the Dick Clark restaurant.

'Let's do it,' said Slava. 'This should be interesting, no? The kids make it a challenge.'

'No,' Zoya said. 'The kids make it insane. Wait until the Wolf hears about this. He'll have puppies. That's American slang, by the way.'

Chapter Twenty-Five

The name of the woman who'd been purchased was Audrey Meek. She was a celebrity and had founded a highly successful line of women's fashions and accessories called *Meek*. It was her mother's maiden name, and the one she still used herself.

The Couple watched her closely, tailed her into the parking garage without creating suspicion. They finally jumped her as she was putting her Neiman Marcus and Hermès and other shopping bags into a shiny black Lexus SUV with New Jersey plates.

'Children, run! Run away!' Audrey Meek struggled fiercely as Zoya tried to stuff an acrid-smelling gauzy cloth over her nose and mouth. Soon she saw circles, stars and bright colors for a couple of dramatic seconds. Then she finally passed out in Slava's powerful arms.

Zoya peered around the parking garage. It was nothing much to look at – cement walls with number/letter marks. Nobody anywhere near them. Nobody noticing anything wrong, even though the children were yelling and starting to cry.

'Leave my mommy alone!' Andrew Meek shouted and threw punches at Slava, who only smiled at the boy.

'Good little fellow,' he applauded. 'Protect your mama. She would be proud of you. I am proud of you.'

'Let's go, stupid!' shouted Zoya. As always, she was the one who took care of all the important business. It had been that way since she was growing up in the Moskovskaya oblast outside Moscow, and Zoya had decided she couldn't bear to be either a factory worker or a prostitute.

'What about the kids? We can't leave them here,' said Slava.

'*Leave* them. That's what we're supposed to do, you idiot. We *want* witnesses. That's the plan. Can't you keep anything straight?'

'In the garage? Leave them here?'

'They'll be fine. Or not. Who the hell cares. C'mon. We must go. Now!'

They drove off in the Lexus wagon with the target, Audrey Meek, unconscious on the backseat, and her two children wailing uncontrollably in the parking garage. Zoya drove at a moderate speed around the mall's plaza, then turned on to the Dekalb Pike.

They traveled only a few minutes to the Valley Forge Station Park, where they switched cars.

Then another eight miles to a remote parking area where they changed vehicles yet again.

Then off to New Hope in the Bucks County area of Pennsylvania. Soon, Mrs Meek would meet the Art Director, who was madly in love with her. He must have been – he had paid $250,000 for the pleasure of her company, whatever that might be.

And there had been witnesses to the abduction – a screw-up – *on purpose*.

PART TWO

FIDELITY, BRAVERY, INTEGRITY

Chapter Twenty-Six

No one had been able to figure out the Wolf yet. According to information from Interpol and also the Russian police, he was a no-nonsense, hands-on operator, but one who had originally been trained as a policeman. Like many Russians, he was able to think in very fluid, commonsense terms. That native ability was sometimes given as the reason the Mir space station was able to stay in space so long. The Russian cosmonauts were simply better than the Americans at figuring out everyday problems. If something unexpected went wrong in the spacecraft, they *fixed* it.

And so did the Wolf.

On that sunny afternoon, he drove a black Cadillac Escalade to the northern section of Miami. He needed to see a man named Yeggy Titov about some security matters. Yeggy liked to think of himself as a world-class website designer and cutting-edge engineer. He had a doctorate from Cal-Berkeley and never let anyone forget it. But Yeggy was just another pervert and creep with delusions of

grandeur and an 'attitude'; a really bad attitude.

The Wolf banged on the metal door of Yeggy's apartment in a high-riser overlooking Biscayne Bay. He was wearing a skullcap and a Miami Heat windbreaker, just in case anyone saw him visiting.

'All right, all right, hold your urine!' Yeggy shouted from inside. It took him another couple of minutes to finally open up. He had on blue jean shorts and a tattered, faded-black novelty-store sweatshirt with Einstein's grinning face on it. Quite the kidder, that Yeggy.

'I told you not to make me come and see you,' the Wolf said, but he was smiling broadly, as if he were making a big joke. So Yeggy smiled too. They had been business associates for about a year – which was a long time for anyone to put up with Yeggy.

'Your timing is perfect,' he said.

'How lucky for me,' said the Wolf as he strolled into the living room and immediately wanted to hold his nose. The apartment was an incredible dump – littered with fast-food wrappers and pizza boxes, empty milk cartons, and dozens, maybe a hundred, old copies of *Novoye Russkoye Slovo*, the largest Russian-language newspaper in the United States.

The odor of filth and decaying food was bad enough, but even worse was Yeggy himself, who always smelled like week-old sausages. The science-man led him into a bedroom off the living-room area – only it turned out not to be a bedroom at all. It was the lab of a very disorganized person. Ugly brown carpeting, three beige CPU boxes on the floor, parts in a corner – discarded heatsinks, circuit boards, hard drives.

'You are a pig,' the Wolf said, then laughed again.

'But a very smart pig.'

In the center of the room was a modular desk. Three flat screen displays formed a semicircle around a well-worn rumble chair. Behind the display screens was a fire hazard of intertwined cables. There was only one outside window, the blind permanently drawn.

'Your site is *very* secure now,' Yeggy said. 'Primo. One hundred per cent. No possible screw-ups. The way you like it.'

'I thought it was already secure,' the Wolf replied.

'Well now it's more secure. You can't be too careful these days. Tell you what else – I finished the latest brochure. It's a classic, instant classic.'

'Yes, and only three weeks late.'

Yeggy shrugged his bony shoulders. 'So what – wait'll you see my work. It's genius. Can you recognize genius when you see it? *This* is genius.'

The Wolf examined the pages before he said anything to the science-man. The brochure was printed on 8½- by 11-inch glossy paper, bound in a clear report cover with a red spine. Yeggy had cranked it out on his HP color laser printer. The colors were electric. The cover looked perfect. The elegance was weird, actually, as if the Wolf were looking at a Tiffany's catalog. It sure didn't look like the work of a man who lived in this shithole.

'I told you that girls number seven and seventeen were

no longer with us. Dead, actually.' The Wolf finally spoke. 'Our boy genius is forgetful, no?'

'Details, details,' said Yeggy. 'Speaking of which, you owe me fifteen thousand cash on delivery. This would be considered delivery.'

The Wolf reached into his suit jacket and pulled out a Sig Sauer 210. He shot Yeggy twice between the eyes. Then, for laughs, he shot Albert Einstein between the eyes too.

'Looks like you are no longer with us either, Mr Titov. Details, details.'

The Wolf sat at a laptop computer and fixed the sales catalog himself. Then he burned a CD and took it with him. Also several copies of the Russian newspaper *Novoye Russkoye Slovo* that he had missed. He would send a crew to dispose of the body and burn this shithole later. Details, details.

Chapter Twenty-Seven

I skipped a class with a topic on *'Arrest Techniques'* that morning. I figured I probably knew more on the subject than the teacher. I called Monnie Donnelley instead, and told her I needed whatever she had on the white slave trade, particularly recent activity in the US, that might relate to the White Girl case.

Most of the Bureau's crime analysts were housed ten miles away at the Criminal Incident Response Group (CIRG), but Monnie had an office at Quantico. Less than an hour later, she was at the doorway of my no-frills cubicle. She held out two disks, and looked proud of herself.

'This should keep you busy for a while. I concentrated on white women only. Attractive. Recent abductions. I also have a lot on the crime scene in Atlanta. I expanded the circle to get a read on the mall, owner, employees, the neighborhood in Buckhead. I have copies for you of the police and the Bureau's investigative reports. All the things you asked for. You *do* your homework, don't you?'

'I'm a student of the game. I prepare as best I can. Is that so unusual? Here at Quantico?'

'Actually, it is for agents who come to us from police departments or the armed forces. They seem to like to work out in the field.'

'I like field work too,' I admitted to Monnie, 'but not until I've narrowed it some. Thank you for this, *all* of this.'

'Do you know what they say about you, Dr Cross?'

'No. What do they say?'

'That you're close to psychic. Very imaginative. Maybe gifted. You can think like a killer. That's why they put you on White Girl right away.' She remained in the doorway. 'Listen. Some unasked-for advice if I may. You shouldn't piss off Gordo Nooney. He takes his little orientation games seriously. He's also basically a bad guy. And, he's *connected*.'

'I'll remember that.'

I nodded. 'So there are *good* guys too?'

'Absolutely. You'll see that most of the agents are real solid. Good people, the best. All right, well, happy hunting,' Monnie said. Then she left me to my reading, lots and lots of reading. Too much.

I started off with a couple of abductions – both in Texas – that I thought could be related to those in Atlanta. Just reading the accounts got my blood boiling again, though. Marianne Norman, twenty, had disappeared in Houston on 6 August, 2001. She'd been staying with her college sweetheart in a condo owned by his grandparents. Marianne and Dennis Turcos were going to be seniors at Texas Christian that fall and planned to be married in the spring of '02. Everybody said they were the nicest kids in the world.

Marianne was never seen or heard from after that night in August. On 30 December of that year, Dennis Turcos put a revolver to his head and killed himself. He said he couldn't live without Marianne, that his life ended when she disappeared.

The second case involved a fifteen-year-old runaway from Childress, Texas. Adrianne Tuletti had been snatched from an apartment in San Antonio where three girls involved in prostitution were said to live. Neighbors in the complex reported having seen two suspicious-looking people, a male and a female, entering the building on the day that Adrianne disappeared. One neighbor thought it might be the girls' parents who had come to bring their daughter home, since the fifteen-year-old was never seen or heard from again.

I looked at her picture for a long moment – she was a pretty blonde and looked as if she could have been one of Elizabeth Connelly's daughters. Her parents were elementary schoolteachers back in Childress.

Around one o'clock that afternoon, I got more bad news. The worst kind. A fashion designer named Audrey Meek had been abducted from the King of Prussia Mall in Pennsylvania. Her two young children had witnessed the kidnapping. *That* piece of information stunned me. The children had told the police that the abductors were a man and a woman.

I started to get ready to travel to Pennsylvania. I called Nana and she was supportive for a change. Then I got a message from Nooney's office. *I wasn't going to Pennsylvania.*

I was expected at my classes that afternoon.

The decision had obviously come from the top, and I didn't understand what was happening. Maybe I wasn't supposed to.

Maybe all of this was a test?

Chapter Twenty-Eight

'**D**o *you know what they say about you, Dr Cross? That you're close to psychic. Very imaginative. Maybe gifted. You can think like a killer.*' Those were Monnie Donnelley's words to me that very morning. If that was true, why had I been taken off the case?

I went to my classes in the afternoon but I was distracted, maybe angry. I suffered a little angst: *what was I doing in the FBI? What was I becoming?* I didn't want to fight the system in Quantico, but I'd been put in an impossible position. The next morning I had to be ready for my classes again: Law; White Collar Crime; Civil Rights Violations; Firearms Practice and a practical exercise.

I was sure that I'd find the subject 'Civil Rights Violations' interesting, but a couple of missing women named Elizabeth Connelly and Audrey Meek were out there somewhere. Maybe one or both of them were still alive. Maybe I could help find them – if I was so goddamn gifted.

I was finishing breakfast with Nana and Rosie the cat at

the kitchen table when I heard the morning paper *plop* on the front porch.

'Sit. You eat. I'll get it,' I told Nana as I pushed my chair away from the table.

'No argument from this corner,' Nana said and sipped her tea with great little-old-lady aplomb. 'I have to conserve myself, you know.'

'Right.'

Nana was still cleaning every square inch of the house, inside and out, and cooking most of the meals. A couple of weeks ago I'd caught her hanging on to an extension ladder, cleaning out the gutters on the roof. 'It's not a problem,' she hollered down to me. 'My balance is excellent and I'm light as a parachute.' Come again?

The *Washington Post* hadn't actually reached the porch. It lay open halfway up the sidewalk. I didn't even have to stoop down to read the front page.

'Awhh hell,' I said. 'Damn it.'

This wasn't good. It was awful, actually. I almost couldn't believe what I was seeing.

The headline was a shocker: ABDUCTIONS OF TWO WOMEN MAY BE CONNECTED. Worst of all, the rest of the story contained very specific details that only a few people in the FBI knew. Unfortunately, I was one of them.

The story told about a couple – a man and woman – who had been seen at the most recent kidnapping in Pennsylvania was key. I felt sick in the pit of my stomach. The eyewitness account given by Audrey Meek's children was information that we didn't want released to the press.

Somebody had leaked the story to the *Post*; somebody had also connected the dots for them. Other than maybe Bob Woodward, nobody at the newspaper could find it out by themselves. They weren't that smart.

Who had leaked information to the *Post*?

Why?

It didn't make sense. Was somebody trying to sabotage the murder investigation? Who?

Chapter Twenty-Nine

I didn't walk Jannie and Damon to school that morning. I sat out on the sunporch with the cat and played the piano – Mozart, Brahms. I had the guilty thought that I should have gotten up earlier and helped out at St Anthony's soup kitchen. I usually pitch in a couple of mornings a week, often on Sundays. *My church*.

Traffic was terrible that morning and the frustrating ride down to Quantico took me a little over an hour and twenty minutes. I imagined Senior Agent Nooney standing at the front gates, waiting impatiently for me to arrive. At least the ride gave me time to think over my current situation. I decided the best course of action, for now anyway, was to go to my classes. Keep my head down. If Director Burns wanted me on White Girl, he'd get word to me. If not, then fine.

That morning the class centered on what the Bureau called a 'practical application exercise'. We had to investigate a 'fictitious' bank robbery, including interviews with victims and tellers. The instructor was another very competent SSA named Marilyn May.

About half an hour into the exercise, Agent May notified the class of a fictitious automobile accident about a mile from the bank. We proceeded as a group to Hogans Alley to investigate the accident, and to see if it had any connection to the bank robbery. I was being conscientious, but I'd been involved in actual investigations like this for the past dozen years, and it was hard for me to take it too seriously, especially since some of my classmates conducted interviews according to the instructional manual. I thought maybe they'd watched cop shows on television too often. Agent May seemed amused at times herself.

As I stood around the accident scene with a new buddy who had been a captain in the army before going into the Bureau, I heard my name spoken. I turned to see Nooney's administrative assistant. 'Senior Agent Nooney wants to see you in his office,' he said.

Oh Christ, what now? This guy is nuts! I was thinking as I walked quickly to Administration. I hurried upstairs to where Nooney was waiting.

'Shut the door, please,' he said. He was seated behind a scarred oak desk, looking as if someone close to him had died.

I was getting hot under the collar. 'I'm in the middle of an exercise.'

'I know what you're doing. I wrote the program and the schedule,' he said. 'I want to talk to you about the front page of today's *Washington Post*,' he went on. 'You see it?'

'I saw it.'

'I spoke to your former chief of detectives this morning.

He told me that you've used the *Post* before. He said you have friends there.'

I tried hard not to roll my eyes. 'I used to have a good friend at the *Post*. He was murdered. I don't have friends there anymore. Why would I leak information about the abductions? What would I gain?'

Nooney pointed a rigid finger my way. He raised his voice. 'I know how you work. And I know what you're after – you don't want to be part of a team. Or to be controlled or influenced in any way. Well, it's not going to happen that way. We don't believe in golden boys, or special situations. We don't think that you're more imaginative or creative than anyone else in your class. So get back to your exercise, Dr Cross. And wise up.'

Without saying another word I left the office fuming. I returned to the fake accident scene which Agent Marilyn May soon neatly connected to the fake robbery that had been staged in Hogans Alley. Some program that Nooney had written. I could have done a better one in my sleep. And yeah, now I was mad. I just didn't know whom I was supposed to be mad at. I didn't know how to play this game.

But I wanted to win.

Chapter Thirty

A nother *purchase* had been made – a large one.

That night, the Couple entered a bar called The Halyard, on the water in Newport, Rhode Island. The Halyard was different from most of the gay clubs in Newport's so-called Pink District. There was the occasional glimpse of a bad-ass boot or spike-studded wristband, but most of the men who frequented the place sported tousled hairdos and boating dress, and the ever-popular Croakie-attached sunglasses.

The DJ had just selected a Strokes tune and several couples were dancing the night away. The Couple fit in, which is to say that they didn't stand out. Slava wore a baby blue T-shirt and Dockers, and had gelled his longish black hair. Zoya had on a raffish sailing cap and made herself up to look like a pretty young male. She had succeeded beyond her own expectations for she had already been hit on.

She and Slava were looking for a certain physical 'type', and they had found a promising prospect soon after they arrived. His name, they would learn later, was Benjamin

Coffey, and he was a senior at Providence College. Benjamin had first become aware that he was gay while serving as an altar boy at St Thomas in Barrington, Rhode Island. No priest ever touched or abused him while he was there, or even came on to him, but he discovered a like-minded altar server, and they became lovers when they were both fourteen. The two had continued to meet through high school, but then Benjamin moved on.

He was still keeping his sex life a secret at Providence College, but he could be himself in the Pink District. The Couple watched the very handsome boy as he chatted up a thirtysomething bartender, whose toned muscles were set off by the track lighting over his head.

'The boy could be on the cover of *GQ*,' said Slava. 'He's the one.'

A strapping man in his fifties approached the bar. Close behind him were four younger males and a woman. Everyone in the group was wearing white ducks and blue Lacoste shirts. The bartender turned away from Benjamin and shook hands with the older man, who then turned to introduce his companions. 'David Skalah. Crew. Henry Galperin. Crew. Bill Lattanzi. Crew. Sam Hughes. Cook. Nora Hamerman. Crew.'

'And this,' the bartender said, 'is Ben.'

'It's Benjamin,' the boy corrected, and smiled brilliantly.

Zoya snuck a look at Slava and the two of them couldn't help grinning. 'The boy is just what we want,' she said. 'He's like a cleaned-up version of Brad Pitt.'

He was definitely the physical 'type' that the client had

specified: slender, blond, boyish, still probably a teenager, luscious red lips, intelligent-looking. That was a must – *intelligence*. And the buyer wanted no part of 'chicken hawks', young boys who sold themselves on the street.

Ten minutes or so passed, then the Couple followed Benjamin to the bathroom, which was white on white and sparkling clean. Illustrations of nautical knots had been drawn on the walls. There was a table elaborately set with colognes, mouthwashes, a teak box filled with amyl nitrite poppers.

Benjamin headed into one of the stalls and the Couple pushed in after him. It was a tight squeeze.

He turned when he felt a hard shove. 'Taken,' he said. 'I'm in here. Jesus, are you two stoned? Give me a break.'

'Arm or leg?' said Slava, and laughed at his own joke.

They forced him to his knees. 'Hey, hey,' he called out in alarm. 'Somebody help me. Somebody!'

A gauzy cloth was pressed tightly against his nose and mouth, and he became unconscious. Then the Couple lifted Benjamin up and supported him on either side, carrying him from the bathroom as if they were buddies helping someone who'd passed out.

They took him out a back door to a parking lot filled with convertibles and SUVs. The Couple didn't care if they were seen, but they were careful not to hurt the boy. No bruises. He was worth a lot of money. Somebody wanted him badly.

Another purchase.

Chapter Thirty-One

The buyer's name was *Mr Potter*.

It was the code name he used when he wanted to make a purchase from *Sterling*, when he and the seller communicated for any reason. *Potter* was very happy with Benjamin and he'd told this to the Couple when they dropped the package at his farm in Webster, New Hampshire, which had a population of a little more than fourteen hundred – a place where no one bothered you. Ever. The farmhouse he owned there was partially restored, with white antique wood shingling, two stories, a new roof. About a hundred yards behind it sat a red barn, the 'guest house'. This was where Benjamin would be kept, where the others before him had been stored as well.

The house and barn were surrounded by more than sixty acres of woods and farmland, which had belonged to Potter's family, and now were his. He didn't live on the farm, but in Hanover, fifty-two miles away, where he toiled as an assistant professor of English at Dartmouth.

God, he couldn't take his eyes off Benjamin. Of course, the boy couldn't see him. Couldn't speak. Not yet. A hood made of burlap completely covered his face. He was gagged, and his hands and legs were bound by police handcuffs.

Other than that, Benjamin wore nothing but a sliver of silver thong, which looked precious on him. The sight of the very handsome young man took Potter's breath away for the third or fourth or tenth time since he'd taken possession of him. The maddening thing about teaching at Dartmouth these past five years was: *you could watch, but you could not touch the boys who went there.* It was frustrating beyond belief to be that close to his heart's desire, but now – it almost seemed worth it. Benjamin was his reward. For *waiting.* For *being good.*

He moved close to the boy, inches at a time. Finally, he slid his hand through the waves of thick blond hair. Benjamin jumped! He actually shivered and shook uncontrollably. That was nice.

'It's all right . . . to be afraid,' Potter whispered. 'There's a strange joy to be found in fear. Trust me on that, Benjamin. I've been there. I know exactly what you're feeling now.'

Potter could barely stand it! This was just too much of a great thing, a dream come true. He had been denied this forbidden pleasure – and now here was this absolutely perfect, beautiful, stunning young man.

What was this? Benjamin was trying to speak through his gag and hood. Potter wanted to hear the boy's sweet voice, to see his luscious mouth move, to look into his eyes. He bent forward and kissed the place where the boy's mouth ought to be. He actually felt Benjamin's lips underneath, their softness.

Then Mr Potter couldn't stand it for one second more. His fingers fumbling, incoherent whispers seeping from his mouth, his body shaking as if he had palsy, he lifted off the hood and looked at Benjamin's face.

He also let the boy see him.

'May I call you Benjy?' he whispered.

Chapter Thirty-Two

A nother of the captives – *Audrey Meek* – watched this obscene deviate, possibly an *insane* captor, as he calmly and coolly fixed her breakfast. She was bound by rope, *loosely*, but she couldn't run. She couldn't believe any of this was happening, *had* happened, and presumably would continue happening. She was being held in a nicely furnished cabin – *somewhere, who knew where* – and she was still flashing back to the incredible moment when she had been grabbed at the King of Prussia Mall, when they yanked her away from Sarah and Warren. *Dear God, were the children all right?*

'My children?' Audrey asked again. 'I have to know for sure they're all right. I want to talk to them. I won't do anything you ask until I speak to them. Not even eat.'

Another uncomfortable silent moment passed, and then the *Art Director* chose to speak.

'Your children are just fine. That's all I'll tell you,' he said. 'You should eat.'

'How could you know my children are all right?' she sniffed. 'You can't.'

'Audrey, you're in no position to make demands. Not anymore. That life is behind you.'

He was tall, maybe six feet two and well-built, with a thick, bushy black beard and flashing blue eyes that seemed intelligent to her. She guessed that he was around fifty. He'd told her to call him *Art Director*. No rhyme or reason for the name, not yet anyway, nor any other explanation for what had happened so far.

'I was concerned myself, so I called your house. The children are there with your nanny and husband. I promise. I wouldn't lie to you, Audrey. I'm different from you in that respect.'

Audrey shook her head. 'I'm supposed to trust you? Your word?'

'I think it would be a good idea, yes. Why not? Who else can you trust out here? Yourself of course. And me. That's all there is. You're miles and miles away from anybody else. It's just us two. Please get used to it. You like your scrambled eggs a little soft, right? Fluffy? Isn't that the word you use?'

'Why are you *doing* this?' Audrey asked, getting braver since he hadn't actually threatened her yet. 'What are the *two* of us doing here?'

He sighed. 'All in due time, Audrey. For now, let's just say it's an unhealthy obsession. It's more complicated, actually, but let's leave it at that for now.' She was surprised by the answer – he *knew* he was a freaking nutcase, didn't he? Was that good or bad, though, that he knew exactly what he was doing?

'I'd like to keep you free like this as much as possible. I

don't want you kept in bondage, for God's sake. Not even the ropes. Please don't try to run away, or it won't be possible. Okay?'

He seemed so reasonable at times. *Seemed*. Christ! Wasn't this the most insane thing? Of course it was. But insane things happened all the time to people.

'I want to be your friend,' he said as he served her breakfast – the eggs cooked just so, twelve-grain toast, herbal tea, boysenberry jam. 'I've cooked all the things you like. I want to treat you like you deserve. You can trust me, Audrey. Start by trusting me just a little bit . . . Try your eggs. Fluffy. They're delish.'

Chapter Thirty-Three

I was marking time at Quantico and I didn't like it much. I attended my classes the next morning, then an hour of fitness training. At noon, I went to the Dining Hall Building to see what Monnie Donnelley had collected so far on White Girl. She had a small, cramped cubicle on the third floor. On one wall was a collage of photos and photocopies of bits of evidence from brutally violent crimes arranged in an eye-catching cubist's fantasy.

I rapped my knuckles against her metal nameplate before entering the cube.

Monnie turned and smiled when she saw me standing there. I noticed glossy photos of her sons and a funny portrait of Monnie, the sons, and also one of Pierce Brosnan as debonair, sexy James Bond. 'Hey, look who's back for more punishment. You can tell by the size of my digs that the Bureau doesn't yet realize that this is the Information Age, what Bill Clinton used to call The Third Way. You know the joke – the Bureau supports yesterday's technology tomorrow.'

'Any information for me?'

Monnie swiveled back to her computer, an IBM. 'Let me print up a few of these choice pieces for your burgeoning collection. I know you like hard copies. Dinosaur.'

'It's just the way I work.'

I had asked around about Monnie and heard the same thing everywhere: she was bright, an incredibly hard worker, woefully under-appreciated by the powers at Quantico. I'd also found out that Monnie was a single mother of two, and struggling to make ends meet. The only 'complaint' against her was that she worked too hard, brought stuff home just about every night and weekends.

Monnie shuffled together a thick batch of pages for me. I could tell she was obsessive by the way she evened out all the pages. They had to be just so.

'Anything pop out at you?' I asked.

She shrugged. 'I'm just a researcher, right? More corroboration. Upscale, white women who've been reported missing in the last year or so. The numbers are out of whack, way too high. A lot of them are attractive blondes. Blondes *do not* have more fun in these instances. No particular regional skew, which I want to look into more. Geographic profiling? Sometimes it can pinpoint the exact locus of criminal activity.'

'No obvious regional discrepancies so far. That's too bad. Anything in terms of the victims' appearances? *Any* patterns at all?'

Monnie clucked her tongue, shook her head. 'Nothing sticks out. There are women missing in New England, the

South, Far West. I'll check into it more. The women are described as very attractive for the most part. And *none* of them have been found. They go missing, they stay missing.'

She looked at me for a few uncomfortable seconds. There was sadness in her eyes. I sensed that she wanted out of this cubicle.

I reached down for the pages. 'We're trying. I made a promise to the Connelly family.'

There was a flicker of humor in her light green eyes. 'You keep your promises?'

'Try,' I said. 'Thanks for the pages. Don't work too hard. Go home and see your kids.'

'You too, Alex. See your kids. You're working too hard already.'

Chapter Thirty-Four

N ana and the kids, not to mention Rosie the cat, were lying in wait for me on the front porch when I got home that night. Their cranky body language and the sullen looks on their faces weren't good signs. I figured I knew why everybody was so happy to see me. *You always keep your promises?*

'Seven-thirty. It's getting later and later,' Nana said and shook her head. 'You mentioned we might go see *Drumline* at the movies. Damon was excited.'

'It's orientation,' I told her.

'Exactly,' Nana said and the frown on her face deepened. 'Wait until the real stuff starts up. You'll be coming home at midnight again. If at all. You have no life. You have no love life. All those women who like you, Alex – though God knows why. Let one of them *catch* you. Let somebody in. Before it's too late.'

'Maybe it's too late already.'

'Wouldn't surprise me.'

'You're tough,' I said and plopped down on the porch

steps next to the kids. 'Your Nana is tough as nails. Still light out,' I said to them. 'Anybody want to play hoops?'

Damon frowned and shook his head. 'Not with Jannie. No way that's gonna happen.'

'Not with the big *superstar* Damon!' Jannie smirked. 'Even though Diana Taurasi could kick his butt at O-U-T.'

I got up and headed inside. 'I'll get the ball. We'll play O-U-T.'

When we returned from the park, Nana had already put little Alex to bed. She was back sitting on the porch. I'd brought a pint of Pralines and Cream and a pint of Oreos and Cream. We ate, then the kids wandered up to their rooms to sleep, or study, or mess around on the Internet.

'You're becoming hopeless, Alex,' Nana pronounced as she sucked the last ice cream off her spoon. 'That's all I can say to you.'

'You mean consistent. And dedicated. That's getting harder to find. You like that Oreos and Cream, don't you?'

She rolled her eyes. 'Maybe you ought to catch up with the times, son. Duty isn't everything anymore.'

'I'm here for the kids. And even for you, old woman.'

'Never said you weren't. Well, not lately anyway. How's Jamilla?'

'We've both been busy.'

Nana nodded her head, up and down, up and down, like one of those dolls that people keep on the dashboards of their automobiles. Then she pushed herself up and started to gather the ice-cream dishes the kids had left around the porch.

'I'll get those,' I told her.

'Kids should get them. They know better too.'

'They take advantage when I'm around.'

'Right. Because they know you feel guilty.'

'For what?' I asked. 'What did I do? What am I missing here?'

'Now *that* is the main question you have to answer, isn't it? I'm going in to bed. Goodnight, Alex. I love you. And I do like Oreos and Cream.'

Then she muttered, 'Hopeless.'

'Am not,' I said to her back.

'Are too,' she spoke without turning. She *always* gets the last word.

I eventually moseyed up to my office in the attic and made a phone call I'd been dreading. But I'd made a promise.

The phone rang and then I heard a man's voice say, '*Brendan Connelly*.'

'Hello, Judge Connelly, this is Alex Cross,' I said. I heard him sigh, but he said nothing, so I continued. 'I don't have any specific good news about Mrs Connelly yet. We have over fifty agents active in the Atlanta area, though. I'm calling because I told you I'd keep in touch and to reassure you that we're working.'

Because I made a promise.

Chapter Thirty-Five

Something about the abductions wasn't tracking for me. The early kidnappings had been committed carefully, then suddenly the abductors began to get sloppy. The pattern was inconsistent. Why? What did it mean? What had changed about the abductions? If I could figure that out, we might have a break.

The next morning, I got to Quantico about five minutes before the Director touched down in a big, black Bell helicopter. The news that Burns was on the grounds circulated quickly. Maybe Monnie Donnelley was right about one thing, this *was* the Information Age, even inside the Bureau, even at Quantico.

Burns had ordered an emergency meeting, and I was informed that I was to come. *Maybe I was back on the case?* The Director acknowledged a couple of agents when he entered the conference room in the Admin Building. His eyes never made contact with mine, and, once again, I wondered what he was doing here. Did he have news for us? What kind of news would warrant a visit from him?

He sat in the first row as the Behavioral Analysis Unit Chief, Dr Bill Thompson, walked to the front of the room. It was becoming clear that Burns was here as an observer. But why? What did he want to observe?

An administrative assistant to Dr Thompson passed out stapled documents. At the same time, the first slide of a PowerPoint presentation was projected on a wall screen. 'There's been another kidnapping,' Thompson announced to the group. 'It occurred Thursday night in Newport, Rhode Island. There's been a sea change here. The victim was a *male*. To our knowledge, he's the first male that they've taken.'

Dr Thompson gave us the details, which were also projected on the wall screen. An honor student at Providence College, Benjamin Coffey, had been abducted from a bar called The Halyard in Newport. It appeared that the abductors were both males.

A team.

And they had been spotted again.

'Anyone?' asked Thompson once he had given us the basics. 'Reactions? Comments? Don't be shy. We need input. We're nowhere on this.'

'Pattern's definitely different,' an analyst volunteered. 'Abduction *at a bar*. Male taken.'

'How can we be so sure of that at this point?' Burns spoke up from the front of the room. 'What *is* the pattern here?' he asked.

Burns's question was met with silence. Like most chief executives he had no idea of his own power. He turned and looked around at the group. His eyes finally settled on mine. 'Alex? What *is* the pattern?' he asked. 'You have any ideas?'

The other agents were watching me. 'Are we certain it was two males at the club?' I asked. 'That's the first question I have.'

Burns nodded in agreement. 'No, we are *not* sure, are we? One of them had on a sailor's cap. Could have been the woman from King of Prussia. Do you agree with the opinion voiced about the disconnection between this abduction and the others? Has the pattern been broken?'

I considered the question, trying to get in touch with my gut reaction to what I'd heard so far.

'No,' I finally said. 'There doesn't even have to be a behavioral pattern. Not if the abduction team is working for money. I'm inclined to think they probably are. I don't see these as crimes of passion. But what bothers me are the mistakes. Why are they making mistakes? That's the key to everything.'

Chapter Thirty-Six

Lizzie Connelly had no sense of time anymore, except that it seemed to be moving very slowly, and that she was pretty sure she was going to die soon. She would never see Gwynne, Brigid, Merry or Brendan again and that made her incredibly sad. *She was definitely going to die.*

After she was locked away in the small closet-room, she'd spent no time feeling sorry for herself, or worse, feeling panic, letting it rule her for whatever time she had left. Certain things were obvious to her, but the most important was the reality that this horrible monster wasn't going to let her go. Ever. So she had spent countless hours plotting her escape. But, realistically, she knew that it wasn't likely to happen. She was bound with leather straps, and though she'd tried every possible maneuver, every twist and turn, she'd never be able to break loose. Even if she did, by some miracle, she could never overpower him. He was probably the strongest man she'd ever seen, twice as powerful as Brendan, who had played football in college.

So what could she do? Maybe try something during a

bathroom or food break – but he was so attentive and careful. At the very least, Lizzie Connelly wanted to die with dignity. Would the monster let her? Or would he want her to suffer? She thought about her past history quite a lot, and took comfort in it. Her growing-up years in Potomac, Maryland, spending nearly every spare hour at a nearby stable. College at Vassar in New York. Then the *Washington Post*. Her marriage to Brendan, the good times, and the bad. The kids. All leading up to that fateful morning at Phipps Plaza. What a cruel joke life had played on her.

During her last few hours locked up in the dark, she'd been trying to remember how she had gotten through other terrifying experiences. She thought that she knew: with faith; with humor; and with a clear understanding that knowledge was power. Now, Lizzie tried to remember specific examples . . . anything that might help.

When she had been eight years old she'd needed surgery to correct a straying eye. Her parents were always 'too busy' so her grandparents had taken her to the hospital. As she watched them leave, tears had streamed from her eyes. When a nurse came in and saw the tears, Lizzie pretended that she'd bumped her head. And somehow she got past the lonely, terrifying incident. *Lizzie survived*.

Then when she was thirteen there was another terrifying incident. She was returning from a weekend with a friend's family in Virginia, and had fallen asleep in the car. When she woke up she was groggy and confused and completely covered with blood. She remembered staring out into the gloomy darkness and slowly beginning to understand.

There'd been an automobile accident while she was asleep. A man from another car involved in the accident lay in the street. He wasn't moving – but Lizzie believed she *heard* him tell her *'not to be afraid'*. He said that she could stay on earth, or leave. It was her decision – no one else's. She had chosen to live.

'It's my choice,' Lizzie whispered in the blackness of the closet. 'It's my choice to live or die, not his. Not the Wolf's. Not anybody else's.

'I choose to live.'

Chapter Thirty-Seven

The next morning, just about everybody attached to the White Girl task force had been assembled in the main conference hall at Quantico. We hadn't been told much yet, just that there was breaking news, which was good; there had already been too much bureaucracy and wheel-spinning for me.

Senior Agent Ned Mahoney from HRT arrived when the room was already filled. He walked to the front, turned and faced us. His intense, gray-blue eyes went from row to row, and he seemed more pumped up than usual.

'I have an announcement. Good news for a change,' Mahoney said. 'There's been a significant break. Word just came down from Washington.' Mahoney paused, then he continued. 'Since this past Friday, agents from our office in Newark have been monitoring a suspect named Rafe Farley. The suspect is a repeat sex offender. He did four years in Rahway Prison for breaking into a woman's apartment, beating and raping her. At the time, Farley claimed that the victim was a girlfriend from where he worked.

What alerted us to Farley is that he went into an Internet chat room and had a lot to say about Mrs Audrey Meek. Too much. He knew details about Mrs Meek, including facts about her family in the Princeton area, her house there, even the physical layout inside.

'The suspect also knew precisely how and when Mrs Meek was abducted at the King of Prussia Mall. He knew that her car was used, what kind of car it was, and that the children were left behind.

'In a subsequent visit to the chat room, Farley provided specific details that even we don't have. He claimed that she was knocked out with a specific drug and then taken to a wooded area in New Jersey. He left it vague as to whether Audrey Meek is alive or dead.

'Unfortunately, the suspect hasn't gone to visit Mrs Meek during the period we've been watching him. It's been nearly two days. We believe it's possible he may have spotted the surveillance. It is our decision, and the Director concurs, that we take Farley down.

'HRT is already on the scene in North Vineland, New Jersey, assisting the local field office and the police. We're going in this morning, probably within the hour. Score one for the good guys,' said Mahoney. 'Congratulations to everyone involved at this end.'

I sat at my seat and applauded with the others, but I had a funny feeling too. I hadn't been involved, or even known about Farley or the surveillance on him. I was out of the loop, and I hadn't felt like this for over a dozen years, not since I started with the police department in D.C.

Chapter Thirty-Eight

A phrase from the briefing kept playing in my head: the *Director concurs . . .* I wondered how long Director Burns had known about the suspect in Jersey, and why he decided not to tell me. I tried not to be disappointed, or paranoid, but still . . . I wasn't feeling good as the meeting broke up to huzzahs from the group of agents.

The trouble was, something felt wrong to me and I had no idea what it was. I just didn't like something about this bust.

I was filing out of the room with the others when Mahoney came ambling up to me. 'The Director asked that you go to New Jersey,' he said, then grinned. 'Come with me to the helipad. I want you there too,' he added. 'If we don't break Farley down immediately, I don't think we'll get Mrs Meek back alive.'

A little less than fifty-five minutes later a Bell helicopter set down at Big Sky Aviation in Millville, New Jersey. Two black SUVs were waiting, and Mahoney and I were rushed to North Vineland, about six miles to the north.

We parked in the lot of an International House of Pancakes restaurant. Farley's house was one point two miles north on Garden Road. 'We're ready to roll on him,' Mahoney told his group. 'I have a pretty good feeling about this one.'

I accompanied Mahoney in one of the SUVs. We wouldn't be part of the six-man HRT team that would go into the house first, but we'd have immediate access to Rafe Farley. Hopefully, we'd find Audrey Meek alive in the house.

In spite of my misgivings, I was starting to get pumped about the take-down. Mahoney's enthusiasm was contagious and any kind of action beats sitting around. At least we were doing something. Maybe we'd get Audrey Meek back.

Just then, we passed by an unpainted, off-white bungalow. I saw broken porch boards and a rusty car and camping stove in the small front yard. 'That's it,' said Mahoney. 'Home sweet home. Let's pull over up there.'

We stopped about a hundred yards up the road, near a stand of red oaks and pines. I knew that a couple of surveillance agents in ghillie suits were already nestled in close to the bungalow. These agents did nothing but surveillance, and wouldn't be involved in the actual bust. There was also a closed-circuit camera aimed at the bungalow and the UNSUB's car, a red Dodge Polaris.

'We think he's sleeping inside,' Mahoney informed me as we jogged through the woods until we had the ramshackle house in view.

'It's almost eleven in the morning,' I said.

'Farley works a late-night shift. He got home at six this a.m. His girlfriend's in there too.'

I didn't say anything.

'What? What are you thinking?' Mahoney asked as we watched the house from a thick stand of woods less than fifty yards away.

'You said he has a girlfriend in the house? That doesn't sound right, does it?'

'I don't know, Alex. According to surveillance, the girlfriend's been there all night. I guess they could be the couple. We're here. My job is to take Rafe Farley down. Let's do it . . . *This is HRT One. I have control. Ready! Five, four, three, two, one. Go. Go!*'

Chapter Thirty-Nine

Mahoney and I watched as the breech team moved quickly on the small, inconsequential-looking house. The six agents were outfitted in black-on-black flight suits and body armor. The side yard was littered with two more junked vehicles, a small car and a Dodge truck, and a lot of spare parts for appliances like refrigerators and air conditioners. There was a standing urinal out back that looked like it came from a tavern.

The house windows were darkened even though it was past eleven. *Was Audrey Meek in there? Was she alive? I hoped that she was. It was a huge break if we got her back now. Especially since everybody thought she was probably dead.*

But something about the raid bothered me.

Not that it mattered now.

There is no 'knock and announce' protocol when HRT is involved. No talking, no negotiating, no political correctness. I watched two agents breech the front door. They started to go inside the suspect's house.

Suddenly, a muffled *boom*. The agents at the front door

went down. One of them didn't get up. The other got up and stumbled back from the house. It was awful to witness, a complete shock.

'Bomb,' said Mahoney in surprise and anger. 'He musta booby-trapped the door.'

By then, the four other agents were inside the house. They had gone in through a back and side door. There were no more explosions so the doors hadn't been booby-trapped. Two HRT agents approached the wounded pair at the front of the house. They pulled away the agent who hadn't moved since the blast.

Mahoney and I ran as fast as we could toward the house. He kept repeating 'fuck' over and over. There were no gunshots coming from inside.

I was suddenly afraid Farley wasn't even in the house. I prayed that Audrey Meek wasn't already dead in there. Everything was feeling so wrong to me. This wasn't how I would have done the raid. The FBI! I had always hated and distrusted these bastards, and now I was one of them.

Then I heard, '*Secure! Secure!*' And '*We have a suspect! We've got him! It's Farley. There's a woman here too!*'

What woman? Mahoney and I barged in through the side door. I saw thick smoke everywhere. The house reeked of the explosive, but also marijuana and greasy cooking smells. We made our way back to a bedroom off a small living room.

A naked man and a woman were spread-eagled on the bare wooden floor of the bedroom. The woman on the floor *wasn't* Audrey Meek. She was heavy, at least forty or fifty pounds overweight. Rafe Farley looked to be close to three hundred pounds, and had hideous clumps of red hair not only on his head but all over his body.

An old poster for the movie *Cool Hand Luke* was taped over a kingsize bed that had no sheets or covers. Nothing else caught my eye.

Farley was screaming at us, his face deeply crimson. 'I have rights! I have goddamn legal rights! You bastards are in real trouble.'

I had a feeling that he might be right, and that if this screaming man had kidnapped Mrs Meek – *she was already dead, and he knew he had nothing to worry about.*

'You're the one in trouble, fat boy!' an HRT agent barked in the suspect's face. 'You too, girlfriend!'

Could this possibly be the couple who had taken Audrey Meek and Elizabeth Connelly?

I didn't see how.

So who in hell were they?

Chapter Forty

Ned Mahoney and I were stuck in a close, dark, pigsty of a bedroom with the suspect, Rafe Farley. The woman, who assured us she *was* his girlfriend, had put on a filthy bathrobe and been taken into the kitchen to be grilled.

We were all angry about what had happened outside. Two agents had been wounded by a booby trap. Rafe Farley was the closest thing we had to a break in the case, or a suspect.

Things kept getting weirder. For starters, Farley *spit* at Mahoney and me until his mouth went dry. It was so strange and crazy that, at one point, Ned and I just looked at each other and started to laugh.

'Think this is fucking *funny*?' Farley rasped from the edge of the bed where he was lodged like a beached whale. We'd made him put on clothes, blue jeans and a work shirt, mostly because we couldn't stand the sight of his flaccid rolls of fat, tattoos of naked women, and a purple dragon that was eating a child.

'You're going down on kidnap and murder charges,' Mahoney snarled at him. 'You injured two of my men. One might lose an eye.'

'You had no right comin' in my house, middle of the night! I have *enemies*!' Farley yelled and spit at Mahoney again. 'You barge in here, 'cause I sell some weed? Or I screw a married broad who likes me more than she likes her old man?'

'Are you talking about Audrey Meek?' I asked.

Suddenly he went quiet. He stared at me, and his face and neck turned bright red. What was this? He wasn't a good actor, and he wasn't real smart either.

'What the hell're you talking about? You been smoking my shit?' Farley stammered. 'Audrey Meek? That chick they kidnapped?'

Mahoney leaned forward. 'Audrey Meek. We know you know all about her, Farley. Where is she?'

Farley's piggy eyes seemed to be getting smaller. 'How the hell would I know where she is?'

Mahoney kept at him. 'You ever been in a chat room called Favorite Things Four?'

Farley shook his head. 'Never heard of it.'

'We have you on tape, asshole,' Ned said. 'You got a lot of 'splaining to do, Lucy.'

Farley looked confused. 'Who the hell is *Lucy*? What are you *talking* about, man? You mean, like, *I Love Lucy*?'

Mahoney was good at keeping Farley off guard. I thought we were working okay together.

'You've got her in the woods somewhere in Jersey. We

have it on tape,' Mahoney yelled, then stamped his foot hard.

'Did you hurt her? Is she all right? Where is Audrey Meek?'

I picked up.

'Take us to her, Farley!'

'You're going back to prison. This time, you don't get out again,' I shouted in his face.

It was as if Farley were finally waking up. He squinted his eyes and stared hard at us. Lord, he smelled, especially now that he was scared.

'Wait a fucking minute. Now I get it. That Internet place? I was just showin' off.'

'What's that supposed to mean?'

Farley slumped down into himself as if we'd been beating him. 'Favorite Four is for freaks to talk. Everybody makes shit up, man.'

'But you *didn't* make up the stuff about Audrey Meek. You *know* things about her. You got it all right,' I said.

'The bitch turns me on. She's a fox. Hell, I collect catalogs from Meek, always have. All those skinny-ass models look like they need a good, *unh, unh, uh!*'

'You knew things about the abduction, Farley,' I said.

'I read the newspapers, watch CNN. Who doesn't? I told you, Audrey Meek turns me on. I *wish* I'd abducted her. You think I'd be sleeping with Cini if Audrey Meek was around here?'

I jabbed an index finger at Farley. 'You knew things that *weren't* in the newspapers.'

He shook his huge head from side to side. Then he said, 'Got a scanner. Listen in on police radios and such. Shit, I didn't kidnap Audrey Meek. I wouldn't have the balls. I wouldn't. I'm all talk, man.'

Mahoney cut in. 'You had the balls to rape Carly Hope,' he said.

Farley seemed to be shrinking inside himself again. 'Nah, nah. It's like I said in court. Carly was a girlfriend. I didn't rape her none. I don't have the balls. I didn't do nothing to Audrey Meek. I'm nobody. *I'm nothing.*'

Rafe Farley stared at us for a long moment. His eyes were bloodshot, everything about him was pathetic. I didn't want to, but I was starting to believe him. *I'm nobody. I'm nothing.* That was Rafe Farley, all right.

Chapter Forty-One

Sterling.
Mr Potter.
The Art Director.
Sphinx.
Marvel.
The Wolf.

The cover names sounded harmless, but the men behind them weren't. During one session, Potter had nicknamed the group Monsters Inc. as a joke, and that was an accurate description. They were monsters, all of them; they were freaks; they were deviates, and worse.

And then there was the Wolf, who was in a whole other class.

The meeting was on a secure website that was inaccessible to outsiders. All messages were encrypted and required a *pair* of keys: one key garbled the information; a second key was needed to recover it. More important, a hand scan was necessary to get on to the site. They were considering using a retinal scan, or possibly an anal probe.

The subject under discussion was the Couple, and what to do about them.

'What the hell does that mean – *what to do about them?*' asked the *Art Director*, who was jokingly called Mr Softee because he could get very emotional, the only one of them who ever did.

'It means just what it sounds like,' answered Sterling. 'There's been a serious breach of security. Now we have to decide what to do about it. There's been sloppiness, stupidity, and maybe worse than that. They were *seen*. It's put us all in danger.'

'What are our options?' the Art Director continued. 'I'm almost afraid to ask.'

Sterling responded instantly. 'Have you read the newspapers lately? Do you have a TV? A *team* of two took a woman in a mall in Atlanta, Georgia. They were spotted. A *team* of two abducted a woman in Pennsylvania – and they were seen. Our options? Do absolutely nothing – or do something extreme. An object lesson is needed – for the other teams.'

'So what are we doing about the problem?' asked Marvel, who was usually spookily quiet, but who could be nasty and dangerous when he was aroused.

'For one thing, I've shut down all deliveries for the moment,' said Sterling.

'Nobody told me about that!' Sphinx erupted. 'I'm expecting a delivery. As all of you know, I paid a price for it. Why wasn't I informed before now?'

No one said anything to Sphinx for several seconds. No

one liked him. Besides, each one of them was a sadist. They enjoyed torturing Sphinx, or anyone else in the group who showed weakness.

'I expect my delivery!' Sphinx insisted. 'I deserve it. You bastards! Fuck you all.' Then he went off-line. In a huff. Typical Sphinx. Laughable, really, except none of them was laughing right now.

'The Sphinxter has left the building,' Potter finally said.

Then Wolf took over. 'I think that's enough idle chat for tonight, enough fun and games. I'm concerned about the news stories. We need to deal with the *Couple* in some decisive manner that satisfies me. What I propose is that we have another team pay them a visit. Is there any disagreement?'

There was none, which wasn't unusual when the Wolf had the floor. They were afraid of him; all of them were petrified of the Russian.

'There is some good news, though,' Potter said then. 'This fuss and attention . . . it is exciting, isn't it? Gets the blood boiling. It's a hoot, right?'

The group shared a laugh. 'You're crazy, Potter. You're mad.'

'Don't you just love it?'

The well-protected chat room was not protected enough.

Suddenly the Wolf said, 'Don't say another word. Not a word! I think someone else is on with us. Wait. They're *off* now. Someone broke into the den, and now they're gone. Who could have gotten in here? Who let them in? Whoever it is, they're dead.'

Chapter Forty-Two

Lili Lynch was fourteen and a half years old, going on twenty-four, and she honestly believed she'd heard everything, until she hacked into the *Wolf's Den*.

The sick bastards in the well-protected-but-not protected-*enough* chat room were all older men, and they were gross and despicable. They liked to talk incessantly about women's private parts, and having *vile* sex with anyone and everything that moved – any age, any gender, human or animal. The men were beyond disgusting, and they made her want to puke. Only then it got a lot worse, and Lili wished she had never even heard of the *Wolf's Den*, never hacked into the highly protected chat room. *They might be murderers!*

And then the leader, Wolf, actually discovered Lili was on the site with them, listening to everything they'd said.

So now Lili knew about the murders, and the kidnappings, everything they fantasized about, and possibly did. *Only she didn't know if any of what she heard was real or not.*

Was it real? Or were they making it all up? Maybe they

were just nasty, sicko bullshitters. Lili almost didn't want to know the truth, and she didn't know what to do about the stuff she'd already overheard. She had hacked on to their site and that was illegal. If she went to the police, she'd be turning herself in. So she couldn't do that. Could she? Especially if the stuff on the site was just fantasies.

So she sat in her room and pondered the unthinkable. Then pondered it again. She felt so bad, so sick to her stomach, so sad, but she was also afraid.

They *knew* she'd hacked on to the Wolf's Den. But did they also know how to find her? If she was them, she'd know how. So were they already on their way to her house?

Lili knew she should go to the police. Maybe the FBI. But she couldn't bring herself to do it. She sat frozen. It was as if she were paralyzed.

When the doorbell rang she just about jumped out of her skin. *'Holy shit! Holy mother! It's them!'*

Lili took a deep breath, then she scurried downstairs to the front door. She looked through the peephole. She could hear her own heart thundering.

Domino's pizza! Jesus!

She'd forgotten all about it. It was a pizza delivery, not killers, at the front door, and suddenly Lili was giggling to herself. She wasn't going to die, after all.

She opened the front door.

Chapter Forty-Three

The Wolf had seldom been angrier and someone had to pay. The Russian had a longstanding hatred for New York City, and the smug and overrated metropolitan area. He found it filthy-dirty, foul beyond imagining, the people rude and uncivilized, even worse than in Moscow. But he had to be there today; it was where the Couple lived, and he had business with them. The Wolf also wanted to play some chess, one of his passions.

Long Island was the general address he had for Slava and Zoya.

Huntington was the specific one.

He arrived in the town just past three in the afternoon. Actually, he did remember the one other time he'd been here – two years after he had arrived in New York from Russia. Cousins of his owned the house and had helped set him up in America. He had committed four murders out here 'on the Island', as the locals called it. Well, at least Huntington was close to Kennedy Airport. He'd be out of New York as soon as possible.

The Couple lived in a typical suburban ranch house. The Wolf banged on the front door and a goateed bull of a man by the name of Lukanov opened it. Lukanov was part of another team, one that worked successfully in California, Oregon, and Washington State. Lukanov had once been a major in the KGB.

'Where are the stupid fucks?' the Wolf asked once he was inside the front door.

The bull Lukanov jerked a thumb toward a semi-darkened staircase behind him, and the Wolf trudged up. His right knee was aching today, and he remembered a time in the eighties when members of a rival gang had broken it. In Moscow that kind of thing was considered a warning. The Wolf wasn't much for warnings himself. He had found the three men who'd tried to cripple him, and broken every bone in their bodies – one by one. In Russia this gruesome practice was called *zamochit*, but the Wolf and other gangsters called it mushing.

He entered a small, sloppily kept bedroom and immediately saw Slava and Zoya, his ex-wife's cousins. The pair had grown up about thirty miles from Moscow. They had been in the army until the summer of '98, then they emigrated to America. They'd been working for him for less than eight months, so he was just getting to know them.

'You live in a garbage dump,' he said. 'I know you have plenty of money. What do you do with it?'

'We have family at home,' said Zoya. 'Your relatives are there too.'

The Wolf tilted his head. 'Awhh, so touching. I had no

idea you had such a big heart of gold, Zoya.' He motioned for the Bull to leave, and said, 'Shut the door. I'll be down when I'm finished in here. It might be a while.'

The Couple were tied up together on the floor. Both were in their underwear. Slava had on shorts patterned with little ducks. Zoya wore a black bra with a matching bikini thong.

The Wolf finally smiled. 'What am I going to do with you two, huh?'

Then Slava began to laugh out loud, a nervous, high-pitched cackling. He had thought they were going to be killed, but this would just be a warning. He could see this in the Wolf's eyes.

'So what happened? Tell me quickly. You knew the rules of the game,' he said.

'Maybe it was getting too easy. We wanted a little more of a challenge. It's our mistake, Pasha. We got sloppy.'

'Never lie to me,' the Wolf said. 'I have my sources. They are everywhere!'

He sat on the arm of an easy chair that looked as if it had been in this hideously ugly bedroom for a hundred years. Dust puffed from the old chair as it took his weight.

'You like him?' he asked Zoya. 'My ex-wife's cousin?'

'I love him,' she said, and her brown eyes went soft. 'Always. Since we were thirteen years old. Forever, I loved him.'

'Slava, Slava,' the Wolf said and walked over to the muscular man on the floor. He bent to give Slava a hug. 'You are my ex-wife's blood relative. And you betrayed me. You sold me out to my enemies, didn't you? Sure you did. How much did you get? A lot, I hope.'

Then he twisted Slava's head as if he were opening a big jar of pickles. Slava's neck *snapped*, a sound that the Wolf had come to love over the years. His trademark in the Red Mafiya.

Zoya's eyes widened to about twice their normal size. But she didn't make a sound, and because of that the Wolf understood what tough customers she and Slava really were, how dangerous they had been to the safety of the organization. 'I'm impressed, Zoya,' he said. 'Let's talk some.'

He stared into those amazing eyes of hers. 'Listen, I'm going to get the two of us some real vodka, Russian vodka. Then I want to hear your war stories,' he said. 'I want to hear what you've done with your life, Zoya. You have me curious now. Most of all, I want to play chess, Zoya. Nobody in America knows how to play chess. One game, then you go to heaven with your beloved Slava. But first vodka and chess, and, of course, I fuck you!'

Chapter Forty-Four

O n account of secrets that Zoya had told him under significant duress, the Wolf had to make one more stop in New York. *Unfortunate.* This meant that he wouldn't be able to catch his flight home out of Kennedy, and he would miss the professional hockey game that night. Regretful, but he knew this was the right thing to do. The betrayal by Slava and Zoya had jeopardized his life, and also made him look bad.

At a little past eleven, he entered a club called the Passage in the Brighton Beach section of Brooklyn. The passage looked like a dump from the street, but inside it was beautiful, very ornate, almost as nice as the best places in Moscow.

He saw people he knew from the old days: Gosha Chernov, Lev Denisov, Yura Fomin and his mistress. Then he spotted his darling Yulya. His ex-wife was tall and slender, with large breasts he'd bought for her in Palm Beach, Florida. Yulya was still beautiful in the right light, not so much changed since Moscow, where she had been a dancer since she was fifteen.

She was sitting at the bar with Mikhail Biryukov, the latest king of Brighton Beach. They were directly in front of a mural of St Petersburg, which was very cinematic, thought the Wolf, a typical Hollywood visual cliché.

Yulya saw him coming, and she tapped Biryukov. The local *pakhan* turned and looked, and the Wolf *closed* on him fast. He slammed a black king down on the table. 'Checkmate,' he roared, then laughed and hugged Yulya.

'You're not even happy to see me?' he asked the couple. 'I should be hurt.'

Biryukov grunted. 'You are a mystery man. I thought you were in California.'

'Wrong again,' said the Wolf. 'By the way, Slava and Zoya say hello. I just saw them out on Long Island. They couldn't make the trip here tonight.'

Yulya shrugged – such a cool little bitch. 'They mean nothing to me,' she said. 'Distant cousins.'

'Or me either, Yulya. Only the police care about them now.'

Suddenly he grabbed Yulya by the throat and lifted her out of her bar seat with one arm. 'You told them to fuck me over, didn't you? You must have paid them a lot!' he screamed in her face. 'It was you. And *him!*'

With dazzling speed, the Wolf pulled an ice pick from his sleeve and stuck it into Biryukov's left eye. The gangster was blinded, and dead in an instant.

'No . . . Please.' Yulya struggled to get out a few words. 'You can't do this. Not even you!'

Then the Wolf addressed everyone in the nightclub. 'You are all witnesses, are you not? *What?* Nobody helps her? You're afraid of me? Good – you should be. Yulya tried to get revenge on me. She was always stupid as a cow. Biryukov – he was just a dumb, greedy bastard. *Ambitious!* The godfather of Brighton Beach! What is that? He wanted to be *me!*'

The Wolf lifted Yulya even higher in the air. Her long legs kicked violently and one of her red mules went flying, scooting under a nearby table. Nobody picked up the shoe. Not a person in the club moved to help her. Or to see if Mikhail Biryukov was still alive. Word had already circulated that the madman in the front of the passage was the Wolf.

'You are witnesses to what happens – if *anyone* ever crosses me. You are witnesses! So you've had a warning. Same as in Russia. Same as now in America.'

The Wolf took his left hand out of her hair and wrapped it around her throat. He twisted hard and Yulya's neck broke. *'You are witnesses!'* he screamed in Russian. 'I killed my ex-wife. And this rat Biryukov. You saw me do it! So go to hell.'

And then the Wolf stomped out of the nightclub. No one did a thing to stop him.

And no one talked to the New York police when they came.

Same as in Russia.
Same as now in America.

Chapter Forty-Five

B enjamin Coffey was being held in a dark root cellar under the barn where he'd been brought – *what was it now – three, maybe four days ago?* Benjamin couldn't remember exactly, couldn't keep track of the days.

The Providence College student had nearly lost his mind, until he made an amazing discovery in the solitary confinement of the cellar. He found God, or maybe *God found him*.

The first and most startling thing Benjamin felt was God's presence. God accepted him, and maybe it was time for him to accept God. He learned that God understood him. But why couldn't he understand the first thing about God? It didn't make sense to Benjamin, who'd attended Catholic schools from kindergarten up to his senior year at Providence, where he studied philosophy and also art history. Benjamin had come to another conclusion in the darkness of his 'prison cell' under the barn. He'd always thought that he was basically a good person, but now he knew that he wasn't; and it didn't have anything to do with his sexuality, as his hypocritical Church would have him think. The way he figured it, a bad person was someone who habitually caused harm to others. Benjamin was guilty of that by his treatment of his parents and siblings, his classmates, his lovers, even his so-called best friends. He was mean-spirited, always acted superior, and continually inflicted unnecessary pain. He had acted like this ever since he could remember. He was cruel, a snob, a martinet, a sadist, a complete piece of shit. He'd always justified his bad behavior, because other people had caused him so much pain.

So was that why things had turned out like this? Maybe. But what was truly astonishing to Benjamin was the realization that if he ever got out of this alive – he probably *wouldn't change*. In fact, he believed he would use this experience as an excuse to continue being a miserable bastard for the rest of his life. *Cold, cold, I'm so cold*, he thought. *But God loves me unconditionally. That never changes either*. Then Benjamin realized that he was incredibly confused, and crying, and had been for a long time, at least a day. He was shivering, babbling nonsense to himself, and he didn't know what he really thought about anything. Not anymore, he didn't.

His mind kept shifting back and forth. He did have good friends, *great* friends, and he'd been an okay son; so why were all these terrible thoughts shuttling through his head? Because he was in hell? Was that it? Hell was this foul-smelling, claustrophobic root cellar under a decaying barn somewhere in New England, probably New Hampshire or Vermont. Was that right?

Maybe he was supposed to repent and couldn't be set free until he did? Or maybe this was it – for eternity.

Suddenly he remembered something from Catholic grade school in Great Barrington, Rhode Island. A parish priest had tried to explain an eternity in hell to Benjamin's sixth-grade class. 'Look across the river at that mountain,' the priest had said. 'Now imagine that every thousand years the tiniest sparrow transports what it can carry *in its beak* across the river from the mountain. When that tiny sparrow has transported the entire mountain to this side of the river, that, boys and girls, would just be the *beginning* of eternity.' But Benjamin didn't really believe the priest's little fable, did he? Fire and brimstone forever? Somebody would find him soon. Somebody would guide him out.

Unfortunately, he didn't completely believe that either. How could anyone find him here? They wouldn't. God, the police had lucked out finding the Washington sniper, and Malvo and his uncle weren't very smart. Mr Potter was.

He had to stop crying soon because Potter was angry with him already. He'd threatened to kill him if he didn't stop, and, *oh God, that was why he was crying so hard now*. He didn't want to die, not when he was just twenty-one and had his whole life ahead of him.

An hour later? Two hours? Three? He heard a loud noise above him, and began to cry again. Now Benjamin couldn't stop sobbing, shaking all over. He was sniveling too. He'd sniffed and sniveled since pre-school. *Stop sniveling, Benjamin. Stop it! Stop it!* But he couldn't stop.

Then the trapdoor opened! Someone was coming down.

Stop the crying, stop the crying, stop it! Stop it this instant! Potter will kill you.

Then the most unbelievable thing happened, a turn of events that Benjamin would never have expected.

He heard a deep voice – not *Potter*'s.

'Benjamin Coffey? Benjamin? This is the FBI. Mr Coffey, are you down there? This is the FBI.'

He was shaking worse now, and sobbing so hard he thought he might choke behind the gag. Because of the gag, he *couldn't* call out, couldn't let the FBI somehow know that he was down here.

The FBI found me! It's a miracle. I have to signal them. But how? Don't leave! I'm down here! I'm right here!

A flashlight illuminated his face.

He could see a person behind the light. A silhouette. Then the full face peered out of the shadows.

Mr Potter was frowning down at him from the trapdoor. Then he stuck out his tongue. 'I told you what was going to happen. Didn't I tell you, Benjamin? You did this to yourself. And you're so *beautiful*. God, you're perfect in every other way.'

His tormentor came down the stairs. He saw a battered sledgehammer in Potter's hand. A heavy farm tool. Waves of fear washed over Benjamin. 'I'm a lot stronger than I look,' Potter said. 'And you've been a very bad boy.'

Chapter Forty-Six

M r Potter's real name was Homer O. Taylor, and he was an assistant professor in the English department at Dartmouth. Brilliant to be sure, but still an assistant, a *nobody*. His office was a small but cozy one in the turret at the northwest corner of the Liberal Arts building. He called it his 'garret', the place where a nobody would labor in lonely solitude.

He had been up there most of the afternoon with the door locked, and he was fidgeting. He was also grieving for *his beautiful dead boy, his latest tragic love – his third!*

Part of Homer Taylor wanted to hurry back to the barn at the farm in Webster to be with Benjamin, just to watch over the body for a few more hours. His Toyota 4-Runner was parked outside, and he could be there in forty-five minutes if he pushed it. *Benjamin, dear boy*, why couldn't you have been good? Why did you bring out the worst in me, when there was so much to love?

Benjamin had been such a beauty, and the loss that Taylor felt now was horrifying. And not only the physical and emotional drain – there was the great financial loss. Five years ago, he'd inherited a little over two million dollars. It was going too fast. Much too fast. He couldn't afford to play like this – but how could he ever stop now?

He wanted another boy already. He needed to be loved. And to love someone. Another Benjamin, only not an emotional wreck as the poor boy had been.

So he stayed in his office for the entire day to avoid an excruciating hour-long tutorial at four o'clock. He pretended to be marking term papers for his Wednesday classes, in case someone knocked, but he never looked at a single page.

Instead, he obsessed.

He finally contacted Sterling around seven o'clock. 'I want to make another purchase,' he said.

Chapter Forty-Seven

I visited Sampson and Billie one night and had a great time with them, talking about babies and scaring big, bad John Sampson as much as I could. I tried to talk to Jamilla at least once a day. But White Girl was starting to heat up, and I knew what that meant. I was probably about to get lost in the case.

A married couple, Slava Vasilev and Zoya Petrov, had been found murdered in the house they rented on Long Island. We had learned that the husband and wife had come to the United States two years before. They were suspected of bringing Russian and other Eastern European women here for the purpose of prostitution, but also to bear children who would be sold to affluent couples.

Agents from our New York office were all over the murder scene on Long Island. Photographs of the two victims had been shown to the high school students who'd seen the Connelly abduction, as well as to Audrey Meek's children, and eyewitnesses at The Halyard in Newport, Rhode Island. Several of them identified the couple as the kidnappers. I wondered why the bodies had been left there? As examples? For whom?

Monnie Donnelley and I regularly met at seven before I had to attend orientation classes for the day. We were still analyzing the Long Island murders. Monnie was pulling together everything she could find on the husband and wife, as well as other Russian criminals working in the US, the so-called *Red Mafiya*. She was hot-wired into the Organized Crime Section over at the Hoover Building, and also the Red Mafiya squad in the Bureau's New York office.

'I brought "everything" bagels from D.C.,' I said as I entered her cube at ten minutes past seven that morning. 'Best in the city. According to Zagat anyway. You don't seem too excited.'

'You're late,' Monnie said without looking up from her computer screen. She'd mastered the droll, deadpan-delivery style favored by hackers.

'These bagels are worth it,' I said. 'Trust me.'

'I don't trust anybody,' Monnie replied.

She finally glanced up at me and smiled. Nice smile, worth the wait. 'You know that I'm kidding, right? It's just a tough-girl act, Alex. Give with the bagels.'

I laughed. 'I'm used to cop humor.'

'Oh, I'm *honored*,' she muttered, deadpan again, as she looked back at the glowing computer screen. 'He thinks I'm a cop, not just a desk jockey. You know, they started me in *fingerprinting*. The absolute bottom.'

I liked Monnie, but I had the sense that she needed a lot of support. I knew she'd been divorced for about two years.

She'd majored in Criminology at Maryland, where she had also pursued another interesting passion – studio arts. Monnie still took classes in drawing and painting, and, of course, there was the mural in her cube.

She yawned. 'Sorry. I watched *Alias* with the boys last night. That will be grandma's problem when she has to get them up this morning.'

Monnie's home life was another thing we had in common. She was a single parent, with two young kids, and a doting grandmother who lived less than a block away. The grandmother was her ex-husband's mother, which told the story of the marriage. Jack Donnelley had played basketball at Maryland, where he and Monnie met. He was a big drinker in college, and it got worse once he graduated. Monnie said he'd never recovered from being all-everything in a Pennsylvania high school, and then just another guard for the Maryland Terrapins. Monnie was five foot even, and joked that she hadn't played any kind of ball at Maryland. She told me her nickname in high school was Spaz.

'I've been reading all about women being traded and sold from Tokyo to Riyadh,' she said as she chewed a bagel. 'Breaks my heart and it pisses me off. Alex, we're talking some of the worst slavery in history. What's *with* you men?'

I looked at her. 'I don't buy and sell women, Monnie. Neither do any of my friends.'

'Sorry. I'm carrying around a little extra baggage because of Jack the Rat and a few other husbands I know.' She looked down at her computer screen. 'Here's a choice quote for today. Know what the Thai Premier said about the thousands of women from his country sold into prostitution? *"Thai girls are just so pretty."* And here's the Premier on ten-year-old girls being sold. *"Come on, don't you like young girls, too?"* I swear to God, he said that.'

I sat down next to Monnie and peered at her computer screen. 'So now somebody's opened a lucrative market for suburban white women. Who? And where are they working out of? Europe? Asia? The US?'

'The murdered couple could be a break for us. *Russians*. What do you think?' she asked.

'Could be a ring operating out of New York. Brighton Beach. Or maybe they're headquartered in Europe? The Russian mob is set up just about everywhere these days. It's not "The Russians are Coming" anymore. They're here.'

'I kind of like the Russians for this,' Monnie went on. Then she started to spit out information. 'The Solntsevo gang is the largest crime syndicate in the world right now. Did you know that? They're big here too. Both coasts. The Mafia has basically collapsed in their country. They smuggled close to a hundred billion out of Russia and a lot of it came here. You know, we've got major task forces working in L.A., San Francisco, Chicago, New York, D.C., Miami. The Reds *bought* banks in the Caribbean and Cyprus. Believe it or not, they've taken over prostitution, gambling, money laundering in Israel. In Israel!'

I finally got a few words in. 'I spent a couple of hours last night reading the files from Anti-Slavery International. The Red Mafiya comes up there too.'

'I'll tell you one other thing.' She looked at me. 'That kid who was grabbed in Newport. I *know* it's a different pattern, I get it, but I do believe he's part of this. What do you think?'

I nodded. So did I. And I also thought that Monnie had great street smarts for somebody who rarely left the office. So far, she was the best person I'd met at the Bureau, and here we were in her tiny cube trying to solve *White Girl*.

Chapter Forty-Eight

I had never really stopped being a student since my days at Johns Hopkins, and it had served me well in the Washington P.D., even given me a certain mystique. Hopefully, it would be the same in the Bureau, though it hadn't been so far. I set myself up with a supply of black coffee and started in on the Russian mob research. I needed to know everything about them, and Monnie Donnelley was a willing accomplice.

I made notes along the way, though I usually remember most of what is important enough and don't need to write it down. According to the FBI files, the Russian mob was now more diverse and powerful in America than La Cosa Nostra. Unlike the Italian Mafia, the Russians were organized in loose networks which cooperated, but weren't dependent on one another. At least not so far. A major benefit was that the loose style of organization avoided RICO Mafia prosecutions by the government. No conspiracies could be proved. There were two distinctly different types of Russian mobsters. The 'knuckle draggers' were into extortion, prostitution and racketeering, and their particular crime group was called the *Solntsevo*. The second type of Russian mobster operated at a more sophisticated level – often securities fraud and money laundering. These were the neocapitalist criminals, called the *Izmailovo*.

For the moment, I decided to concentrate on the first group, the low-lifes, especially the brigades involved with prostitution. According to the Bureau's Organized Crime Section report, the prostitute business operated 'a lot like major-league baseball'. A group of prostitutes could actually be 'traded' from an owner in one city to one in another. As a footnote, a survey conducted among seventh-grade girls in Russia listed prostitution as among their top-five choices for when they grew up. Several historical anecdotes in the file had been inserted to represent the mob mentality: *smart and ruthless*. According to one story, Ivan the Terrible had commissioned St Basil's Cathedral to rival, even surpass, the great churches of Europe. He was pleased with the result, and invited the architect to the Kremlin. When the artist arrived, his blueprints were burned and his eyes poked out, thus ensuring that he could never create a finer cathedral for anyone else.

There were several more contemporary examples in the report, but that was how the Red Mafiya worked. It was what we were up against if the Russians were behind *White Girl*.

Chapter Forty-Nine

Something incredible was about to happen.

It was a gorgeous afternoon in eastern Pennsylvania, the leaves just beginning to turn bright shades of crimson and gold. The Art Director found himself lost in a storm of dazzling colors, and their reflections sliding back and forth across his windshield were mesmerizing. *Am I doing the right thing now?* he had asked himself several times during the ride. He thought that he was.

'You have to admit that it's beautiful,' he said to the bound passenger in his Mercedes G Class SUV.

'It is,' said Audrey Meek. She was thinking that she'd believed she would never see the outdoors again, never smell fresh grass and flowers. So where was this madman taking her with her hands tied? They were driving *away* from his cabin. Going where? What did it mean?

She was terrified, but trying not to show it. *Small talk*, she told herself. *Keep him talking.*

'You like this G Class?' she asked, and immediately knew it was an insane question, just insane.

His tight smile, but especially his eyes, told her that he thought so too. And yet, he answered politely. 'I do, actually. At first I thought it was the final proof that rich people are incredibly stupid. I mean, it's kind of like putting a Mercedes logo on a wheelbarrow, and then paying triple for it. But I do like the oddness of the vehicle, the rigid lines of the design, the gizmos like lockable differentials. Of course, I'll have to get rid of this one now, won't I?'

Oh God, she was afraid to ask why, but maybe she knew already. She'd seen the car he drove. Maybe someone else had too. But she had also seen his face, so he wasn't really making sense. Or was he?

Suddenly Audrey found that she couldn't talk at all. No words would come out of her mouth, which was very dry. This self-professed nice guy, who said he wanted to be her friend but who had raped her half a dozen times, was going to kill her very soon. And then what? Bury her out here in the beautiful woods? Dump her body in a gorgeous lake with a heavy weight attached to it?

Tears formed in Audrey's eyes, and her brain buzzed as if there were a short in the circuit. She didn't want to die. Not now, not like this. She loved her children, her husband, Georges, and even her company. It had taken her so long, so much sacrifice and hard work, to get her life right. And now this had to happen, this fluke, this incredibly bad luck.

Suddenly the Art Director turned sharply on to a narrow dirt road, then sped down it much too fast. Where was he going? Why so fast? What was at the end of the road?

But apparently they weren't going all the way to the end! He was braking.

'My God, no!' Audrey screamed. 'No! Please! Don't!'

He stopped the car but let the engine run.

'Please,' she pleaded. 'Oh please . . . don't do this. Please, please, please. You don't have to kill me.'

The Art Director merely smiled. 'Give us a hug, Audrey. Then get out of the car before I change my mind. You're free. I'm not going to hurt you. You see, I love you too much.'

Chapter Fifty

There was a break in *White Girl*. One of the women had been found – alive.

I was rushed to Bucks County, Pennsylvania, in one of the two Bell helicopters kept at Quantico for emergencies. A few senior agents had told me that they'd never been up in one of the helicopters. It didn't sit too well with them. Now here I was becoming a regular during my orientation period. There were benefits to being on the Director's fast track.

The sleek black Bell set down in a small field in Norristown, Pennsylvania. During the flight I found myself thinking of a recent orientation class. We'd burned fingernail clippings so that everybody would know what a DOA smelled like. I already knew, and I didn't relish experiencing it again. I didn't think there would be any DOAs on this trip to Pennsylvania. Unfortunately, that turned out to be wrong.

Agents from the field office in Philadelphia were there to meet the helicopter and accompany me to where

Audrey Meek had been brought for questioning. So far there'd been no announcement to the press, though her husband had been notified and was on his way to Norristown.

'I'm not exactly sure where we are right now,' I said as we rode to a local state troopers' barracks. 'How far is this from where Mrs Meek was abducted?'

'We're five miles,' said one of the agents from Philly. 'It would take about ten minutes by car.'

'Was she held captive near this area?' I asked. 'Do we know yet? What exactly *do* we know?'

'She told the state police that the abductor brought her here early this morning. She's not sure of the directions but thinks they rode for well over an hour. Her wristwatch had been taken away from her. He kept some of her clothing too. Even a small bottle of perfume called *Meek One*.'

I nodded. 'Was she blindfolded during the ride? I assume that she was.'

'No. That's odd, isn't it? She saw her captor several times. Also his vehicle. He didn't seem to care one way or the other.'

That was a genuine surprise to me. It didn't track, and I said so.

'Stump the stars,' said the agent. 'Isn't that what this case is about so far?'

The state trooper barracks occupied a redbrick building tucked back from the highway. There wasn't any activity outside, and I took that as a good sign. At least I had beaten the press there. No one had leaked the story so far.

I hurried inside the barracks to meet Audrey Meek. I was eager to find out how she had survived against all odds, the first woman who had.

Chapter Fifty-One

My very first impression was that Audrey Meek didn't look at all like herself, not as she did in any of her publicity. Not now anyway, not after her terrible ordeal. Mrs Meek was thinner, especially in the face. Her eyes were dark blue, but the sockets appeared hollowed-out. She had some color on both cheeks.

'I'm FBI Agent Alex Cross. It's good to see you safe,' I said in a quiet voice. I didn't want to interview her right now, but it had to be done.

Audrey Meek nodded and her eyes met mine. I had the sense that she knew how lucky she was.

'You have some color in your cheeks. Did you get that today?' I asked her. 'While you were in the woods?'

'I don't know for sure, but I don't think so. He took me outside for walks every day he held me captive. Considering the circumstances, he was often considerate. He made my meals, good ones for the most part. He told me he'd been a chef at one time in Richmond. We had long talks almost every day, really long talks. It was so strange, everything about it. There was one day in the middle when he wasn't at the house at all. I was petrified he'd left me there to die in the woods. But I didn't really believe he would.'

I didn't interrupt her. I wanted to let Audrey Meek tell her story, without any pressure or steering from me. It was astonishing to me that she had been released. It didn't happen very often in cases like this one.

'Georges? My children?' she asked. 'Have they arrived yet? Will you let me see them if they're here?'

'They're on their way,' I said. 'We'll bring them in as soon as they arrive. I'd like to ask a few questions while everything is still fresh in your mind. I'm sorry about this. There may be other missing people, Mrs Meek. We think that there are.'

'Oh God,' she whispered. 'Let me try to help then. If I can, I will. Ask your questions.'

She was a brave woman and she told me about the kidnapping, including a description of the man and woman who had grabbed her. It fit the late Slava Vasilev and Zoya Petrov. Then Audrey Meek took me through the ritual of the days that she was held captive by the man who called himself the Art Director.

'He said he liked to wait on me, that he enjoyed it immensely. It was as if he was used to being subservient. But I sensed he also wanted to be my friend. It was so terribly weird. He'd seen me on TV and read articles about Meek, my company. He said he admired my sense of style and the way I didn't seem to have too many airs about myself. He made me have sex with him.' Audrey Meek was holding herself together so well. Her strength amazed me, and I wondered if that was what her captor had admired.

'Can I get you water? Anything?' I asked.

She shook her head. 'I saw his face,' she said. 'I even tried to draw it for the police. I think it's a good likeness. It's him.'

This was getting stranger by the moment. Why would the Art Director let her see him, then release her? I'd never known anything like it, not in any other kidnapping case.

Audrey Meek sighed, and nervously clasped and unclasped her hands as she continued.

'He admitted that he was obsessive-compulsive. About cleanliness, art, style, about loving another human being. He confessed several times that he adored me. He was often derogatory about himself. Did I tell you about the house?' she asked. 'I'm not sure what I said here – or to the officers who found me.'

'You didn't talk about the house yet,' I said.

'It was covered with some material, like a heavy-duty cellophane. It reminded me of event art. Like Christo. There were dozens of paintings inside. Very good ones. You ought to be able to find a house covered in cellophane.'

'We'll find it,' I agreed. 'We're looking now.'

The door to the room where we were talking opened a crack. A trooper in a brimmed hat peeked in, then he opened the door wide and Audrey Meek's husband, Georges, and her two children burst inside. It was such an unbelievably rare moment in abduction cases, especially one in which someone has been missing for nearly a week.

The Meek children looked afraid at first. Their father gently urged them forward and unbelievable joy took over. Their faces were wreathed in smiles and tears, and there was an incredible group hug that seemed to last for ever.

'Mommy, Mommy, *Mommy*!' the smaller child shrieked and clung to her mother as if she'd never let go of her again.

My eyes filled, and then I went to the worktable. Audrey Meek had made two drawings. I looked at the face of the man who had held her captive for a week. He looked very ordinary, like anybody you'd meet on the street.

The Art Director.

Why did you let her go? I wondered.

Chapter Fifty-Two

We got another possible break around midnight. The police had information about a house covered with a plastic material in Ottsville, Pennsylvania. Ottsville was about sixty-five miles away, and we drove there in several cars in the middle of the night. It was tough duty at the end of a long day, but nobody was complaining too much.

Ottsville was about seven miles from Erwinna, Pennsylvania, where a covered bridge crossed the Delaware River to New Jersey. Unfortunately, the ride from the bridge was on narrow, winding roads and took over twenty minutes.

When we arrived, the scene reminded me of my past life in D.C. – officers used to wait for me there too. Three sedans and a couple of black vans were parked along the heavily wooded country road around a bend from a dirt lane that led to the house. Ned Mahoney and I met up with the local sheriff, Eddie Lyle.

'Lights are all out in the house,' Mahoney sniffed as we approached what was actually a renovated log cabin. The only access to the secluded property was the dirt road. His HRT teams were waiting on his command to 'go'.

'It's nearly two,' I said. 'He might be waiting on us, though. I think there's something desperate about this guy.'

'Why's that?' Mahoney wanted to know. 'I need to hear.'

'He let her go. She saw his face, and the house, the car too. He must have known we'd find him here.'

'My people know what they're doing,' the sheriff interrupted, and sounded offended that he was being ignored. I didn't much care what he thought – I had seen a local, inexperienced rookie cop blown away in Virginia one time. '*I* know what I'm doing too,' the sheriff added.

I stopped talking to Mahoney and stared at Lyle. 'Hold it right there. We don't know what's waiting for us inside the house, but we do know this – he knew we'd find this place and come for him. Now you tell your men to stand down. FBI HRT goes in first! You're backup for us. *Do you have a problem with that?*'

The sheriff's face reddened and he thrust out his chin. 'I sure as hell do, but it doesn't mean fuck-all, does it?'

'No, it doesn't matter at all. So tell your men to stand down. You stand down too. I don't care how good you think you are.'

I started walking forward again with Mahoney, who was grinning, and not trying to hide it. 'You're a hot ticket, man,' he said. A couple of his snipers had been watching the cabin from less than fifty yards away. I could see that it had a gabled roof with a dormer on the loft level. Everything was dark inside.

'This is HRT One. Anything going on in there, Kilvert?' Mahoney spoke into his mike to one of the snipers.

'Not that I can see, sir. What's the take on the UNSUB?' Mahoney looked at me.

My eyes moved slowly across the cabin, and the front and side yards. Everything looked neat, well-maintained, and seemed to be in good repair. Power lines led to the roof.

'He *wanted* us to come here, Ned. That can't be good.'

'Booby trap?' he asked. 'That's how we plan to proceed.'

I nodded. 'That's how I would go. If we're wrong it'll give the locals some yuks!'

'Fuck the local yokels,' said Mahoney.

'I agree with that. Now that I'm not a local anymore.'

'Hotel and Charlie teams, this is HRT One,' Mahoney spoke into his mike. 'This is control. On the ready. Five, four, three, two, one, *go!*'

Two HRT teams of seven rose up from 'phase line yellow,' which is the final position for cover and concealment. They passed 'phase line green' on the way to the house. After that there was no turning back.

HRT's motto for this kind of action is 'speed, surprise and violence of action'. They are very good at it, better than anything the Washington P.D. has to offer. Within a matter of seconds, the Hotel and Charlie teams were inside the cottage where Audrey Meek had been kept captive for over a week. Then Mahoney and I burst in through the back door and into the kitchen. I saw *stove, refrigerator, cabinets, table.*

No Art Director.

No resistance of any kind.

Not yet.

Mahoney and I moved ahead cautiously. The living-room area had a wood-burning stove, a striped, contemporary-style couch in beige and brown, several club chairs. A big chest covered by a dark green afghan. Everything was tasteful and organized.

No Art Director.

Canvases were everywhere. Most had been finished. Whoever had done the paintings was talented.

'Secure!' I heard. Then a shout – '*In here!*'

Mahoney and I raced down a long hallway. Two of his men were already inside what looked to be the master bedroom. There were more painted canvases, lots of them, fifty or more.

A nude body lay sprawled across the wooden floor. The look on the face was grotesque, tortured. The dead man's hands were tightly wrapped around his own throat – as if he were strangling himself.

It was the man Audrey Meek had drawn for us. He was dead, and his death had been horrible. Most likely poison of some kind.

Papers lay scattered on the bed. Alongside them, a fountain pen.

I bent and began to read one of several notes:

To whomever—

As you know by now, I am the one who held Audrey Meek captive. All I can say is that it is something I had to do. I believe I had no choice; no free will in the matter. I loved her since the first time I saw her at one of my exhibitions in Philadelphia. We talked that night, but of course she didn't remember me. No one ever does (until now anyway). What is the rationale behind an obsession? I have no idea, not a clue, even though I obsessed on Audrey for over seven years of my life. I had all the money I would ever need, and yet it meant nothing to me. Not until I got the opportunity to take what I really wanted, what I needed. How could I resist – no matter the price? A half-million dollars seemed like nothing to be with Audrey, even for these few days. Then a strange thing. Maybe a miracle. Once we spent time together, I found that I loved Audrey too much to keep her like this. I never harmed her. Not in my own mind anyway. If I hurt you, Audrey, I'm sorry. I loved you very much, this much.

One sentence kept repeating inside my head after I finished reading. *Not until I got the opportunity to take what I really wanted, what I needed.* How had that happened? Who was out there – fulfilling the fantasies of these madmen?

Who was behind this? It sure wasn't the Art Director.

PART THREE

WOLF TRACKS

Chapter Fifty-Three

I didn't get back to Washington until almost ten the following night, and I knew I was in trouble with Jannie, probably with everybody in the house except little Alex and the cat. I'd promised we would go to the pool at the Y and now it was too late to go anywhere except to sleep.

Nana was sitting over a cup of tea in the kitchen when I came in. She didn't even look up. I bypassed a lecture and headed upstairs in the hopes that Jannie might still be awake.

She was. My best little girl was sitting on her bed surrounded by several magazines, including *American Girl*. Her old favorite bear, Theo, was propped in her lap. Jannie had gone to sleep with Theo since she was less than a year old, when her mother was still alive.

In one corner of the room Rosie the cat was curled up on a pile of Jannie's laundry. One of Nana's jobs for her and Damon was that they start doing their own laundry.

I had a thought about Maria now. My wife was kind and courageous, a special woman who'd been shot in a mysterious drive-by incident in Southeast that I'd never been able to solve. I never closed the file. Maybe something would turn up. It's been known to happen. I still missed her almost every day. Sometimes I even say a little prayer. *I hope you forgive me, Maria. I'm doing the best I can. It just doesn't seem good enough sometimes, good enough to me anyway. We love you dearly.*

Jannie must have sensed I was there, watching her, talking to her mother. 'I thought it was you,' she said.

'Why is that?' I asked.

She shrugged. 'I just did. My sixth sense is working pretty good lately.'

'Were you waiting up for me?' I asked as I slipped into her room. It had been our one guest bedroom, but last year we had converted it to Jannie's. I had built the shelving for the clay menagerie from her 'Sojourner Truth period': the stegosaurus, a whale, black squirrel, a panhandler, a witch tied to a stake, as well as dozens of her favorite books.

'I wasn't waiting up, no. I didn't expect you home at all.'

I sat down on the edge of the bed. Framed over it was a copy of a Magritte painting of a pipe with the caption: *This is not a pipe.* 'You're going to torture me some, huh?' I said.

'Of course. Goes without saying. I looked forward to some pool-time all day.'

'Fair enough.' I put my hand on top of hers. 'I'm sorry. I'm really sorry, Jannie.'

'I know. You don't have to say that, actually. You don't have to be sorry. Really you don't. I understand what you do is important. I get it. Even Damon does.'

I squeezed my girl's hands in mine. She was so much like Maria. 'Thank you, sweetie. I needed that tonight.'

'I know,' she whispered. 'I could tell.'

Chapter Fifty-Four

The Wolf was in Washington, D.C. on a business trip that night. He had a late dinner at the Ruth's Chris Steak House on Connecticut Avenue near Dupont Circle.

Joining him was Franco Grimaldi, a stocky, thirty-eight-year-old Italian capo from New York. They talked about a promising scheme to build Tahoe into a gambling mecca that would rival Vegas and Atlantic City; they also talked about pro hockey, the latest Vin Diesel movie, and a plan the Wolf had to make a billion dollars on a single job. Then the Wolf said he had to leave. He had another meeting in Washington. Business rather than pleasure.

'You seeing the President?' Grimaldi asked.

The Russian laughed. 'No. He can't get anything done. He's all *stronzate*. Why should I see him? He should see *me* about Bin Laden and the terrorists. I get things done.'

'Tell me something,' Grimaldi asked, before the Wolf left. 'The story about Palumbo out in the max-security prison in Colorado. You did that?'

The Wolf shook his head. 'A complete fairy tale. I am a

businessman, not a low-life, not some butcher. Don't believe everything you hear about me.'

The Mafia head watched the unpredictable Russian leave the steak house, and he was almost certain the man had killed Palumbo, and also that the President ought to contact the Wolf about Al Qaeda.

Around midnight, the Wolf got out of a black Dodge Viper in Potomac Park. He could see the outline of an SUV across Ohio Drive. The roof light blinked on and a single passenger got out. *Come to me, pigeon,* he whispered.

The man who approached him in Potomac Park was FBI and worked in the Hoover Building. His carriage was stiff and herky-jerky like that of so many government function-aries. There was no confident G-man swagger. The Wolf had been warned that he couldn't buy a useful agent, and then he couldn't trust the information if he did. But he hadn't believed that. Money always bought things, and it always bought people – especially if they had been passed over for promotions and raises; this was as true in America as it had been in Russia. If anything, it was more true here where cynicism and bitterness were becoming the national pastimes.

'So is anybody talking about me up on the fifth floor of the Hoover?' he asked.

'I don't want to meet like this. Next time, you run an ad in the *Washington Times*.'

The Wolf smiled, but then he jabbed a finger into the federal agent's jaw. 'I asked you a question. Is anybody talking about me?'

The agent shook his head. 'Not yet, but they will. They've connected the murdered couple on Long Island to Atlanta, and to the King of Prussia Mall.'

The Wolf nodded. 'Of course they have. I understand that these people of yours aren't stupid. They're just very limited.'

'Don't underestimate them,' the agent warned. 'The Bureau is changing. They're going to come after you with everything they have.'

'It won't be enough,' said the Wolf. 'And besides, maybe I'll come after them – with everything I have. I'll huff, and I'll puff, and I'll blow their house down.'

Chapter Fifty-Five

The next night I got home before six o'clock. I had a sit-down dinner with Nana and the kids, who were surprised, but clearly thrilled that I was home so early.

The telephone rang toward the end of the meal. I didn't want to answer it. Maybe somebody else had been grabbed, but I didn't want to deal with it. Not tonight.

'I'll get it,' said Damon. 'It's probably for me. Some *girlfriend*.' He snatched the ringing telephone off the kitchen wall, flipped it from one hand to the other.

'You *wish* it was a girl,' taunted Jannie from the table. 'Dinnertime. It's probably somebody selling insurance or a bank loan. They always call at dinner.'

Then Damon was pointing at me, and he wasn't smiling. He didn't look so good either, as if he'd suddenly gotten a little sick to his stomach. '*Dad*,' he said in a low voice, 'it's for you.'

I got up from the table and took the phone from him.

'You okay?' I asked.

'*It's Mrs Johnson*,' Damon whispered.

My throat felt constricted as I took the receiver. Now I was the one who felt a little sick, but also confused. 'Hello? This is Alex,' I said.

'It's Christine, Alex. I'm in Washington. For a few days. I'd like to see little Alex while I'm here,' she said, and I almost felt it was a prepared speech.

I felt my face flush. *Why are you calling here? Why now?* I wanted to say, but didn't. 'Do you want to come over tonight? It's a little late, but we could keep him up.'

She hesitated. 'Actually, I was thinking about tomorrow. Maybe around eight-thirty, quarter to nine in the morning? Would that be all right?'

I hesitated, then I said, 'That would be fine, Christine. I'll be here.'

'Oh,' she said, then fumbled her words a little. 'You don't have to stay home for me. I heard you were working for the FBI.'

My stomach clenched. Christine Johnson and I had split up over a year ago, mainly because of the nature of the murder cases I worked. She had actually been abducted because of my work. We finally found her in a shack in a remote area of Jamaica. Alex was born there. We were never the same after that. I never knew Christine was pregnant at the time. I felt it was my fault. Several months ago she'd moved to Seattle. It had been Christine's idea that Alex stay with me. She'd been seeing a psychiatrist, and said she wasn't emotionally fit to be his mother. Now she was in D.C. *'for a few days'.*

'What brings you back to Washington?' I finally asked.

'I wanted to see our son,' she said, her voice going very soft. 'And some other friends of mine.' I remembered how much I had loved her, and probably still did on some level, but I was resigned to the fact that we wouldn't be together. Christine couldn't stand my life as a cop; and I couldn't seem to give it up.

'All right, well, I'll be over at around eight-thirty tomorrow,' she said.

'I'll be here,' I said.

Chapter Fifty-Six

E ight-thirty on the button.

A shiny silver Taurus, a rental car from Hertz, pulled up in front of our house on Fifth Street.

Christine Johnson got out, and though she looked a little severe with her hair pulled back in a tight bun, I had to admit that she was still a beautiful woman. Tall and slender, with distinct, sculpted features that I couldn't make myself forget. Seeing her again made my heart catch in spite of what had happened between us.

Suddenly I was edgy, but also tired. Why was that? I wondered how much energy I'd lost in the past year and a half. A doctor friend from Johns Hopkins has a half-serious theory that our lifelines are written on the palms of our hands. He swears he can chart stress, illnesses, general health. I visited him a few weeks ago and Bernie Stringer said I was in excellent physical shape, but that my lifelines had taken a beating in the last year. That was partly because of Christine, our relationship, and the eventual break-up.

I was standing behind the protective screen of the front

door, with Alex in my arms. I stepped outside as Christine approached the house. I saw that she was wearing heels and a dark blue suit.

'Say hi,' I said to Alex and waved one of his arms at his mother.

It was so strange, so completely unnerving to see Christine like this again. We had such a complicated history. Much of it was good, but what was bad, was very bad. Her husband had been killed in her house during a case I was working on. I had nearly been responsible for her death. Now we were living thousands of miles apart. Why was she in D.C. again? To see little Alex of course. But what else had brought her?

'Hello, Alex,' she said and smiled, and for a dizzying instant, it was as if nothing had changed between us. I remembered the first time I had seen her, when she was still the principal at the Sojourner Truth School. She'd taken my breath away. Unfortunately, I guess, she still did.

Christine knelt at the foot of the stairs, and spread her arms. 'Hi, you handsome guy,' she said to little Alex.

I set him down and let him decide what to do next. He looked up at me, and laughed. Then he chose Christine's beckoning smile, chose her warmth and charm – and ran right into her arms.

'Hello, baby,' she whispered. 'I missed you so much. You've grown so big.'

Christine hadn't brought a gift, no bribes, and I liked that. It was just her, no tricks or gimmicks, but that was enough. In seconds, Alex was in her arms, laughing and talking up a storm. They looked good together, mother and son.

'I'll be inside,' I said after I watched them for a moment. 'Come in when you want. There's fresh coffee. Nana's. Breakfast if you haven't eaten.'

Christine looked up at me, and she smiled again. She looked so happy holding The Boy, our small son. 'We're fine for the moment,' she said. 'Thank you. I'll come in for coffee. Of course I will.' Of course. Christine had always been so sure about everything, and she hadn't lost any of her confidence.

I stepped back inside and nearly bumped into Nana, who was watching from just beyond the screen door.

'Oh, Alex,' she whispered, and didn't have to say any more than that. I felt as if a knife had been plunged into my heart. It was the first twist, and just the first of many. I shut the front door and left them to have their private time.

Christine brought little Alex inside after a while, and we all sat in the kitchen and drank coffee and she watched our son drinking his apple juice. She talked about her life out in Seattle; mostly about work at a school out there, nothing too personal or revealing. I knew she had to be nervous and stressed, but I never saw it.

And then Christine showed the kind of warmth that could melt a heart. She was looking at little Alex. 'What a sweetheart he is. What a sweet, darling little boy. Oh, Alex, my little Alex, how I missed you. You have no idea.'

Chapter Fifty-Seven

*C*hristine Johnson in D.C. again.

Why had she come back now? What did she want with us?

The questions throbbed in my head, but also deep inside my heart. They made me afraid, even before I had a clear idea what to fear. Of course, I had a suspicion – *Christine had changed her mind about little Alex.* That was it, had to be. Why else would she be here? She certainly hadn't come back to see me. Or had she?

I was still on I-95, but just minutes away from Quantico when Monnie Donnelley got through to me on my cell. Miles Davis played on the radio in the car. I'd been trying to chill before I got to work.

'You're late again,' she said, and though I knew it was a joke, it still cut me some.

'I know, I know. I was out partying last night. You know how it is.'

Monnie got right to it. 'Alex, did you know they grabbed a couple more suspects last night?'

Them again. I was so surprised that I didn't answer Monnie right away. I hadn't been told anything about a bust!

'I guess not,' Monnie answered her own question. 'It took place in Beaver Falls, Pennsylvania. Joe Nameth's old hometown? Two UNSUBS in their forties, ran an adult bookstore, sort of named after the town. The press got a hold of it a few minutes ago.'

'Did they find any of the missing women?' I asked Monnie.

'Don't think so. It's not in the news reports. Nobody seems to know for sure here.'

I didn't understand. 'Do you know how long they were under surveillance? Forget it, Monnie, I'm getting off 95 right now. I'm almost there. I'll see you in a couple of minutes.'

'Sorry to ruin your day so early,' she said.

'It was already ruined,' I muttered.

We worked straight through the day, but at seven, we still didn't have very good answers to several questions about the takedown in Pennsylvania. I knew a few things, mostly unimportant details, and it was frustrating. The two men had criminal records for selling pornography. Agents from the field office in Philly had gotten a tip that the two of them were involved in a kidnapping scheme. It was unclear *who* in the FBI's chain of command knew about the suspects, but there seemed to have been an internal communication breakdown of the sort I had been hearing about years before I arrived at Quantico.

I talked with Monnie a couple of times during the day, but my buddy Ned Mahoney never called me about the bust; Burns's office didn't try to contact me either. I was shook. For one thing, there were reporters out in the parking lot at Quantico. I could see a *USA Today* van and a CNN truck from my window. Very strange day. Odd and unsettling.

Late in the afternoon, I found myself thinking about Christine Johnson's visit to the house. I kept playing back the scene of her holding the baby, playing with Alex. I wondered if I could believe that she'd come to D.C. just to see him and a few of her old friends. It made my heart ache to think about losing 'the big boy', as I always called him. *The big boy!* What a joy he was to me, and the kids, and to Nana Mama. What an unbearable loss it would be. I just couldn't imagine it. Nor could I imagine being Christine, and not wanting him back.

Before I left for the night, I forced myself to pick up the phone and make a call that I was dreading. Judge Brendan Connelly answered after a few rings. Thinking about little Alex made me remember the promise I'd made.

'It's Alex Cross,' I said. 'Just wanted to check in with you. Tell you about the news stories you've been seeing today.'

Judge Connelly asked me if his wife had been found, if there was *any* news about Lizzie.

'They didn't find her yet. I don't think those two men were involved with your wife. We're still very hopeful that we'll find her.'

Abruptly he began to mutter words that I couldn't make

out. After listening to him for a few seconds, trying to make sense of it, I told him I'd keep him informed. If someone informed me.

After the difficult phone call, I just sat at my desk. Suddenly, I realized I'd forgotten something else – *my class had graduated today!* We were officially agents. The others in my class had gotten their credentials, or 'creds', as well as their assignments. Right now, cake and punch were being served in the lobby of the Hall of Honor. I didn't bother to go to the party. Somehow, it seemed inappropriate to attend. I went home instead.

Chapter Fifty-Eight

How much time did she have left now?

A day? Hours?

It almost didn't matter, did it? Lizzie Connelly was learning to accept life as it came; she was learning who she was – inside; and how to keep herself in balance.

Except, of course, when she was frightened out of her mind.

Lizzie called them her 'swimming dreams'. She had been an avid swimmer ever since she was four years old. The repetition of stroke after stroke, kick after kick, could always put her in another place and time, on autopilot, let her escape. So that was what she was doing now in the closet-room where she was being kept.

Swimming.

Escaping.

Reach, slightly cupped hand, S-figure with her arms, pull at the top, *grab* the water. Tip through to the belly button, then down through the bottom of her swimsuit. Swoosh, swoosh, kick, kick, feeling hot inside, but the water was cooling, refreshing, invigorating. Feeling empowered because she was feeling stronger.

She had been thinking about escape for much of the day, or what she thought of as a day anyway. Now she began to get serious about other things.

She reviewed what she knew about this place – the Closet – and the vicious, horrifying man who kept her. The Wolf. That was what the bastard called himself. *Why the Wolf?*

She was somewhere in a city. She was almost sure the city was in the south, and fairly large, lots of money in the surrounding area. Maybe it was Florida, but she didn't know why she thought that. Maybe she had overheard something and it only registered in her subconscious? She'd definitely heard voices in the house when there had been large parties or, occasionally, smaller get-togethers. She believed that her vermin captor lived alone. Who could possibly live with such a horrible monster? No woman could.

She knew some of his pathetic habits by heart. He usually turned on the TV when he came home: sometimes ESPN, but more often CNN. He watched the news constantly. He also liked detective shows such as *Law and Order*, *CSI*, *Murder/Homicide*. The TV was always on, late into the night.

He was physically large and strong, and he was a sadist – but also careful about not hurting her badly, not so far anyway. Which meant – what did it mean? – that he planned to keep her around for a while more?

If Lizzie Connelly could stand it here for another minute. If she didn't flip out and make him so angry that he'd snap her neck, as he'd threatened to several times a day. *'I'll snap your little neck. Like this! You don't believe me? You should believe me, Elizabeth.'* He always called her Elizabeth, not Lizzie. He told her that Lizzie wasn't a beautiful enough name for her. *'I'll break your fucking neck, Elizabeth!'*

He knew who she was and quite a bit about her, and also about Brendan, Brigid, Merry and Gwynnie. He promised that if she made him angry he'd not only hurt her, but he'd do the same to her family. 'I'll go back to Atlanta. I'll do it for kicks, just for fun. I live for that kind of thing. I could murder your whole family, Elizabeth.'

Ironically, he was desiring her more and more – she could certainly tell when a man got like that. So she *did* have some control over him, didn't she? *How about that. So fuck you too, buddy!*

Sometimes he would leave her binds slightly looser and even give her free time to walk around in the house. Tied up of course – on a kind of chain leash that he would hold in his hands. It was so demeaning. He told her that he knew she'd be thinking that he was getting kinder and gentler – but not to get any stupid ideas.

Well, what the hell else could she do *except* get ideas? There was nothing for her to do all day in the dark by herself. She was—

The closet door swung open violently! Then it slammed against the wall outside.

The Wolf screamed in Lizzie's face. 'You were *thinking*

about me, weren't you? You're starting to get *obsessive*, Elizabeth? I'm in your thoughts *all the time*.'

Damn it, he was right about that.

'You're even glad for the company. You miss me, don't you?'

But he had that wrong, dead wrong.

She hated the Wolf so much that Lizzie contemplated the unthinkable: she could kill him. Maybe that day would come.

Imagine that, she thought. *God, that is what I want to do – kill the Wolf myself. That would be the greatest escape of all.*

Chapter Fifty-Nine

That same night the Wolf had a meeting with two professional hockey players at Caesars in Atlantic City, New Jersey. The suite where he stayed had gold-foil wallpaper everywhere, windows facing the Atlantic, a hot tub in the living room. Out of respect for his guests, who were big stars, he wore an expensive, chalk-stripe Prada suit.

His contact happened to be a wealthy cable TV operator, who arrived at the Nero suite with the hockey players Alexei Dobrushkin and Ilia Teptev in tow. Both were members of the Philadelphia Flyers. They were top defensemen who were considered to be tough guys, because they were big men who moved quickly and could do a lot of damage. The Wolf didn't believe the hockey players were that tough, but he was a huge fan of the game.

'I love American-style hockey,' he said as he welcomed them with a broad smile and an extended hand.

Alexei and Ilia nodded his way, but neither of the hockey players shook his hand. The Wolf was offended, but he didn't reveal his feelings. He smiled some more and figured that the hockey players were too stupid to understand who he was. Too many wooden sticks to the skull.

'Drinks anyone?' he asked his guests. 'Stolichnaya? Whatever you like.'

'I'll pass,' said the cable operator, who seemed incredibly self-important, but a lot of Americans were that way.

'Nyet,' Ilia said with disinterest, as if his host were a hotel barman, or a waiter. The hockey player was twenty-two years old, born in Voskrensh, Russia. He was six foot five with close-cropped hair, stubble not quite amounting to a beard, a block of a head sitting on an enormous neck.

'I don't drink Stoly,' said Alexei, who, like Ilia, wore a black leather jacket with a dark turtleneck underneath. 'Maybe you have Absolut? Or some Bombay Gin?'

'Of course,' the Wolf nodded cordially. He walked to the suite's mirrored wet bar where he made the drinks, and decided what to do next. He was starting to enjoy this. It was different. No one here was afraid of him.

He plopped down on the pillowed couch between Ilia and Alexei. He looked back and forth into their faces, smiling broadly again. 'You've been away from Russia for a long time, no? Maybe too long,' he said. 'You drink Bombay Gin? You forget your manners?'

'We hear you're a real tough man,' said Alexei, who was in his early thirties and obviously lifted weights, a lot of weights, and often. He was around six feet, but over two hundred and twenty pounds.

'No. Not really,' said the Wolf. 'I am just another American businessman these days. Nothing very special.

Not tough anymore. So, I was wondering, do we have a deal for the game with Montreal?'

Alexei looked over at the cable guy. 'Tell him,' he said.

'Alexei and Ilia are looking for a little more action than what we originally talked about,' he said. 'You understand what I'm saying? *Action?*'

'Aahhh,' said the Wolf and grinned broadly. 'I love action,' he said to the businessman. 'I love *shalit* too. Means *mischief* in my country. *Shalit.*'

He was up off the couch faster than anyone would have thought possible. He'd pulled out a small lead pipe from beneath the couch cushion and cracked it across Alexei Dobrushkin's cheek. Then he swung it off the bridge of Ilia Teptev's nose. The two hockey stars were bleeding like pigs in seconds.

Then, and only then, did the Wolf take out his gun. He held it between the eyes of the cable operator. 'You know, they're not such tough guys as I thought. I can tell about these things in a few seconds,' he said. 'Now, down to business. One of the two big bears *will* allow a score by Montreal in the first period. The other will miss a play for a score in the second. Do you understand? The Flyers will lose the game in which they're favored. Understood?

'If, for any reason, this doesn't happen, then everybody dies. Now let yourselves out. I look forward to the game. As I said, I love American-style hockey.'

The Wolf began to laugh as the big hockey stars stumbled out of the Nero suite. 'Nice meeting you Ilia, Alexei,' he said as the door shut. 'Break a leg.'

Chapter Sixty

A huge task force meeting was held in the SIOC Suite on the fifth floor of the Hoover Building, which was considered sacred ground in the Bureau. SIOC is the Strategic Information Operations Center, and the central suite was where most of the really important powwows were held, from Waco to September 11.

I had been invited, and I wondered whom I had to thank for it. I arrived at around nine and had to be brought in by an agent who manned the front desk.

I saw that the SIOC Suite consisted of four rooms, three of which were filled with state-of-the-art workstations, probably for researchers and analysts. I was led into the last large conference room. The focal point was a long glass-and-metal table. On the walls were clocks set to different time zones, several maps, half a dozen TV monitors. A dozen or so agents were already inside the room, but it was quiet.

Stacy Pollack finally arrived and the outside doors were shut. The head of SIOC introduced the agents who were present, as well as two visitors from the CIA. Pollack had a reputation inside the Bureau for being a no-nonsense administrator who didn't suffer fools, and who got results. She was thirty-one years old, and Burns loved her.

The TV monitors on the wall told the latest story: live-action film was up and running on the major networks. *Beaver Falls, Pennsylvania,* said the super.

'That's old news. We have a new problem,' announced Pollack from the front of the room. 'We're not here because of the screw-up at Beaver Falls. This is *internal,* so it's worse. Folks, we think we've learned the name of the person responsible for the leaks out of Quantico.'

Then Pollack looked right at me. 'A reporter at the *Washington Post* denies it, but why wouldn't he? The leaks come from a Crime Analyst named Monnie Donnelley. You're working with her, aren't you, Dr Cross?'

Suddenly the SIOC Suite room seemed very small and constricting. Everyone had turned toward me.

'Is this why I'm here?' I asked.

'*No,*' said Pollack. 'You're here because you're experienced with sexual-obsession cases. You've been involved with more of them than anyone else in the room. But *that* wasn't my question.'

I thought carefully before I answered. 'This *isn't* a sexual-obsession case,' I told Pollack. 'And Monnie Donnelley *isn't* the leak.'

'I'd like you to explain *both* of those statements,' Pollack challenged me immediately. 'Please, go ahead. I'm listening with great interest.'

'I'll do my best,' I said. 'The abductors, the group or ring behind the kidnappings, are in this for the money. I don't see any other explanation for their actions. The slain Russian couple on Long Island are a key. I don't think we should be looking at past sex offenders as our focus. The question should be, who has the resources and expertise to abduct men and women for a price, and probably a very large price? Who has experience in this area? Monnie Donnelley knows that and she's an excellent analyst. She's not the leak to the *Post*. What would she have to gain?'

Stacy Pollack looked down and shuffled some of her papers. She didn't comment on anything I'd said. 'Let's move on,' she said.

The meeting resumed without any further discussion of Monnie and the charges against her. Instead, there was a lengthy discussion of the Red Mafiya, including new information that the couple murdered on Long Island definitely had connections to Russian gangsters. There were also rumors of a possible mob war about to break out on the East Coast, involving the Italians and Russians.

After the larger meeting, we broke off into smaller groups. A few agents took workstations. Stacy Pollack pulled me aside.

'Listen, I wasn't accusing you of anything,' she said. 'I wasn't suggesting that you're involved in the leaks, Alex.'

'So who accused Monnie?' I asked.

She seemed surprised by the question. 'I won't tell you that. Nothing is official yet.'

'What do you mean, "nothing is official yet"?' I asked.

'No action has been taken against Ms Donnelley. We will probably pull her off this investigation, though. That's all I have to say on the subject for now. You can go back to Quantico now.' I guess I'd been dismissed.

Chapter Sixty-One

I called Monnie as soon as I could, and told her what had happened.

She got furious – as she should. But then Monnie took hold of herself. 'All right, so now you know – I'm not as controlled as I look,' she said. 'Well, fuck them. I didn't leak anything to the Washington press, Alex. That's absurd. Who would I tell – our paperboy?'

'I know you didn't,' I said. 'Listen, I have to stop at Quantico, then how about I take you and your boys for a quick meal tonight. Cheap,' I added and she managed to sniffle out a laugh.

'All right. I know a place. It's called the Command Post Pub. We'll meet you. The boys like it there a lot. You'll see why.'

Monnie told me how to get to the pub, which was close to Quantico on Potomac Avenue. After I made a stop at my temporary office at Club Fed, I drove over to meet her and her two boys. Matt and Will were just eleven and twelve. They were big dogs, though, like their father. Both were already close to six feet.

'Mom says you're okay,' said Matt as he shook hands with me.

'She said the same about you and Will,' I told him. Everybody laughed at the table. Then we ordered guilty pleasures – burgers, chicken wings, cheese fries, which Monnie figured she deserved after her ordeal. Her sons were well mannered and easy to be with, and that told me a lot about Monnie.

The pub was an interesting choice. It was cluttered with Marine Corps memorabilia including officers' flags, photos, and a couple of tables with machine-gun rounds in them. Monnie said that Tom Clancy had mentioned the bar in *Patriot Games*, but in the novel he said there was a picture of George Patton on the wall, which upset everybody at the bar, especially since Clancy had made a career out of being in the know. The Command Post was a *Marines* bar, not Army.

When we were leaving, Monnie took me aside. A few Marines were going in and out. They gawked a little at us. 'Thank you, thank you, Alex. This means a lot to me,' she said. 'I know denials don't mean a damn thing, but I *did not* leak information to the *Washington Post*. Or to Rush Limbaugh. Or O'Reilly either. Or anyone fucking else. Never happened, never will. I'm true blue to the end, which apparently could be near.'

'That's what I told them at the Hoover Building,' I said. 'The true blue part.'

Monnie rose on her toes and kissed me on the cheek. 'I owe you big time, mister. You should also know, you're impressing the hell out of me. Even Matt and Will seemed neutral to positive, and you're one of the enemy to them – grown-ups.'

'Keep working the case,' I told her. 'You have exactly the right attitude.'

Monnie looked puzzled, but then she got it. 'Oh yeah, I do, don't I. *Fuck them*.'

'It's the Russians,' I said before I left her at the door of the Command Post. 'It has to be. We've got that much right.'

Chapter Sixty-Two

Two people very much in love. Often a beautiful thing to watch. But not in this case, not on this starry night in the hills of central Massachusetts.

The devoted lovers' names were Vince Petrillo and Francis Deegan, and they were juniors at Holy Cross College in Worcester, where they had been inseparable since their first week as freshmen. They'd met in the Mulledy Dorm on Easy Street and had rarely been apart since. They'd even worked at the same fish restaurant the past two summers in Provincetown. When they graduated, they planned to be married, then do the grand tour through Europe.

Holy Cross is a Jesuit school which, justly or unjustly, has some reputation for being homophobic. Offending students can be suspended or even expelled under the *Breach of Peace* rule, which forbids 'conduct which is lewd or indecent'. The Catholic Church does not actually condemn 'temptation' toward members of the same sex, but homosexual acts are often considered 'intrinsically perverted' and constitute a 'grave moral disorder'. Because the Jesuits could be hard on homosexual relationships, among the students anyway, Vince and Francis kept theirs as private and secret as they could. In recent months, though, they figured their relationship probably wasn't a very big deal, especially given the other scandals among the Catholic clergy.

The Campus Arboretum at Holy Cross had long been a hangout for students who wanted to be alone, and who sometimes had romantic intentions. The garden area boasted over a hundred different kinds of trees and shrubs, and overlooked downtown Worcester, 'Wormtown,' as it was sometimes called by students.

That night Vince and Francis, dressed in athletic shorts, T-shirts, and matching royal-purple-and-white baseball caps, strolled down Easy Street to a brick patio and lawn area known as Wheeler Beach. It was crowded, so they continued on to find a quiet spot in the Arboretum.

There they lay on a blanket under a nearly full moon and a sky studded with stars. They held hands and talked about the poetry of W.B. Yeats, whom Francis adored, and Vince, a pre-med student, tolerated as best he could. The two men were an unusual couple physically. Vince was just over five foot seven and weighed one-eighty. Most of it was solid, due to his obsessive weight-lifting at the gym, but it was obvious he had to work hard to keep the weight off. He had curly black hair that framed a soft, almost angelic face which wasn't too different from his baby pictures, one of which his lover carried in his wallet.

Francis could make either sex drool; and that was Vince's private joke when they were among co-eds, 'drool fools'.

Francis was six foot one, trim, without an ounce of fat. His white-blond hair was cut in the same style he had adopted as a sophomore at Christian Brothers Academy in New Jersey. He adored Vince with all his heart, and Vince worshipped him.

They came for Francis, of course.

He had been scouted, and purchased.

Chapter Sixty-Three

The three burly men were dressed in loose jeans, work boots and dark windbreakers. They were hoodlums. In Russian they were called *baklany*, or *bandity*. Scary demons wherever you met up with them; monsters from Moscow let loose in America by the Wolf.

They parked a black Pontiac Grand Prix on the street, then climbed the hill to the main campus at Holy Cross.

'Ебаные холмы, ненавижу!' *Fucking hills, I hate them.* One of them was short of breath and complained about the steepness of the hill.

'Заткнись, мудак!' *Quiet, asshole*, said group leader Maxin, who liked to call himself a personal friend of the Wolf's, though of course he wasn't. No *pakhan* had real friends, but especially not the Wolf. He only had enemies, and almost never met those who worked for him. Even in Russia, he had been known as an invisible or mystery man. But here in the US, it was even worse. Virtually no one knew him by sight.

The three thugs watched the college students on the

blanket as they held hands, then kissed and fondled.

'Kiss like girls,' said one of the Russian men with a nasty laugh.

'Not like any girls I ever kiss.'

The three of them laughed and shook their heads in disgust. Then the hulking leader of the team strode forward, moving very fast, given his weight and size. He silently pointed toward Francis, and the two other men pulled the boy away from Vince.

'Hey, what the hell is this?' Francis started to yell, but was stopped by a wide strip of insulating tape pressed over his mouth, cutting off all sound for help.

'Now you can scream,' said one of the smirking hoods. 'Scream like a girl. But nobody hears you anymore.'

They worked together quickly. While one thug wrapped more black tape around Francis's ankles, the other bound his wrists tightly behind his back. Then he was stuffed inside a large duffel bag, the sort used to carry athletic equipment such as baseball bats or basketballs.

The leader, meanwhile, took out a thin, very sharp stiletto knife. He slit the heavy-set boy's throat, just like he used to kill pigs and goats back in his home country. Vince hadn't been purchased, but he might have seen the abduction team. Unlike the Couple, these men would never play their own little games, or betray the Wolf, or disappoint him. There would be no more mistakes. The Wolf had been explicit on that, clear in a dangerous way that only he could be.

'Take the pretty boy. Quickly,' said the leader of the team as they hurried back to their car. They tossed the bulging bag into the trunk of the Pontiac and got out of town.

The job was perfect.

Chapter Sixty-Four

Here was the deal as Francis saw it now, as he tried to be calm and logical about it. *Nothing that had happened to him could possibly have happened!* He couldn't have been abducted a few hours ago by three absolutely terrifying men at the Arboretum on the campus of Holy Cross. *It just couldn't have happened!* Nor could he have been transported in the trunk of a late-model black sedan for four, maybe five hours, to God only knows where.

Most important, Vince couldn't be dead. That was what he had been told. But it couldn't have happened. *It didn't happen.*

So all of this had to be an impossibly bad dream, a nightmare of the sort that Francis Deegan hadn't experienced since he was maybe three or four years old. And this man standing before him now, this absurd caricature with curly tufts of white-blond hair around the side of his balding head, dressed in a tight, black leather body suit — well, *he couldn't be real either. No way.*

'I'm very angry at you! I'm good and pissed!' Mr Potter

yelled right in Francis's face. 'Why did you leave me?' he screeched. 'Why? Tell me why? You must never leave me again! I get very scared without you and you know that. You know how I am. That was thoughtless of you, Ronald!'

Francis had already tried reasoning with the madman – Potter, he called himself, and no, not Harry. Mister Potter! But reasoning didn't work. He'd told the raving lunatic several times that he had never seen him before. He wasn't Ronald! Didn't know any Ronalds! That had earned him a series of full-handed slaps across the face, one so hard that it bloodied his nose. The dweeby, Billy Idol-lookalike freak, was a lot stronger than he looked.

So out of desperation, Francis finally whispered an apology to the creep. 'I'm sorry. I'm so sorry. I won't do it again.'

And then Mr Potter was hugging him fiercely and he was crying all over him. Wasn't this too weird? 'Oh God, I'm so glad you're back. I was so *worried* about you. You must never leave me again, Ronald.'

Ronald? Who the hell was Ronald? And who was *Mister Potter?* What was going to happen now? Was Vince really dead? Had he been killed tonight back at the college? All of these questions were exploding inside Francis's throbbing skull. So actually it was easy for him to cry in Potter's arms, and even to hold on to him for dear life. To press his face into the fragrant black leather and whisper over and over again, 'I'm so sorry. I'm so, so sorry. Oh my God, I'm sorry.'

And Potter answered, 'I love you too, Ronald. I adore you. You'll never leave me again, will you?'

'No. I promise. I'll never leave.'

Then Potter laughed, and pulled away sharply from the boy.

'*Francis*, dear *Francis*,' he whispered. 'Who the hell is Ronald? I'm just playing with you, boy. This is just a game of mine. You're in college, you must have figured that much out. So let's play games, Francis. Let's go out to the barn and play.'

Chapter Sixty-Five

I received a strange e-mail from Monnie Donnelley at my temporary office. An update of sorts. She hadn't been suspended, Monnie said. Not yet anyway. Plus, she had some news for me. *Need to see you tonight. Same place, same time. Very important news. – M*

So I arrived at the Command Post Pub just past seven and searched around for Monnie. What was this mysterious news she had? The bar area was crowded with customers, but I spotted her. Easy – she was the only woman. I also figured that Monnie and I might be the only non-Marines in the Command Post.

'I couldn't talk to you over the phone at Quantico. Does that suck or what? Whom do you trust?' she said when I walked up to her.

'You can trust me. Of course I don't expect you to believe that, Monnie. You have news?'

'I sure do. Take a load off. I think I have some good news, actually.'

I took a stool beside Monnie. The bartender came and we

ordered beers. Monnie started up as soon as he walked away. 'I have a good friend at ERF,' she began. 'That's the Engineering Research Facility at Quantico.'

'I know what it is. You seem to have friends everywhere.'

'That's true. I guess not at the Hoover Building, though. Anyway, my friend alerted me to a message the Bureau got a couple of days ago, but dismissed as a crank call. It's about a website called the *Wolf's Den*. Supposedly, you can buy a lover at the Den, as in, have someone abducted. The site is supposed to be impossible to hack into. That's the catch.'

'So how did he get in? Our hacker.'

'*She's* a genius. I suspect that's why she was ignored. Want to meet her? She's fourteen years old.'

Chapter Sixty-Six

Monnie had an address for the hacker in Dale City, Virginia, only about twelve miles from Quantico. The agent who'd fielded the original call hadn't followed up very well, which bothered us, so we figured the agent wouldn't mind if we did his job for him.

I wasn't actually planning on taking Monnie along, but she wouldn't have it. So we dropped her SUV off at her house, and she rode with me to Dale City. I'd already called ahead and spoken to the girl's mother. She sounded nervous, but she said she was glad the FBI was finally coming to talk to Lili. She added, 'Nobody can ignore Lili for long. You'll see what I mean.'

A young girl in black coveralls answered the front door, and I assumed it was Lili, but that turned out to be wrong. Annie was the twelve-year-old sister. She certainly looked fourteen. She beckoned, and we stepped into the house.

'Lili is in her laboratory,' said Annie. 'Where else?'

Then Mrs Lynch appeared from the kitchen and we introduced ourselves. She had on a plain white blouse and

THE BIG BAD WOLF

a green corduroy jumper. She was holding a greasy spatula, and I couldn't help thinking how casual the domestic scene was. Especially if what Lili thought she had come upon was actually true. Had a fourteen-year-old found a possible trail that would lead us to the kidnappers? I'd heard of cases solved in stranger ways. But still . . .

'We call her Dr Hawking. Like Stephen Hawking? Her I.Q. is up there,' said her mom, waving the cooking utensil upward for emphasis. 'Smart as she is, Lili lives on Sprite and Pixie Stix. There's nothing I can do to influence her dietary habits.'

'Is it all right if we talk to Lili now?' I asked.

Mrs Lynch nodded. 'So I guess you're taking this seriously. That's so wise with Lili. She's not making any of this up, believe me.'

'Well, we just want to talk to her. To be on the safe side. We're not sure that this is anything, really.' Which was true enough.

'Oh, it's something,' said Mrs Lynch. 'Lili never makes a mistake. She hasn't so far anyway.'

She pointed the spatula down the hall. 'Second door on the right. She left it unlocked for a change, because she's expecting you. She instructed us to stay out of it.'

Monnie and I headed down the hallway. 'They have no idea what this could be, do they?' she whispered. 'I almost hope it's nothing. A false lead.'

I knocked once on a wooden door that sounded hollow.

'It's open,' came a high-pitched female voice. 'Come.'

I opened the door and looked in on a pine bedroom

suite. Single bed, rumpled cow-pattern sheets, posters from MIT, Yale and Stanford up on the walls.

Seated behind a blue halogen lamp at a laptop was a teenage girl – dark hair, eyeglasses, braces on her teeth. 'I'm all set up for you,' she said. 'I'm Lili of course, of course. I've been working on a decryption angle. It comes down to finding flaws in the algorithms.'

Monnie and I both shook Lili's hand, which was very small and seemed as fragile as an eggshell.

Monnie began, 'Lili, you said in your e-mail to us that you had information that could help with the disappearances in Atlanta and Pennsylvania.'

'Right. But you found Mrs Meek already.'

'You hacked on to a very secure site? That's right, isn't it?' Monnie asked.

'I sent out some stealth UDP scans. Then IP spoofing. Their rootserver bit on the false packets. I planted a source-code for the sniffer. Finally hacked in using DNS poisoning. It's a little more complicated, but that's the basic idea.'

'I get it,' Monnie said. Suddenly I was very glad she was there with me at the Lynch house.

'I think they know I was on with them. Actually, I'm sure of it,' said Lili.

'How do you know that?' I asked Lili.

'They said so.'

'You didn't get into too many specifics with Agent Tiezzi. You said you *thought* someone might be "for sale" at the site.'

'Yeah, but I blew it, didn't I? Agent Tiezzi didn't believe

me. I also admitted I was fourteen, and a girl. How dumb of me, right?'

'I won't hold it against you,' Monnie said and smiled kindly.

Lili finally cracked a smile too. 'I'm in big trouble, aren't I? Actually, I know that I am. They might already know *who* I am.'

I shook my head. 'No, Lili,' I said to her. 'They don't know who you are, or where you are. I'm sure they don't.'

If they did, you'd already be dead.

Chapter Sixty-Seven

It was so eerie and strange, being in the young wunder-kind's room – with her life, and her family members' lives, possibly in great danger. Lili had been a little coy in her message to the Bureau, so I understood how the tip might have fallen through the cracks. Also, she *was* four-teen years old. But now that we'd met and spoken to Lili one-to-one, I was sure that she had something real that could help us.

She'd heard them talking.

Someone had been purchased while she'd listened.

She was afraid for herself, and for her family.

'Do you want to go on-line with them?' Lili suddenly asked in an excited voice. 'We could! See if they're together now. I've been working on some cool anonymizing soft-ware. I think it will work. Not sure though. Well, yeah, it'll work.'

She smiled broadly, showing those beautiful braces.

I could see in her eyes that she wanted to prove some-thing to us.

'Is this a good idea?' Monnie leaned in and asked me.

I pulled her aside, I lowered my voice. 'We have to move her and the family anyway. They can't stay here now, Monnie.'

I looked over at Lili. 'Okay. Why don't you try to get on-line with them again. Let's see what they're up to. We'll be right here with you.'

Lili talked constantly as she went through the various steps to get the site's passwords and encrypted protection. I didn't understand any of what the fourteen-year-old had to say, but Monnie got most of it, and she was enthusiastic, supportive, but mostly impressed.

Suddenly, Lili looked up in alarm. 'Something's all wrong here.' She went back to her computer.

'Oh shit! God damn them!' she swore. 'Those *creeps*. I can't believe this.'

'What's happened?' Monnie asked. 'They changed the keys, didn't they?'

'Worse,' Lili said and kept tapping out commands very rapidly. 'Much, much worse. Awhh horsespit. I can't believe it.'

She finally turned away from the glowing screen of her laptop.

'First, I couldn't even *find* the site. They set up this very cool, very dynamic network – it was in Detroit, Boston, Miami, bouncing all over the place. Then when I did find it, I couldn't get on. *Nobody* can get into the site except them.'

'Why is that?' Monnie asked. 'What happened between a couple of days ago and now?'

'They installed an *eye-scan*. It's almost impossible to fool. The whole thing is run by this guy who calls himself Wolf. Wolf's a very scary dude. He's Russian. Like a wolf from Siberia. I think he's even smarter than I am. And that's fucking smart.'

Chapter Sixty-Eight

The next day I worked in the Strategic Information and Operations Center (SIOC) conference rooms on the fifth floor of the Hoover. So did Monnie Donnelley, who still felt as if she were in limbo. We were keeping what we had found out quiet so that we could check out a few things. The main room was humming around us. The abductions were the major media story now. The Bureau had taken an incredible amount of heat in the past few years; they needed a win. *No,* I thought, *we needed a win.*

A lot of important Bureau people were at the group meeting late that night: they included the heads of the Behavioral Analysis Unit-east and BAU-west, the unit chief of the Child Abduction Serial Murder Investigative Resource Center (CASMIRC), the head of Innocent Images in Baltimore, an FBI unit dedicated to finding and eliminating sexual predators on the Internet. Stacy Pollack led the discussion again; and she was clearly in charge of the case.

In spite of all the heavies present, the briefing was non-eventful, since not much had happened that day.

'I want to get approval for a reward, maybe half a million,' said Jack Arnold, who ran BAU-east. No one commented on the proposal. Several agents went on making notes or using their laptops. Actually, it was de-spiriting.

'I think I have something.' I finally spoke from the back of the room.

Stacy Pollack looked my way. A few heads popped up, reacting to the group's silence more than anything. I rose at my seat.

The FNG had the floor. I introduced Monnie, just to be cute. Then I told them about the Wolf's Den and our meeting with fourteen-year-old Lili Lynch. I also mentioned the Wolf, who, according to Monnie's findings, might be a Russian gangster by the name of Pasha Sorokin. His pedigree was hard to trace, especially before he moved out of the USSR. 'If we can get inside the Den somehow, I think we'll find out something about the missing women. In the meantime, I think we need to put more heat on some of the sites already identified by Innocent Images. It seems logical that the pervs using the Wolf's Den might visit other porn sites too. We need help. If the Wolf turns out to be Pasha Sorokin, we'll need a lot of help.'

Suddenly Stacy Pollack was interested. She led a discussion in which both Monnie and I were given the third degree. It was clear that we threatened some of the other agents in the room. Then Pollack made a decision.

'You can have resources,' she said. 'We'll watch the porn sites, twenty-four, seven. Thing is, we have nothing better at this point. I want our Russian group out of New York on this, too. I can't quite believe Pasha Sorokin would be personally involved in this, but if he is, it's huge. We've been interested in Sorokin for six years! We're very interested in the Wolf.'

Chapter Sixty-Nine

During the next twenty-four hours, over thirty agents were assigned to surveillance of fourteen different porn sites and chat rooms. It had to be one of the most lurid 'stakeouts' ever. We didn't know exactly whom we were looking for – other than anyone who happened to mention a site called Wolf's Den, or possibly the Wolf. In the meantime, Monnie and I were gathering all the information we could about the Red Mafiya, and especially about Pasha Sorokin.

At four that afternoon, I had to leave. The timing couldn't have been much worse, but there wouldn't have been any good time for this. I'd been asked to attend a preliminary meeting with Christine Johnson's lawyers at the Blake Building in the Dupont Circle area. Christine was coming after little Alex.

I arrived at a little before five-thirty and had to fight the tide of office workers streaming from an unusual twelve-story structure, which actually rounded the corner where Connecticut Avenue met L. I checked the downstairs registry and saw that the tenants in the building included Mazda, Barron's, the National Safety Council, several law offices, including Mark, Haranzo, and Denyeau which represented Christine.

I trudged to the elevator bank and pushed a button. Christine wanted custody of Alex Jr. Her attorney had arranged for this meeting in the hopes of eventually resolving things without going to court or possibly resorting to Alternative Dispute Resolution. I had talked to my attorney in the morning and decided not to have him present since this was an 'informal' meeting. I tried to have only one thought as I rode the elevator to the seventh floor: *do what is best for little Alex*. No matter what, or how it might make me feel.

I got off at seven and was met by Gilda Haranzo who was slim and attractive, dressed in a charcoal suit with a white silk blouse knotted at the throat. My lawyer had competed against Ms Haranzo and told me she was good, and also 'on a mission'. She was divorced from her physician husband and had custody of their two children. Her fees were high, but she and Christine had gone to Villanova together and were friends from back then.

'Christine is already in the conference room, Alex,' she said after introducing herself. Then she added, 'I'm sorry it's come to this. This case is difficult. There are no bad people involved. Will you please follow me?'

'I'm sorry it's come to this too,' I said. I wasn't so sure that there weren't any bad guys, though. We'd see soon enough.

Ms Haranzo led me to a mid-size room with gray

carpeting and light blue fabric walls. There was a glass table with six toney, black leather chairs in the center of the room. The only things on the table were a pitcher of iced water, some glasses, and a laptop computer.

A row of tall windows looked out on a view of Dupont Circle. Christine was standing near the windows, and she didn't speak as I entered. Then she walked over to the table and sat in one of the leather chairs.

'Hello, Alex,' she finally said.

Chapter Seventy

Gilda Haranzo slid into her seat behind her laptop, and I chose a spot across from Christine at the glass conference table. Suddenly, the loss of little Alex seemed very real to me. The thought took my breath away. Whether it was a good decision or not, fair or unfair, Christine had walked away from us, moved thousands of miles away and hadn't been to see him once. She'd knowingly relinquished her parental rights. Now she'd changed her mind. And what if she changed her mind again after that?

Christine spoke again. 'Thank you for coming here, Alex. I'm sorry about the circumstances. You must believe that I'm sorry.'

I didn't know what to say. It wasn't that I was mad at her, but – well, maybe I was angry. I'd had little Alex for so long, and I couldn't stand the thought of losing him now. My stomach was dropping like an elevator in free fall. The experience was like seeing your child run into the street, about to have a serious accident, and not being able to stop it from happening, not being able to do a thing. I sat there very quietly, and I held in a primal scream that would have shattered all the glass in the office.

Then the meeting began. The informal get-together. With no bad people in the room.

'Dr Cross, thank you for taking the time to come here,' Gilda Haranzo said and threw a cordial smile my way.

'Why wouldn't I come?' I asked.

She nodded and smiled again. 'We all want this problem to be settled amicably. You've been an excellent caregiver and no one disputes that.'

'I'm his father, Ms Haranzo,' I corrected.

'Of course. But Christine is able to take care of the boy now, and she is the mother. She's also a primary school principal in Seattle.'

I could feel my face and neck flushing. 'She left Alex with me.'

Christine spoke up. 'That isn't fair, Alex. I told you that you could take him for now. Our arrangement was always meant to be temporary.'

Ms Haranzo asked, 'Dr Cross, isn't it true that your eighty-two-year-old grandmother takes care of the child most of the time?'

'We all do,' I said. 'And besides, Nana wasn't too old when Christine left to go to Seattle. She's extremely capable and I don't think you'd ever want Nana on the witness stand.'

The lawyer continued. 'Your work takes you away from home frequently, doesn't it?'

I nodded. 'Occasionally, it does. But Alex is always well cared for. He's a happy, healthy, bright child, smiles all the time. And he's loved. He's the center of our household.'

Ms Haranzo waited for me to finish, then she started in again. Suddenly, I felt as if I were on trial here. 'Your work, Dr Cross. It's dangerous. Your family has been put in grave danger before. Also, you've had intimate relationships with women since Ms Johnson left. Isn't that so?'

I sighed. Then I slowly rose from the leather chair. 'I'm sorry, but this meeting is over. Excuse me. I have to get out of here.' But at the door, I turned back to Christine. 'This is wrong.'

Chapter Seventy-One

I had to get out of there and put my mind somewhere else for a while. I returned to the Hoover Building and no one seemed to have missed me. I couldn't help thinking that some of these agents squirreled away in the home office had no idea how crimes were solved in the real world. They almost seemed to believe that you fed data into computers and eventually it spit out a killer. *It happens on the street! Get out of this windowless 'crisis' room with all the bad air. Work the sidewalks!* I wanted to shout.

But I didn't say a word. I sat at a computer and read the latest on the Russian mob. I didn't see any promising connections. Plus, I couldn't really concentrate after my meeting at Christine's lawyers'. Eventually, I packed up my things and left the Hoover Building.

Nobody seemed to notice me leave. And then I wondered – *is that such a bad thing?*

When I got home, Nana was waiting at the front door. I was just walking up the steps when she opened the door and came outside. 'You watch little Alex, Damon. We'll be back in a while,' she called through the screen.

Nana limped down the front stairs and I followed her. 'Where are we going?' I asked.

'We're going for a drive,' she said. 'You and I have some things to talk about.'

Oh shit.

I got back in the old Porsche and started it up. Nana flopped down in the passenger seat.

'Drive,' she said.

'Yes, Miss Daisy.'

'Don't give me any of your lip either, or your sorry attempts at wit.'

'Yes ma'am.'

'That's a good example of your lip.'

'I know it is, ma'am.'

I decided to head out west toward the Shenandoah Mountains, a pretty ride and one of Nana's favorites. For the first part of the drive, we were both fairly quiet, unusual for the two of us.

'What happened at the lawyers'?' Nana finally asked as I turned on to Route 66.

I gave her the long version, probably because I needed to vent. She listened very quietly, then she did something unusual for her. Nana actually cursed. 'The *hell* with Christine Johnson. She's wrong about this!'

'I can't completely blame Christine,' I said. As much as I didn't want to, I could see her side of things.

'Well, I do. She left that sweet little baby and went to

Seattle. She didn't have to go that far away. Her decision. Now she has to live with it.'

I glanced over at Nana. Her face was screwed tight. 'I don't know if that would be considered an enlightened point of view these days.'

Nana waved away what I'd said. 'I don't think these days are all that enlightened. You know I believe in women's rights, mothers' rights, all of that, but I also believe you have to be held responsible for your actions. Christine walked away from that little boy for all this time. She walked away from her responsibility.'

'You through?' I asked.

Nana had her arms folded tightly across her chest. 'I am. And it felt good, real good. You ought to try it sometime. Vent, Alex. Lose control. Let it out.'

I finally had to laugh. 'I had the radio blasting all the way home from work, and I was yelling half the time. I'm more upset than you are, Nana.'

For once – and I don't ever remember this happening before – she actually let me have the last word.

Chapter Seventy-Two

Jamilla called that night around eleven o'clock – eight o'clock her time. I hadn't spoken to her for a few days, and to be truthful, now wasn't the best time. Christine's visit to D.C. and then the meeting with her lawyer had me tense and messed-up. Shook. I tried not to show it, but that was wrong too.

'You never write, you never call,' Jamilla said and laughed in her usual loose and engaging way. 'Don't tell me you're already wrapped up in a case for the Bureau? You are, aren't you?'

'A big, nasty one, yeah. I'm sort of in and out of it,' I told Jam, then quickly explained what was happening, and what *wasn't*, at the Hoover Building, including my mixed emotions about being with the Bureau – all the stuff in my life that *didn't really matter right now*.

'You're the new guy on the block,' she said. 'Give it some time.'

'I'm trying to be patient. It's just that I'm not used to this wasted motion, the wasted resources.'

I heard her laugh. 'That, and you're used to being the center of attention, don't you think? You've been a star, Alex.'

I smiled. 'You're right, you're right. That's part of it.'

'You saw the Bureau from the other side of the fence. You *knew* what you were getting yourself into. Didn't you know?'

'I guess I should have, sure. But I listened to a lot of promises that were made when I signed up.'

Jamilla sighed. 'I know, I'm not being very sympathetic, empathetic, whatever. One of my faults.'

'No, it's me.'

'Yeah,' she laughed again. 'It is. I never heard you so down and out. Let's see what we can do to bring you up.'

We talked about the case she was working on, then Jamilla asked about each of the kids. She was interested as always. But I was in a sour mood, and I couldn't shake it. I wondered if she could tell, and then I got my answer.

'Well,' Jam said, 'I just wanted to see how you were. Call if you have any news. I'm always here for you. I miss you, Alex.'

'I miss you too,' I said.

Then Jamilla broke the connection with a soft, 'Bye.'

I sat there shaking my head back and forth. Shit. What an ass I am sometimes. I was blaming Jamilla for what had happened with Christine, wasn't I? How dumb was that?

Chapter Seventy-Three

'Hi there. I missed you,' I said and smiled. 'And I'm sorry.'

Five minutes after Jamilla hung up, I called her back to try and make amends.

'You should be sorry, you poop. Glad to see your famous antennae are still working all right,' she said.

'Not so hard to figure out. The crucial evidence was right before my eyes. That was the shortest phone talk we've ever had. Probably the most uncomfortable and frustrating too. I had one of my famous *feelings* about it.'

'So what's the matter, boy scout? Is it the job or is it something else? Is it me, Alex? You can tell me if it is. I have to warn you, though, I carry a gun.'

I laughed at her joke. Then I took a breath, before I let it out slowly. 'Christine Johnson is back in town. It gets worse from there. She came for little Alex. She wants to take him away, to get custody, probably take him to Seattle.'

I heard a sharp intake of breath, then. 'Oh, Alex, that's terrible. *Terrible.* Did you talk to her about it?'

'I sure did. I was at her lawyers' this afternoon. Christine finds it hard to be tough, her lawyer doesn't.'

'Alex, has Christine seen the two of you together? How you are with him? You're like that old movie, *Kramer vs. Kramer*. Dustin Hoffman and that cute little boy?'

'No, she hasn't really watched us together, but I've seen her with Alex. He turned on the charm. Welcomed her back without any recriminations. Little traitor.'

Jamilla was angry now. 'Little Alex *would*. Always the perfect gentleman. Like his father.'

'That, plus – she is his mother. The two of them have a history, Jam. It's complicated.'

'No it isn't. Not for me, not for anybody with a brain. She left him, Alex. Separated herself by three thousand miles. Stayed away for over two years. What's to say she won't do it again? So what are you going to do now?'

That was the big question, wasn't it?

'What do you think? What would you do?'

Jam sniffed out a laugh. 'Oh, you know me – I'd fight her like hell.'

I finally smiled. 'That's what I'm going to do. I'm going to fight Christine like hell.'

Chapter Seventy-Four

The phone calls weren't over for the night. As soon as I got off with Jamilla, and we're talking sixty seconds here, the infernal contraption started to ring again. I wondered if it was Christine. I really didn't want to talk about Alex right now. What would she want to say to me – and what could I say to her?

The phone wouldn't stop ringing, though. I looked at my watch. Saw it was past midnight. Now what? I hesitated before I finally snatched it up.

'Alex Cross,' I said.

'Alex. This is Ron Burns. Sorry to call you so late. I'm just flying into D.C. from New York. Another conference on counterterrorism, whatever the hell that's supposed to mean right now. Nobody seems to know exactly how to fight the bastards, but everybody has a theory.'

'Play by their rules. Of course, that would inconvenience a few people,' I said. 'And it's sure not politically or socially correct.'

Burns laughed. 'You go to the heart of the matter,' he said.

'And you aren't timid about your ideas.'

I said, 'Speaking of which . . .'

'I know you're a little pissed,' he said. 'I don't blame you after what's been happening. The Bureau runaround, everything you were warned about. You have to understand something, Alex. I'm trying to turn around a very slow-moving ocean liner. In the Potomac. Trust me for a little longer. By the way, *why are you still in D.C.*? Not up in New Hampshire?'

I blinked, didn't understand. 'What's in New Hampshire? Oh shit, don't tell me.'

'We have a suspect. Nobody told you, did they? Your idea about tracking the mentions of the Wolf's Den on the Internet worked. We got somebody!'

I couldn't believe what I was hearing now, at midnight. 'Nobody told me. I've been home since I left work.'

There was silence at his end. 'I'm going to make a couple of calls. Get on a plane in the morning. They'll be *expecting* you in New Hampshire. Believe me, they will be expecting you. And Alex, trust me a little longer.'

'Yeah, I will.' A *little* longer.

Chapter Seventy-Five

It seemed both unlikely and peculiar, but a respected assistant professor of English at Dartmouth was the subject of the FBI surveillance in New Hampshire. He had recently gone into a chat room called *Taboo* and bragged about an exclusive website where anything could be bought *if you had enough money.*

An agent at SIOC had monitored the strange conversation with Mr Potter . . .

BOYFRIEND: EXACTLY HOW MUCH IS ENOUGH MONEY TO BUY 'ANYTHING'?

POTTER: MORE THAN YOU HAVE, MY FRIEND. ANYWAY, THERE'S AN EYESCAN TO KEEP OUT RIFF-RAFF LIKE YOURSELF.

THE PACKAGE: WE'RE HONORED THAT YOU'RE SLUMMING WITH US TONIGHT.

POTTER: THE WOLF'S DEN IS ONLY OPEN ABOUT TWO HOURS A WEEK. NONE OF YOU ARE INVITED, OF COURSE.

It turned out that Mr Potter was the moniker used by Dr

Homer Taylor. Guilty or not, Dr Taylor was in a world of trouble right now. Twenty-four agents, four two-person teams working eight-hour shifts, were watching every step he took in Hanover. During the work week, he lived in a small Victorian house near the college and walked back and forth to classes. He was a thin, balding, proper-looking man who wore English-made suits with bright-colored bow ties and purposefully uncoordinated suspenders. He always looked very pleased to be himself. We'd learned from college authorities that he was teaching Restoration and Elizabethan drama as well as a Shakespeare seminar that semester.

His classes were extremely popular and so was he. Dr Taylor had the reputation of being available to his students, even ones who weren't actually taking his courses. He was also known for his quick wit and nasty sense of humor. He often played to standing room, which he called 'full houses', and frequently acted out scenes, both the male and female parts.

It was assumed that he was gay, but no one was aware of any serious relationships the professor had. He owned a farm about fifty miles away in Webster, New Hampshire, where he spent most weekends. Occasionally, Taylor went to Boston or New York, and he'd spent several summers in Europe. There had never been an incident with a student, though some of the males called him 'Puck', a few openly to his face.

The surveillance on Taylor was difficult, given the college-town atmosphere. So far, it was believed that our agents hadn't been spotted. But we couldn't be certain of that. Taylor hadn't been seen doing much beyond teaching his classes, and returning home.

The second day that I was in Hanover, I was in a surveillance car, a dark blue Crown Vic, along with an agent named Peggy Katz. Agent Katz had been raised in Lexington, Massachusetts. She was a very serious person whose main hobby seemed to be an avid interest in professional basketball. She could talk about the NBA or WNBA for hours, which she did during our surveillance time together.

The other agents on with us that night were Roger Nielsen, Charles Powiesnik and Michelle Bugliarello. Powiesnik was the senior agent in charge. I wasn't really sure where I fit in, but they all knew I'd been sent in by Washington, and by Ron Burns himself.

'The good Doctor Taylor is going out. Could be interesting,' Katz and I heard over our two-way late that night. We couldn't actually see his house from where we were parked.

'He's coming your way. You pick him up first,' said agent-in-charge, Powiesnik.

Katz turned on the headlights, and we pulled up to a street corner. Then we waited for Taylor to pass. His Toyota 4-Runner appeared a moment later.

'He's going out toward I-89,' she reported in. 'Proceeding at about forty-five, keeping within the speed limit, which makes him suspicious in my book. Maybe headed to his farm in Webster. Kind of late for picking tomatoes, though.'

'We'll have Nielsen precede him on I-89. You stay behind.

Michelle and I will be right with you,' said Powiesnik.

That sounded familiar to me, and apparently to Agent Katz since she muttered 'right' as soon as she signed off.

Once he exited off 89, Taylor made turns on a couple of narrow side roads. He was doing close to sixty.

'Seems to be in a little more of a hurry now,' Peggy said.

Then Taylor's Toyota veered off on to a drive that appeared to be dirt. We had to stay back or be spotted. Fog lay low over the farmlands, and we proceeded slowly until we could safely park on the side of the road. The other FBI cars hadn't arrived yet, at least we didn't see any of them. We got out of our sedan and headed back into the woods.

Then we could see Taylor's Toyota parked in front of a shadowy farmhouse. A light eventually blinked on inside the house, then another light. Agent Katz was quiet and I wondered if she'd been involved in anything quite as heavy as this before. I didn't think that she had.

'We can see Taylor's Toyota at the house,' she reported in to Powiesnik.

Then she turned to me. 'So now what?' she asked in a whisper.

'It's not up to us,' I said.

'If it was?'

'I'd move in closer on foot. I want to see if that missing kid from Holy Cross is there. We don't know how much danger he's in.'

Powiesnik contacted us again. 'We're going to take a look. You and Agent Cross stay where you are. Watch our backs.'

Agent Katz turned to me and sniffed out a laugh.

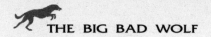

'Powiesnik means – watch our dust, doesn't he?'

'Or, eat our dust,' I said.

'Or suck hind tit,' grumped Katz. Maybe she hadn't seen any action before, but she apparently wanted some now. And I had a feeling Agent Katz might get her wish.

Chapter Seventy-Six

'**O**ver there, heading toward the barn,' I said and pointed. 'That's Taylor. What's he doing?'

'Powiesnik is on the other side of the house. He probably can't see that Taylor is outside,' said Agent Katz.

'Let's see what he's up to.'

Katz hesitated. 'You're not going to get me shot, are you?'

'No,' I said, a little too quickly. This was getting complicated suddenly. I wanted to follow Taylor, but I felt I had to watch out for Katz too.

'Let's go,' Katz finally said, reaching a decision. '*Taylor is out of the house. He's headed southwest,*' she alerted Powiesnik. '*We're following.*'

The two of us hurried forward for a hundred yards or so. We had some ground to make up, and we wanted to keep Taylor in sight. There was a half-moon overhead and that helped, but it was also possible that Taylor might see us coming. We could lose him easily now, especially if he was suspicious.

He didn't seem to be aware of anything going on around

him – at least not so far. Which got me thinking that he was used to sneaking around out here late at night. Not worrying about being seen by anyone. This was his private reserve, wasn't it? I watched him go inside the barn.

'We should call in again,' Katz said.

I didn't disagree completely, but I was nervous about the other agents coming up fast and making noise. How many of them had experience in the field?

'You better call in,' I finally agreed.

It took the other agents a couple of minutes to get to the edge of the woods where we were crouched behind tall brush. Light from inside the barn shone through cracks and holes in the weatherboarding. We couldn't see or hear much from where we were hiding. Finally we could make out Potter crossing the service court and entering the great door of the barn.

Then music blasted from somewhere in the barn. I recognized a choral arrangement by Queen. A sexy lyric about riding a bicycle. Totally whacked at this time of night, playing in the middle of nowhere.

'There's no evidence of violence in his past,' Powiesnik said as he came up and crouched beside me.

'Or kidnapping either,' I said. 'But he might have somebody in that barn. Maybe the kid from Holy Cross. Taylor knew about the Wolf's Den, even the eye scan. I doubt he's an innocent bystander.'

'We're moving on Taylor,' the senior agent ordered. 'He may be armed,' he told the other agents. 'Proceed as if he is.'

He assigned two teams to survey the far side of the barn in case Taylor tried to get out some other way. Powiesnik and Nielsen, along with Agent Katz and myself, were going in the great door that Taylor had entered.

I moved up alongside Powiesnik. 'You okay with this? Going in after him now?'

'It's already been decided,' he said in a tight voice.

So I moved forward, wearing a dark blue windbreaker with *FBI* printed on the back. Queen continued to play loudly in the barn. '*I want to ride my bicycle! Bicycle! Bicycle!*' This was a strange feeling, all of it. The Bureau had excellent resources for getting information; their personnel were certainly booksmart and well trained, but, in the past, I'd always known and trusted only those I went into a dangerous crime scene with.

The wooden barn door hadn't been latched or locked by Taylor. We could see that as we crouched in tall brush a few yards away.

Suddenly the music stopped.

Then I heard loud voices inside. *More than one.* But I couldn't make out what was being said, or who was doing the talking.

'We should take him down. *Now*,' I whispered to Powiesnik. 'We're already committed. We have to go.'

'Don't tell me—'

'I'm *telling* you,' I said.

I wanted to take over from Powiesnik. He was hesitating much too long. Once we had moved close to the barn, we shouldn't have stopped.

'I'll go first. Come in behind me,' I finally said.

Powiesnik didn't overrule me, didn't argue. No one else in the group spoke a word.

I ran very quickly toward the barn, my gun out of my holster. I was there in seconds. The door made a heavy creaking sound when I pulled it open. Bright light escaped outside, splintered into my eyes for a second. *'FBI!'* I yelled at the top of my voice. *FBI! Jesus!*

Taylor looked at me and his eyes filled with surprise, fear. I had a clear shot at him. He'd had no idea he was being followed. He'd been operating in his own private safety zone, hadn't he? I could see that now.

I could also make out someone else illuminated in the shadows of the barn. He was tied with leather bindings to a wooden post that hung from a beam in the hayloft. He had no clothes on. Nothing. His chest and genitals were blood-ied. *But Francis Deegan was alive!*

'You're under arrest . . . Mr Potter.'

Chapter Seventy-Seven

The first interview with Potter took place in the small library he'd built in the farmhouse. It was cozy and tastefully furnished, and gave no hint of the horrible acts going on elsewhere on the property. Potter sat on a dark wood bench with his wrists handcuffed in front of him. His dark eyes boiled over in anger directed at me.

I sat in a straight-backed chair directly across from him. For a long moment we glared at each other, then I let my eyes wander around the room. Bookcases and cabinets had been custom-built and covered every wall. A large oak desk held a computer and printer as well as wooden in/out boxes and stacks of ungraded papers. A green wooden sign behind the desk read: 'Bless This Mess.' There was no hint of the real Taylor, or 'Potter', anywhere.

I noticed authors' names on the spines of the books: Richard Russo, Jamaica Kinkaid, Zadie Smith, Martin Amis, Stanley Kunitz. It was rumored that the Bureau often had an incredible amount of information on a subject *before* an interview was conducted. This was true with Taylor. I already knew about his boyhood spent in Iowa; then his years as a student at Iowa and NYU. No one had suspected he had a dark side. He had been up for promotion and tenure this year, and had been working to finish a book on Milton's *Paradise Lost* as well as an article on John Donne. Drafts of the literary projects were laid out on the desk.

I got up and looked through the pages. *He's organized. He compartmentalizes beautifully*, I was thinking. 'Interesting stuff,' I said.

'Be careful with those,' he warned.

'Oh, sorry. I'll be careful,' I said, as if anything he had to write about Milton or Donne mattered anymore. I continued to look through his books – the *OED*, *Riverside Shakespeare*, Shakespeare and Milton quarterlies, *Gravity's Rainbow*, a *Merck* manual.

'This interrogation is illegal. You must know that. I want to see my lawyer,' he said as I sat down again. 'I demand it.'

'Oh, we're just talking,' I said. 'This is only an interview. We're waiting for a lawyer to get here. Just getting to know you.'

'Has my lawyer been called? Jackson Arnold in Boston?' Taylor said. 'Tell me. Don't fuck with me.'

'As far as I know,' I said. 'Let's see, we busted you at around eight. He was called at eight-thirty.'

Taylor looked at his watch. His dark eyes blazed. 'It's only five o'clock now!'

I shrugged. 'Well, no wonder your lawyer isn't here yet. You haven't even been apprehended. So, you teach English

Lit, right. I liked literature in school, read a lot, still do, but I loved the sciences.'

Taylor continued to glare at me. 'You forget Francis was taken to a hospital. The time is on the record.'

I snapped my fingers and winced. 'Right. Of course it is. He was picked up at a little past nine. I signed the form myself,' I said. 'I have a doctorate, like yourself. In psychology, from Johns Hopkins down in Baltimore.'

Homer Taylor rocked back and forth on the bench. He shook his head. 'You don't scare me, you *fucking asshole*. I can't be intimidated by little people like you. Trust me. I doubt you have a PhD. Maybe from Alcorn State. Or Jackson State.'

I ignored the baiting. 'Did you kill Benjamin Coffey? I think you did. We'll start looking for the body a little later this morning. Why don't you save us the trouble?'

Taylor finally smiled. 'Save you the trouble? Why would I do that?'

'I actually have a pretty good answer. Because you're going to need my help later on.'

'Well then, I'll save you some trouble later on, *after* you help me.' Taylor smirked. 'What are you?' he finally asked. 'The FBI's idea of affirmative action?'

I smiled. 'No, actually I'm your last chance. You better take it.'

Chapter Seventy-Eight

The library in the farmhouse was empty except for Potter and me. He was handcuffed, totally cool and unafraid, glaring menacingly.

'I want my lawyer,' he said now.

'I'll bet you do. I would if I was you. I'd be making a real scene in here.'

Taylor finally smiled. His teeth were badly stained. 'How about a cigarette? Give me *something*.'

I gave him one. I even lit it for him. 'Where did you bury Benjamin Coffey?' I asked again.

'So, you're really the one in charge?' he asked. 'Interesting. The world turns, doesn't it? The worm, too.'

'You know, the calmness gives you away,' I told him. 'You show no fear. Nothing in your eyes. I've seen so many like you. Better, smarter.'

He blew out a smoke ring in my direction. 'To such a skilled interrogator as yourself, such things must be obvious. The calmness I show.'

'So where did you learn about drama, the theater,

English and American literature?'

'You know the answers to that. Iowa. Then NYU. It's on my résumé. I *want* a lawyer.'

'You mentioned the lawyer earlier. You'll be given one. All in good time. So where is Benjamin Coffey? Is he buried out here? I'm sure he is.'

'Then why ask? If you already know the answer.'

'Because I don't want to waste time digging up these fields, or dredging the pond over there.'

'I really can't help you. I don't know a Benjamin Coffey. Of course, *Francis* was here of his own free will. He hated it at Holy Cross. The Jesuits don't like *us*. Well, some of the priests don't.'

'The Jesuits don't like who? Who else is involved with you?'

'You're actually funny, for a police drone. I like a bit of dry humor now and then.'

I stretched my leg out, struck his chest, and knocked his wooden bench over. He hit the floor hard. Banged his head. I could see that it shook him, surprised him anyway. Must have hurt at least a little bit.

'That supposed to scare me?' he asked once he'd gotten his breath. He was angry now, redfaced, veins in his neck pulsing. That was a start. '*I want my lawyer!. . . I'm explicitly asking you for a lawyer!*' he began to yell over and over again. '*Lawyer! Lawyer! Lawyer! Lawyer! Can anyone hear me?*'

Taylor kept yelling at me for over an hour – like some sociopathic kid who wasn't getting his way. I let him scream and curse, until he started to get hoarse. I even went outside and stretched my legs, drank some coffee, chatted with Charlie Powiesnik, who was a pretty good guy.

When I came back inside, *Potter* looked changed. He'd had time to think about everything that had happened at the farm. He knew that we were talking to Francis Deegan, and that we'd find Benjamin Coffey, too. Maybe a few others.

Then he sighed out loud. 'I assume we can make some sort of arrangement to my liking. Mutually beneficial.'

I nodded. 'I'm sure we can make an arrangement. But I need something concrete in return. *How did you get the boys? How did it work?* That's what I need to hear from you.'

I waited for him to answer. Several minutes passed.

'I'll tell you where Benjamin is,' he finally said.

'You'll tell me that, too.'

I waited some more. Took another turn outside with Charlie. Came back to the study.

'I bought the boys from the Wolf,' Potter finally said. 'But you'll be sorry you asked. So will I, probably. He'll make both of us pay. In my humble opinion – and remember, this is just a college professor talking – the Wolf is the most dangerous man alive. He's Russian. Red Mafiya.'

'Where do we find the Wolf?' I asked. 'How do you contact him?'

'I don't know where he is. Nobody does. He's a mystery man. That's his thing, his trademark. I think it turns him on.'

It took several more hours of talking, bargaining and

negotiating, but Potter finally told me some of what I wanted to know about the Wolf, this Russian mystery man who impressed him so. Late in the day, I wrote in my notes – *This makes no sense yet. None of it does, really. The Wolf's plans seem insane. Are they?*

Then I wrote my final thought, at least for the moment.

The brilliance of it may be that it makes no sense.

To us.

To me.

PART FOUR

WOLF TRAP

Chapter Seventy-Nine

S tacy Pollack was a solemn and commanding presence in front of the roomful of agents gathered on the fifth floor of the Hoover Building. It was standing room only for her meeting. I was one of those gathered in the back, but just about everybody knew who I was after our New Hampshire success of bringing in Potter. We had rescued another captive – Francis Deegan was going to be fine. We'd also found the body of Benjamin Coffey, and two other males, unidentified so far.

'Unaccustomed as I am to having things go our way,' Pollack began and got a laugh, 'I'll take this latest development and offer humble thanks to the gods that be. This is a very good break for us. As many of you know, the Wolf has been a key target on our Red Mafiya list, probably *the* key target. He's rumored to be into everything – weapon sales, extortion, sports fixing, prostitution, the white-slave market. His name seems to be Pasha Sorokin and he seems to have learned his trade on the outskirts of Moscow. I say seems, because nothing is a sure thing when it comes to this guy. Somehow he maneuvered his way into the KGB, where he lasted three years. He then became a *pakhan* in the Russian Underworld, a boss, but decided to emigrate to America. Where he completely disappeared.

'We actually believed for a while that he was dead. Apparently not, at least if we can believe Mr Potter. Can we believe him?' Pollack gestured in my direction.

I stayed in my seat. I knew I'd already drawn enough attention.

'I think we can believe Potter. He knows that we need him; he definitely understands what he has to offer us – a possible lead to Sorokin. He also warned me that the Wolf will *come after us*. His mission is to be the top gangster in the world. According to Potter, that's what the Wolf is.'

'So why the white-slave market?' one of the ASACs asked. 'There's not that much money in it. It's risky. What's the point? Sounds like bullshit to me. Maybe we've been had.'

'We don't know why he acts the way he does. It's troubling, I agree. Maybe it's his roots, his patterns,' an agent from the New York office's Russia group spoke. 'He's always had his fingers in whatever he could. It goes back to his days on the streets of Moscow. Also, the Wolf likes women himself. He's kinky.'

'I don't think he *likes* them,' said a woman agent from D.C. 'Honestly, Jeff.'

The New York agent continued. 'There's a rumor that he walked into a club in Brighton Beach about a week ago and wasted one of his ex-wives. That's his style. He once sold a couple of his female cousins from the home country on the slave market. The thing to remember about Pasha Sorokin is that he has no fears. He expected to die young in Russia. He's surprised that he's still alive. He likes it on the edge.'

Stacy Pollack took the floor again. 'Let me tell you a couple of other stories to give you a sense of who we're dealing with. It *seems* that Pasha manipulated the CIA to get him out of Russia originally. That's right, the CIA transported him here. He was supposed to give them all sorts of information, but he never delivered. When he first got to New York, he sold babies out of an apartment in Brooklyn. According to the stories, in one day alone, he sold six babies to suburban couples for ten thousand dollars apiece. More recently he swindled a Miami bank out of two hundred million. He likes what he does, and he's obviously good at it. And now we know an Internet site he visits. We may even be able to get on the site. We're working on it. We're as close to the Wolf as we've ever been. Or so we like to believe.'

Chapter Eighty

The Wolf was in Philadelphia that night, birthplace of a nation, though not his nation. He never showed it but he was anxious, and he liked the emotional charge it gave him.

It made him feel more alive. He also liked it that he was invisible, that no one knew who he was, that he could go anywhere, do anything he wanted to do. Tonight, he was watching the Flyers play Montreal at the First Union Center in Philly. The hockey game was one he had arranged to have fixed, but nothing had happened so far, which was why he was anxious, but also very angry.

As the second period was winding down the score was 2-1. Flyers! He was seated at center ice, four rows back behind the penalty boxes, close to the action. To distract himself he watched the crowd – a mix of yuppies in business suits and loosened ties and blue-collar types in oversized Flyers jerseys. Everybody seemed to have plastic tubs of nachos and twenty-ounce cups of beer.

His eyes shifted back to the game. Players flashed around

the rink at dazzling speeds, making a slashing sound as the blades of their skates tore into the ice. *C'mon, c'mon. Do something!* he urged.

Then suddenly he saw Ilia Teptev out of position. There was the shotgun crash of ninety miles an hour slapshot as it left the stick. Goal – Canadians! The crowd erupted with insults: 'You suck, Ilia! You throwing this game?'

Then the announcer came over the PA. 'Canadian goal by number eighteen, Stevie Bowen. Time of goal, nineteen minutes and thirty-two seconds.'

The period ended like that, 2-2. The Zamboni chugged out resurfacing the ice between periods. More beer and more nachos were consumed. And the resurfaced ice became a slick glass sheet once again.

For the next sixteen minutes, the game was knotted at 2-2. The Wolf wanted to garrote Teptev and Dobrushkin. Then the Canadian center, Bowen, plowed through a half-hearted check and burst into the Flyer zone. He dropped a pass along the right boards. *A shot! Wide!* Recovered by Alexei Dobrushkin – who settled behind his own net with the puck.

He skated to his right – then snapped a pass across the ice – *across the goal mouth* – and it was picked off by Bowen. Bowen slapped the puck into the corner of the net.

Goal – Canadians!

The Wolf smiled for the first time that night. Then he turned to his companion, his seven-year-old son, Dimitri, which would have surprised everyone who supposedly knew him.

'Let's go, Dimmie, the game's over. The Canadians will win. Just like I told you they would. Didn't I tell you?'

Dimitri wasn't convinced about the outcome, but he knew better than to argue with his father. 'You were right, Daddy,' said the boy. 'You're always right.'

Chapter Eighty-One

That night at eleven-thirty I planned to enter the Wolf's Den for the first time. I needed the help of Mr Potter, though. Homer Taylor had been moved to Washington for the purpose. *I needed his eyes.*

The two of us sat close together, Taylor in cuffs, in an operation room on the fifth floor of the Hoover. The professor was nervous, and I guessed that he was having second thoughts about our arrangement with respect to the Wolf. 'Don't think that he won't get to you. He's relentless. He's *crazy*,' he warned me again.

'I've avoided crazy men before,' I said. 'We still have a deal?'

'We do. What choice do I have? But you'll regret it. So will I, I'm afraid.'

'We're going to protect you.'

His eyes narrowed. 'So you say.'

The night had been a busy one already. The top computer experts at the Bureau had tried password-cracking software to get into the Wolf's Den. So far, everything had failed. So had a 'brute force' attack that can often decode encrypted data by feeding in combinations of letters and numbers. Nothing had worked. We needed Mr Potter to get inside. We needed his eyes. The blood-vessel patterns of the retina and the pattern of flecks on the iris offered unique methods of identification. Scanning involved a low-intensity light source and an optical coupler.

Potter set one eye up to the device and then focused on a red dot. An impression was taken and then sent on. Seconds later, we had access.

This is Potter, I typed as Taylor was led out of the operations room. He would be transferred to Lorton Federal Prison for the night, then taken back to New England. I put him out of my mind, but I wouldn't be able to forget his warning about the Wolf.

We were just talking about you, said someone with the username *Master Trekr.*

I wondered why my ears were buzzing, I typed, and wondered if I was communicating with the Wolf for the first time. Was he on-line? If so, *where was he? What city?*

I was center stage in the operation room used by SIOC. More than a dozen agents and technicians were gathered around me. Most were on computers too. The scene looked like a very high-tech classroom.

Master Trekr: Weren't really talking about you, Potter. UR paranoid. Same as it ever was.

I looked at the other user names.

Sphinx 3000.

ToscaBella.

Louis XV.

Sterling 66.

No Wolf. Did that mean he wasn't on-line in the Den? Or was he *Master Trekr*? Was he observing me now? Was I passing his test?

I need a replacement for 'Worcester', I typed. Potter had told me that Francis Deegan's code name was 'Worcester'.

Sphinx 3000: Take a number. We were talking about my package, my delivery. It's my turn. You know that, you fruitcake.

I didn't respond at first. This was my first test. Would Potter apologize to Sphinx 3000? I didn't think he would. More likely, he'd come back with a caustic reply. Or would he? I chose to say nothing for now.

Sphinx 3000: Fuck U too. I know what UR thinking. U kinky bastard. As I was saying before I was interrupted. I want a Southern belle, the more hung up on herself, the more self-absorbed she is, the better. I want an ice goddess, who I plan to shatter. Totally into herself. She wears Chanel and Miu Miu and Bulgari Jewelry. Even to the shopping mall. Heels of course. I don't care if she's tall or short. Beautiful face. Pert tits.

ToscaBella: How original.

Sphinx 3000: Fuck original, and sorry to repeat myself, but fuck U. Give me that old-time rock-and-roll music. I want what I want, and I've earned it.

Sterling 66: Anything else? This Southern belle of yours? In her twenties? Thirties?

Sphinx 3000: That'd be good. All or any of the above.
Louis XV: Teens?
Sphinx 3000: That'd be good too.
Sterling 66: How long do you plan to keep her around?
Sphinx 3000: One glorious night of ecstasy and wild abandon . . . Just one night.
Sterling 66: And then?
Sphinx 3000: I'm going to dispose of her. Now, do I get my goddess?

There was a pause.

No answer came from anyone.

What was going on? I wondered.

Of course U do, answered Wolf. *Just be careful, Sphinx. Be very careful. We're being watched.*

Chapter Eighty-Two

I wasn't sure how to react to the Wolf, or his message to Sphinx. Should I speak now? Did he know we were on to him? How could he?

Sterling 66: Now what's your problem, Mr Potter?

This was my chance. I wanted to try and draw out Wolf if I could. But could I pull it off? I was aware that everyone was watching me in the operation room.

I don't have a problem, I typed. *I'm just ready for another boy. U know I'm good for it. Haven't I always been?*

Sterling 66: UR ready for another boy? U just recently received 'Worcester'. Less than a week ago.

I typed: *Yes, but he's left us.*

Sphinx 3000: That's very funny. UR so cute, Potter. Such a cute psycho-killer.

Sphinx didn't like Potter, did he? I had to assume the feeling was mutual. I typed, *I love u too. We should get together and bond in person.*

Sterling 66: When U say 'he's left us', I assume U mean that he's dead?

Potter: Yes, the dear boy passed. I'm over my grieving though. Ready to move on.

Sphinx 3000: Hilarious.

This bickering was starting to get on my nerves. Who the hell were these sick bastards? Where were they? Besides cyberspace?

I have someone in mind. I've been watching him for a while, I typed

Sphinx 3000: I'll bet he's gorgeous.

I typed: *Oh, he is. One of a kind. The love of my life.*

Sterling 66: U said that about Worcester. What city?

I typed: *Boston. Cambridge, actually. He's a student at Harvard. Working for his doctorate. Argentinian, I believe. Rides polo ponies in the summer.*

Sterling 66: Where did U bump into this one, Potter?

The next tidbit I'd gotten from Homer Taylor himself. *Actually, I did bump into him. He's so firm.*

Sphinx 3000: Where did you meet him? Tell, tell.

I typed: *I was at Harvard for a symposium.*

Sterling 66: On?

I typed: *Milton. Of course.*

Sterling 66: He was attending?

I typed: *No – I literally bumped into him. In the men's room. I watched him for the rest of the day. Found out where he lived. Been studying him for three months.*

Sterling 66: So why did U purchase Worcester?

I knew the question was coming. *Impulse,* I typed. Then, *But this boy in Cambridge, that's true love. Not a casual thing.*

Sterling 66: So U have a name? An address?

I typed: *I do. And I have my checkbook.*

Sterling 66: Worcester won't be found? UR certain?

I could hear *Potter's* voice in my head as I typed. *Good lord, no. Not unless someone goes swimming in my septic tank.*

Sphinx 3000: Gross, Potter. I love it.

Sterling 66: Well, if U have checkbook in hand.

Wolf: No. We'll wait on this. It's too soon, Potter. We'll get back to you. As always, I've enjoyed our talk, but I have other matters to attend to.

Wolf signed off. He was gone. Shit. He'd come and gone, just like that. The mystery man as always. Who was this bastard?

I stayed on-line, chatting with the others for a few minutes – expressing my disappointment at the decision, my eagerness to make a purchase. Then I left the site too.

I looked around the operation room at my colleagues. A few began to clap, partly mocking me, but mostly it was congratulatory. Cop-to-cop stuff. Almost like old times. I felt marginally accepted by the others in the room. For the first time, actually.

Chapter Eighty-Three

We waited to hear from the Wolf again. Everyone in the overcrowded room wanted to take him down in the worst way. He was a complicated and twisted killer, but, besides that, the FBI needed a win; a lot of people working their asses off needed it. Snaring the Wolf would be a tremendous victory. If we could just find him. And what if we could get all of the other sick bastards too? Sphinx. ToscaBella. Louis XV. Sterling.

Still, something was bothering me a lot. If the Wolf was as powerful and successful as he seemed to be, why was he involved in this at all? Because he'd always been into lots of kinds of crimes? Or because he was a sex freak himself? Was that it, the Wolf was a freak? Where could I go with that line of thinking?

He's a freak, and therefore? . . .

Except for a couple of hours when I went home to see the kids, I remained inside the Hoover Building for the next day and a half. So did a lot of other agents on the case, even Monnie Donnelley who was as emotionally invested in this as anybody. We continued to collect information, especially about Russian mobsters in the States, but mostly we waited for a call from the Wolf's Den to Mr Potter. A yes or a no, a go or a no-go. What was the bastard waiting for?

I talked to Jamilla several times – good talks, also to Sampson, the kids, Nana Mama. I even talked to Christine. I had to find out where her head was at about little Alex. After our talk, I wasn't sure if she knew, which was the most disturbing thing of all. I began to detect an ambivalent tone in her voice when she spoke about raising Alex, even though she said she was prepared to sue for custody. Considering all she'd been through, it was hard for me to stay angry at her.

I would rather have given up my right arm than my little boy, though. Just thinking about it gave me a headache that throbbed continuously and made the long wait for a solution even worse.

The phone on my desk rang around ten on the second evening and I picked up right away. 'Waiting for my call? How's it going?' It was Jamilla, and though she sounded close, she was all the way across country in California.

'Sucks,' I said. 'I'm stuck in a small, windowless room with eight smelly FBI hackers.'

'That good, huh? So I take it the Wolfman hasn't called back with an answer.'

'No. And it's not just that.' I told Jamilla about my phone call with Christine.

She wasn't nearly as sympathetic as I was. 'Who the hell

does she think she is? She walked on her little boy. She was away for all that time.'

'It's more complicated than that,' I said.

'No, it isn't, Alex. You always like to give people the benefit of the doubt. You think people are basically good.'

'I guess I do. That's the reason I can do my job. Because most people *are* basically good and they don't deserve the shit that gets heaped on them.'

Jamilla laughed. 'Well, neither do you. Think about that. Neither does little A, Damon, Jannie, Nana Mama. Not that you asked for my opinion. I'll shut up now. So what *is* going on with the case? Change the subject to something more pleasant.'

'We're waiting on this Russian hood and his creeped-out friends. I still don't understand why he's involved in a kidnapping ring.'

'You're at FBI headquarters, the Hoover cube?'

'Yes, but it's not exactly a cube. It's only seven stories on Pennsylvania Avenue, because of the D.C. building codes. And eleven stories in the back part of the building.'

'Thanks for sharing that. You're starting to sound like a Feebie. I'll bet it feels weird to be in there.'

'No, I just figure I'm on the *fifth* floor. Could be in either part of the building.'

'Ha, ha. No, working the other side, the *dark* side. Being in the *J. Edgar Hoover* Building. *Being* a Feebie. Just thinking about it makes me shiver.'

'The waiting is the same, Jam. The waiting's always the same.'

'At least you have good friends to talk to some of the time. At least you have some nice phone pals.'

'I do, don't I? And you're right, it's easier waiting here with you.'

'I'm glad you feel that way. We need to see each other, Alex. We need to touch each other. There are things we have to talk about.'

'I know that. As soon as this case is over. I promise. I'll be on the first plane.'

Jamilla laughed again. 'Well, get cracking, boy. Catch the big bad Wolf psycho bastard. Otherwise, I'll be on my own plane East.'

'Promise?'

'Promise.'

Chapter Eighty-Four

A dozen or so agents had been sitting around eating thick roast beef sandwiches, German potato salad, and drinking iced tea when contact with the Wolf's Den was made again. 'Roast beef' has a special meaning inside the FBI, but that was another story. The Wolf was calling.

Potter. We've made a decision on your request, the e-mail said. *Get back to us.*

The group continued to eat. We agreed there was no need to get back to the Wolf instantly. It would raise his suspicions if Potter was there waiting for the call. An agent was already playing the part of Dr Homer Taylor in Hanover at Dartmouth. We had spread a lie that the professor had the flu and wouldn't be conducting any classes for the next day or two. Occasionally, 'sightings' of Professor Taylor were arranged at his house – sometimes looking out windows, or sitting out on the front porch. To our knowledge, no one else had inquired about Taylor at Dartmouth, or at his house in Webster. Both locations were being watched closely by agents.

I hoped that the agents in the field knew what the hell they were doing. At this point we had no idea how careful the Wolf was, or whether his suspicions had already been aroused. We didn't know enough about the Russian. Not even if he had someone in the Bureau feeding him information.

It was agreed that I would wait an hour and a half, since I hadn't been on-line when he established contact, and the Wolf would know that. During the past day we'd been unsuccessful in trying to connect the Wolf's Den to an owner or even to one of the other users. This probably meant that a high-level hacker had protected the site well. The Bureau's experts were confident they would break-through, but it hadn't happened yet.

Homer Taylor had been transported to D.C. again, and we used his eyes for the retina scan. Then I sat down at a computer and began to type. I was following the model of communication to the Wolf's Den provided by Homer Taylor as part of our deal.

This is Mr Potter, I began. *Can I have my lover?*

Chapter Eighty-Five

I waited for the Wolf to answer Potter's insane question. We all did.

No response came. Shit. What had I done wrong? I'd gone too far, hadn't I? He was clever. Somehow, he knew what we were up to. But how?

'I'll stay on for a while,' I said as I looked around the room. 'I want what he has to offer. He knows it. I'm supposed to be horny.'

This is Potter, I typed again, a few minutes later.

Suddenly words began to appear on my screen.

I read: *Wolf: That's redundant, Potter. I know who you are.*

I typed some more words in Taylor's strident 'voice'. *UR rude to make me wait like this. U know how I feel, what I'm going through.*

Wolf: How could I? You're the scary freak, Potter, not me.

I typed: *Not so. UR the real freak. The cruellest of all.*

Wolf: Why do you say that? You think I take hostages like you?

My heart raced. What did he mean by that? Did the Wolf have a hostage? Maybe more than one? Could Elizabeth Connelly still be alive after all this time? Or some other hostage? Maybe one we didn't even know about?

Wolf: So tell me something, faggot. Prove yourself to me.

Prove myself? How? I waited for more instruction to come. But it didn't.

I typed: *What do U want to know? UR right – I'm horny. No, not really. I'm in love.*

Wolf: What happened to Worcester? You were in love with him too.

The chat was heading into uncharted waters. I was guessing – hoping I could maintain continuity with things Homer Taylor might have shared before. The other question made me edgy: was this really the Wolf I was speaking to?

I typed, *Francis was incapable of love. He made me very angry. He's gone now, never to be heard from again.*

Wolf: And there will be no repercussions?

I'm careful. Like U. I like my life; I don't want to be caught. And I won't be!!!

Wolf: Does that mean Worcester rests in pieces?

I wasn't sure how to answer. With a cruel joke of my own? *Something like that,* I typed: *UR funny.*

Wolf: Be more specific. Give me the bloody details, Potter. Give!

Is this a test? I don't need this shit.

Wolf: You know it is.

I typed: *The septic tank. I told you that.*

No response came from the Wolf. He was rubbing my nerves raw.

So when do I get my new boy? I typed.

A pause of several seconds.

Wolf: You have the money?

Of course I do.

Wolf: How much do you have?

I felt I knew the correct answer to that, but I couldn't be sure. A week earlier, Taylor had taken one hundred twenty-five thousand dollars from his account with a money manager at Lehman in New York.

One hundred twenty-five thousand. The money isn't a problem. It's burning a hole in my pocket.

No response from Wolf.

I typed: *U told me not to be redundant.*

Wolf: All right then, maybe we'll get you the boy. Be careful! There might not be another!

I typed: *Then there won't be another hundred twenty-five thousand!!!*

Wolf: I'm not worried. There are lots of freaks like you. You'd be amazed.

So. U didn't answer my question before. How is your hostage?

Wolf: I have to go back to work . . . one more question, Potter. Just to be safe. Where did you get your name?

I looked around the room. *Oh Christ.* It was something I hadn't thought to ask Taylor.

A voice whispered close to my ear. Monnie's. 'The young adult books? They call Harry "Mr Potter" at the Hogwarts

School. Maybe? I don't know?'

Was that it? I needed to type something; it had to be the right answer. Was the name from the Harry Potter books? Because he liked young boys? Then something from Taylor's office in the farmhouse flashed in my brain.

My fingers went to the keys. Paused for a second. Then I typed my answer.

This is absurd. The name is from the Jamaica Kinkaid novel – Mr Potter. Fuck U!

I waited for a response. So did everyone else in the room. Finally, it came.

Wolf: I'll get you the boy, Mr Potter.

Chapter Eighty-Six

We were in business again, and I was back working the streets, the way I liked it, the way it used to be.

I had been in Boston several times before, loved the city enough to consider moving there, and was comfortable. For the next two days we shadowed a student named Paul Xavier from his apartment on Beacon Hill, to his classes at Harvard, to the Ritz-Carlton where he was a waiter, to popular clubs like No Borders and Rebuke.

Xavier was the 'bait' we had set out for the Wolf and his kidnapping crew.

Actually, Xavier was being impersonated by a thirty-year-old agent from our field office in Springfield, Massachusetts. The agent's real name was Paul Gautier. Boyishly handsome, tall and slender, with fluffy, light brown hair, he looked like someone in his early twenties. He was armed, but also being closely watched by a minimum of six agents at all times of the day and night. We had no idea how or when the Wolf's team might try to grab him, only that they would.

For twelve hours each day, I was one of the agents

watching and protecting Gautier. I had spoken about the dangers of using 'bait' to try and catch the kidnappers, but nobody had paid attention.

On the second night of surveillance, and according to plan, Paul Gautier went to 'the Fens' along the Muddy River near Park Drive and Boylston Street. Actually called the BackBay Fens it had been imagined by Frederick Law Olmsted who'd also designed the Boston Common and Central Park in New York. In the evening hours after the clubs closed the *real* Paul Xavier often cruised the Fens looking for sexual encounters, which was why we had sent our agent there.

It was dangerous work for all of us, but especially for Agent Gautier. The area was dark and there were no streetlights. The tall reeds along the river were thick and provided cover for pickups and liaisons and kidnappings.

Agent Peggy Katz and I were on the edge of the reeds, which resembled elephant grass. During the past half hour, she had admitted that she *wasn't* really interested in sports, but had learned about basketball and football because she wanted to be able to talk with her male counterparts about *something*.

'Men talk about other things,' I said as I scouted the Fens through night-glasses.

'I know that. I can talk about *money* and *cars* too. But I refuse to talk to you horny bastards about sex.'

I coughed out a laugh. Katz could deliver her lines. She was often wry, with a twinkle, and she seemed to be laughing *with* you, even if you happened to be the butt of her jokes. But I also knew that she was very tough, a real hardliner.

'Why did *you* join the Bureau?' she asked as we continued to wait for Agent Gautier to appear. 'You were doing well with the Washington P.D., right?'

'I was doing just fine.'

I lowered my voice and pointed toward a clearing up ahead. 'Here comes Gautier now.'

Agent Gautier had just left Boylston Street. He was walking slowly across the Fens toward the Muddy River. I knew the area pretty well from an earlier scouting trip. During the day this same section of the park was called the 'Victory Gardens'. Area residents raised flowers and vegetables, and there were signs pleading with night visitors not to trample them.

The team leader, Roger Nielsen, spoke in a whisper that seeped into my earphones. 'Male in the watch cap, Alex. Stout guy. You see him?'

'I've got him.' Watch cap was talking into a microphone on the collar of his sport shirt. He wasn't one of ours, so he must be one of theirs – *the Wolf's*.

I began to scour the crowd for a partner or two. The kidnapping crew? Probably. Who the hell else could it be?

Nielsen said, 'I think he has a mike on. You see it?'

'He's definitely miked. I see another suspicious male. Near the gardens to the left of us,' I said. 'Talking into his collar too. They're moving on Gautier.'

Chapter Eighty-Seven

There were three of them, bulky males, and they began to converge on Paul Gautier. At the same time we moved on them. I had my Glock out, but was I really ready for what might happen in this small, dark park?

The kidnappers were keeping close to Park Drive, and I figured they had a van or truck out on the street. They looked confident and unafraid. They'd done this before: grabbed purchased men and women. They were professional kidnappers.

'Take them now,' I told Senior Agent Nielsen. 'Gautier is at risk.'

'Wait until they grab him,' the response came back. 'We want to do this right. Wait.'

I didn't agree with Nielsen and I didn't like what was happening. Why wait? Gautier was hanging out there too much and the park was dark.

'Gautier is at risk,' I repeated.

One of the men, blond, wearing a Boston Bruins windbreaker, waved to him.

Gautier watched the man approach, nodded his head, smiled. The blond had some kind of small flashlight in his hand. He lit up Paul Gautier's face.

I could hear them talking. 'Nice night for a walk,' Gautier said, then laughed. He sounded nervous.

'The things we do for love,' the blond said.

The two of them were only a few feet apart. The other abductors held back, but not far.

Then the blond whipped a gun out of his jacket pocket. He pushed it against Gautier's face. 'You're coming with me. No one will hurt you. Just walk with me. Make it easy on yourself.'

The two others joined them.

'You're making a mistake,' said Gautier.

'Oh, and why is that?' asked the blond. 'I've got the gun, not you.'

'*Take them. Now,*' came the order from Senior Agent Nielsen.

'FBI! Hands up. Back away from him!' Nielsen shouted as we ran forward.

'*FBI!*' came a second shout. 'Everybody, hands up!'

Then everything went crazy. The other two abductors pulled out guns. The blond held his to Agent Gautier's skull.

'*Back off!*' he screamed. 'I'll shoot him dead! Drop *your* guns. I'll shoot him, I promise you! I don't bluff.'

Our agents continued to move forward – slowly.

Then the worst thing happened – the heavy-set blond shot Agent Paul Gautier in the face.

Chapter Eighty-Eight

Before the shock of the gun blast faded, the three men took off running very fast. Two of them galloped toward Boylston, but the blond who'd shot Paul Gautier sprinted out on to Park Drive.

He was a big man, but he was motoring. I remembered hearing from Monnie Donnelley that great Russian athletes, even former Olympians, were sometimes recruited into the Mafia. *Was blondie a former jock?* He moved like it. The confrontation, the shooting and everything else, reminded me of how little we knew about the Russian mobsters. How did they work; how did they think?

I took off after him, an overload of adrenaline rocketing through my body. I still couldn't believe what had happened. It could have been avoided. Now Gautier was possibly dead, probably dead.

I ran as I shouted, 'Take them alive!' It should have been obvious, but the other agents had just seen Paul Gautier gunned down. I didn't know how much street action, or combat, any of them had seen before. And we desperately needed to question the kidnappers once we caught them.

I was getting winded. Maybe I needed more time in the physical-training classes at Quantico, or maybe it was because I'd spent too much time sitting around inside the Hoover Building these past few weeks.

I chased the blond killer through a tree-lined residential area. A moment later, the trees cleared and the towers of the glittering Prudential Center and the Hancock loomed ahead. I glanced back. Three agents trailed behind, including Peggy Katz, who had her gun out.

Then the man running ahead of me turned on to Boylston Street. He was approaching the Hynes Convention Center with four FBI agents racing behind. I was closing a little ground on him, but not enough. I wondered if maybe we'd gotten lucky: *could this be the Wolf up ahead? He was hands-on, right? If it was – then we had him for murder.* Whoever he was – he was still moving well. A long-distance *sprinter*.

'Stop! We'll shoot!' one of the agents yelled behind me. The blond Russian didn't stop. Suddenly he made a sharp, sliding turn down a side street. It was narrow and darker than Boylston. One-way. I wondered if he'd thought about his escape route before this. Probably not.

The extraordinary thing – he hadn't hesitated when he shot Agent Gautier. *I don't bluff,* he'd said. Who would murder so casually? With so many FBI watching?

The Wolf? He was supposed to be fearless and ruthless, maybe even crazy. *One of his lieutenants? . . . How did the Russians think?*

I could hear his shoes slapping down hard on the

pavement up ahead. I was gaining on the Russian a little, getting a second wind.

Suddenly he whirled around – *and fired at me!*

I threw myself down on the ground fast. But then I was up just as quickly, chasing after him again. I'd clearly seen his face – broad, flat features, dark eyes, late thirties to early forties.

He turned again – planted – fired.

I ducked behind a parked car. Then I heard a scream. I whirled around and saw an agent down. One of the males. Doyle Rogers. The blond turned and started to run again. But I had my second wind and I thought I could catch him. Then what? He was ready to die.

Suddenly a shot rang out behind me! I couldn't believe what I saw. The blond dropped face down, fell flat on his chest and face.

He never moved once he hit the ground. One of the agents behind me had shot him. I turned – and saw Peggy Katz. She was still in a shooting crouch.

I checked on Agent Rogers and found he'd only been hit in the shoulder. He'd be okay. Then I walked back alone toward the Fens. When I got there, I discovered that Paul Gautier was still alive. But the two other kidnappers had gotten away. They'd left their van, but commandeered a car on Park Drive. Our agents had lost them. Bad news, the worst.

The whole operation had blown up in our faces.

Chapter Eighty-Nine

I don't think that I'd felt this bad in all my years with the Washington P.D., maybe in all my years combined. If I hadn't been sure before, I was now. I'd made a mistake in coming over to the FBI. The Bureau did things very differently from anything I was used to. They were by-the-book, by-the-numbers, and then suddenly they *weren't*. They had tremendous resources, and staggering amounts of information, but they were often amateurs on the streets. There was some great personnel; and some incredible losers.

After the shootout in Boston I had driven over to the FBI offices. The agents who gathered there all looked shell-shocked. I couldn't blame them. What a mess. One of the worst I'd seen. I couldn't help feeling that Senior Agent Nielsen was the one responsible, but what did it matter, what good did it do to cast around blame? Two well-intentioned agents had been wounded; one had almost died. Maybe I shouldn't have, but I felt partly responsible. I'd told the senior agent to move in on Paul Gautier faster, but he didn't listen.

The blond man I'd chased down Boylston Street had unfortunately died. Katz's bullet had hit him in the back of the neck, and it had taken out most of his throat. He'd probably died instantly. He carried no identification. His wallet held a little more than six hundred bucks, but not much else. He had tattoos of a snake, a dragon, and a black bear on his back and shoulders. Cyrillic lettering, that no one had deciphered yet. Prison tats. We assumed he was Russian. But we had no name, no identification, no real proof.

Photographs of the dead man had been taken, then sent to Washington. They were checking, so we had little to do in Boston until they called back. A few hours later, a Ford Explorer commandeered by the two other abductors was found in the parking lot of a bank in Arlington, Massachusetts. They had stolen a second vehicle out of the bank lot. By now they'd probably switched it for another stolen car.

A total screw-up in every way. Couldn't have gone worse.

I was sitting in a conference room by myself, my face in my hands, when one of the Boston agents walked in. He pointed an accusatory finger my way. 'Director Burns's office on the line.'

Burns wanted me back in Washington – as simple and direct as that. There were no explanations, or even recriminations about what had happened in Boston. I guess I was to be kept in the dark a while longer about what he really thought, what the Bureau thought, and I just couldn't respect that way of operating.

I got to the SIOC offices in the Hoover Building at six in

the morning. I hadn't slept. The place was humming with activity, and I was glad no one had time to talk about the shooting of the two agents in Boston.

Stacy Pollack came up to me a few minutes after I arrived. She looked as tired as I felt, but she put a hand on my shoulder. 'Everybody here knows that you felt Gautier was in danger and tried to move in on the shooter. I talked to Nielsen. He said it was his decision.'

I nodded, but then I said, 'Maybe you should have talked to me first.'

Pollack's eyes narrowed. But she said nothing more about Boston. 'There's something else,' she finally spoke again. 'We've had some luck. Most of us have been here all night. The money transfer we made to the Wolf's Den . . . we used a contact of ours in the financial world, a banker from Morgan Chase's International Correspondent Unit. We were able to trace the money out of the Caymans. Then we monitored virtually every transaction to US banks with correspondent relationships. Had them screen all inbound wire payment orders. That's where our consultant, Robert Hatfield, said it got tricky. The transaction zipped from bank to bank – New York, then Boston, Detroit, Toronto, Chicago, a couple of others. But we know where the money finally wound up.'

'Where?' I asked.

'Dallas. The money went to Dallas. And we have a name – a recipient for the funds. We're hoping that he's the Wolf. At any rate, we know where he lives, Alex. You're going to Dallas.'

Chapter Ninety

The earliest abduction cases we tracked had occurred in Texas and dozens of agents and analysts went to work investigating them in depth. Everything about the case was larger scale now. The surveillance details on the suspect's house and place of business were the most impressive I had ever seen. I doubted that any police force in the country, with the possible exceptions of New York and Los Angeles, could afford this kind of effort.

As usual the Bureau had done a thorough job finding out everything possible about the man who had received money from us through the Caymans bank. Lawrence Lipton lived in Old Highland Park, a moneyed neighborhood north of Dallas proper. The streets there meandered alongside creeks under a canopy of magnolias, oaks, and native pecans. The grounds of nearly every house were expensively landscaped and most of the traffic during the day belonged to tradesmen, nannies, cleaning services and gardeners.

So far the evidence we'd gathered on Lipton was

contradictory though. He had attended St Marks, a prestigious Dallas prep school and then the University of Texas at Austin. His family, and his wife's, was old Dallas oil money, but Lawrence had diversified and now owned a Texas winery, a venture capital group, and a successful computer software company. The computer connection caught Monnie Donnelley's eye, and mine as well.

Lipton seemed to be such a straight arrow, however. He sat on the boards of the Dallas Museum of Art, and the Friends of the Library. He was a trustee for the Baylor Hospital and a deacon at First United Methodist.

Could he be the Wolf? It didn't seem possible to me.

The second morning I was in Dallas a meeting was held at the field office there. Senior Agent Nielsen remained in charge of the case, but it was clear to everyone that Ron Burns was calling the shots on this from Washington. I don't think any of us would have been too surprised if Burns had shown up for the briefing himself.

At eight in the morning, Roger Nielsen stood before a roomful of agents and read from a clipboard. 'They've been real busy through the night back in Washington,' he said, and seemed neither impressed nor surprised by the effort. Apparently this had become s.o.p. on cases that got big in the media.

'I want to acquaint all of you with the latest on Lawrence Lipton. The most important development is that he doesn't seem to have any known connections to the KGB or any Russian mobs. He isn't Russian. Maybe something will turn up later; or maybe he's just that good at hiding his past. In the fifties, his father moved to Texas from Kentucky to seek his fortune on "the prairie". He apparently found it *under* the prairie, in West Texas oil fields.'

Nielsen stopped and looked around the meeting room, going from face to face. 'There is one interesting recent development,' he went on. 'Among its holdings, Micro-Management owns a company called Safe Environs in Dallas. Safe Environs is a private security firm. Lawrence Lipton has recently put himself under armed guard. I wonder why? Is he worried about us, or is he scared of somebody else? Maybe the big bad Wolf?'

Chapter Ninety-One

I f it wasn't so incredibly terrifying, it would be mind-boggling. Lizzie Connelly was still among the living. She was keeping herself positive by being somewhere else – anywhere but *here in the horrid closet. With this complete madman bursting in two, three, sometimes five times a day.*

Mostly she got lost in her memories. Once upon a time, and it seemed so long ago, she had called her girls 'Merry-Berry', 'Bobbie-doll', names like that. They used to sing 'High Hopes' all the time, and songs from 'Mary Poppins'.

They had endless positive-energy thoughts – which Lizzie called 'happy thoughts', and always shared them with one another, and with Brendan of course.

What else could she remember? What? Anything?

They had so many animals over the years that eventually they gave each one *a number*.

Chester, a black lab with a curly tail like a chow was number 16. The lab would bark constantly, all day and all night until Lizzie merely *showed* him a bottle of Tabasco sauce – his kryptonite. Then he would finally shut up.

Dukie, number 15, was a short-haired, orange calico who Lizzie believed had probably been an old Jewish lady in another life and who was always complaining, 'Oh no, no, no, no.'

Maximus Kiltimus was number 11; Stubbles was number 31; Kitten Little was number 35.

Memories were all that Lizzie Connelly had – because there could be no present for her. None.

She couldn't be here in this horror house.

Had to be somewhere else, anywhere else.

Had to be!

Had to be!

Had to be!

Because he was inside her now.

The Wolf was inside her, in the real world, grunting and thrusting like an animal, violating, raping, for minutes that seemed like hours.

But Lizzie had the last laugh, didn't she?

She wasn't there.

She was somewhere in her memories.

Chapter Ninety-Two

Then he was finally gone, the terrible, inhuman Wolf. Monster! Beast! He'd given her a bathroom break, and food, but now he was *gone*. God, his arrogance in keeping her here in his house! *When is he going to kill me? I'm going mad. Going, going, gone!*

She peered through teary eyes into the pitch-blackness. She'd been bound and gagged again. In a strange way, that was good news. It meant he still wanted her, right?

Good God, I'm alive because I'm desirable to a horrid beast! Please help me, dear God. Please, please, help me.

She thought about her good girls and then she turned her mind toward escape. A *fantasy*, she understood, and therefore *escape* in itself.

By now, she knew this closet by heart, even in total darkness. It was as if she could *see* everything, as if she had night sight. More than anything, she was aware of her own body – *trapped* in here – and her mind – trapped as well.

Lizzie let her hands wander as much as they could. There were clothes in the closet – a male's – *his*. The closest to her was some kind of sport coat with round, smooth buttons. Possibly a blazer? Lightweight, which reinforced her belief that this was a warm-weather city.

Next was a vest. A smallish ball was in one pocket, hard, maybe a golf ball.

What could she do with a golf ball? Could it be a weapon?

A zipper on the pocket. *What could she do with a zipper? She'd like to catch his tattooed dick in it!*

Then a windbreaker. Flimsy. Strong, sickening smell of tobacco on it. And then, her favorite thing to touch, a soft overcoat, possibly cashmere.

There were more 'treasures' in the overcoat's pockets.

A loose button. Scraps of paper. *From a notepad?*

A ballpoint pen, possibly a Bic – *blue, black or red*. Coins – four quarters, two dimes, a nickel. Unless the coins were foreign? She wondered endlessly.

There was also a book of matches, with a shiny cover and embossed letters.

What did the embossed letters say? Would it tell her the city where she was being kept?

Also, a lighter.

A half pack of mints which she knew to be cinnamon because she smelled it on her hands.

And at the bottom of the pocket – lint, so insignificant, yet important to her now.

Behind the overcoat were two bundles of his clothing still covered in plastic from the cleaners. A receipt of some kind on the first packet. Attached by a staple.

She imagined the name of the cleaners, an identification

number in red, *writing* by some dry-cleaning store clerk.

All of it seemed strangely precious to Lizzie – because she had nothing else.

Except a powerful will to live.

And get her revenge on the Wolf.

Chapter Ninety-Three

I was a part of the large surveillance detail near the house in old Highland Park, and I thought we were going to take Lawrence Lipton down soon, maybe within hours. We'd been told that Washington was working with the Dallas police.

I stared absently at the house, a large two-story Tudor on about two and a half acres of very expensive real estate. It looked pristine. A redbrick sidewalk went from the street to an arched doorway, which led inside to a house which looked as if it had a dozen rooms. Interestingly, the big news that day in Dallas was about a fire in Kessler Park that had incinerated a 64,000-square-foot mega mansion. The Lipton spread was less than a third that size, but it was still impressive, or depressing, or both.

It was around nine in the evening. A supervisory agent from the Dallas office, Joseph Denyeau, came on my earphones. 'We just got word from the Director's office. We have to back off immediately. I don't understand it either. The order couldn't be any clearer, though. Pull back!

Everybody head to the office. We need to reconnoiter and talk about this.'

I looked at my partner in the car that night, an agent named Bob Shaw. It was pretty obvious that he didn't understand what the hell had just happened either.

'What was *that*?' I asked him.

Shaw shook his head and rolled his eyes. 'What do I know? We go back to the field office, drink some bad coffee, maybe somebody higher-up explains it to us, but don't count on it.'

It took us only fifteen minutes to get to the field office at that time of night. The Rangers were playing the Angels, and Agent Shaw turned on the game as we rode. We needed to hear something, anything, that seemed a little organized and sane, even a baseball play-by-play on the car radio.

We filed into a conference room at the field office, and I saw a lot of weary, confused and pissed-off agents. Nobody was saying much yet. We'd gotten close to a possible break on this case, and now we'd been ordered to pull back. Nobody seemed to understand why.

The ASAC finally came out of his office and joined the rest of us. Joseph Denyeau looked thoroughly disgusted as he threw his dusty cowboy boots up on a conference table. 'I have *no idea*,' he announced. 'Not a clue, folks. Consider yourselves debriefed.'

So about forty agents waited for an explanation of the night's action, but one didn't come, or wasn't 'forthcoming' as they say. The agent in charge, Roger Nielsen, finally called D.C. and was told they would get back to us. In the meantime, we were to stand down. We might even be sent home in the morning.

Around eleven o'clock Denyeau got another update from Nielsen, and passed it on to us. 'They're working on it,' he said and smiled wryly.

'Working on what?' somebody called from the back.

'Oh hell, I don't know, Donnie. Working on their pedicures. Working on getting all of us to quit the Bureau. Then there'll be no more agents, and, I guess, no more embarrassing screw-ups for the media to write about. I'm going to get some sleep. I'd advise all of you to do the same.'

That's what we did.

Chapter Ninety-Four

We were back at the field office by eight the next morning. Several of the agents looked a little messed-up after the night off. First thing, Director Burns was on the line from Washington. I was pretty sure the Director rarely, if ever, spoke to the troops like this. So why do it now? What was up?

Agents around the room were looking at one another. Brows crinkled, eyebrows arched. No one could fathom why Burns was so involved. Maybe I could. I'd seen the restlessness in him, the dissatisfaction with the ways of the past, even if he couldn't effectively change them all at once. Burns had started as a street cop in Philadelphia and worked his way up to Police Commissioner. Maybe he could change things at the Bureau.

'I wanted to explain what happened yesterday,' he said over the speakerphone. Every agent in the room listened intently, myself included. 'And I also wanted to apologize to all of you. Everything got territorial for a while. The Dallas police, the mayor, even the governor of Texas, were involved. The Dallas police asked that we pull back, because they didn't have full confidence in us. I agreed to the action because I wanted to talk it through with them rather than force our presence there.

'They didn't want mistakes, and they weren't sure that we have the right man. The Lipton family has a good reputation in the city. He's very well connected. Anyway, Dallas was surprised that we listened to their concerns – and now they've backed off again. They respect the team we've assembled.

'We will continue our action against Lawrence Lipton and, believe me, we're going to take that bastard down. Then we're going to take Pasha Sorokin down, the Wolf. I don't want you to worry about past mistakes. Don't worry about mistakes at all. Just do your job in Dallas. I have the utmost confidence in you.'

Burns went off the line and just about every agent's face in the room wore a smile. It was quite magical, actually. The Director had said things that some of them had been waiting years to hear; especially welcome was the news that he believed in their ability, and wasn't worried about mistakes. We were back in the game; we were expected to bring down Lawrence Lipton.

Minutes after the phone call ended, my cell went off. I answered and it was Burns himself. 'So how'd I do?' he asked. I could hear the smile in his voice. I could also almost see the cocky upturn of his lip when he grinned. He, he knew how he'd done.

I walked away from the group and into a far corner of the

room, and told him what he wanted to hear. 'You did good. They're pumped to do the job.'

Burns exhaled. 'Alex. I want you to turn up the heat on this punk. I sold you hard to Dallas as a key member of the team. They bought you, and your reputation. They know how good we think you are. I want you to make Lawrence Lipton very uncomfortable. Do it your own way.'

I found myself smiling. 'I'll see what I can do.'

'And Alex, contrary to what I said to the others, *don't* make any mistakes.'

Chapter Ninety-Five

Don't make any mistakes. It was a hell of an exit line, I had to give him that. Kind of funny, in a sadistic, hard ass way. I was starting to like Ron Burns again. Couldn't help myself. *But did I trust him?*

Somehow, I got the feeling that Burns wasn't that worried about the mistakes, though. He wanted to catch the kidnappers, especially Pasha Sorokin – even if we didn't yet know who he really was, or where he lived. According to his orders, all I had to do was figure out a way to break Lawrence Lipton down, do it in a hurry, and not embarrass the Bureau in any way.

I met with Roger Nielsen on possible next strategies – we had already resumed surveillance on Lawrence Lipton. It was decided that it was time to put real pressure on him, to let him know we were in Dallas, and that we *knew* about him. After Burns's phone call, I wasn't surprised that I had been chosen to confront Lipton.

We decided that I would go and see Lipton at his office in the Lakeside Square Building at the intersection of the LBJ

Freeway and North Central Expressway. The building was twenty stories high with lots of reflective glass. It was practically blinding down on the street as I looked skyward in the Texas sunshine. I walked inside at a little past ten in the morning. Lipton's office suite was on the nineteenth floor. When I got off the elevator, a recorded voice said, 'Howdy.'

I stepped into a large reception area with half an acre of red-wine-colored carpeting, beige walls, dark brown leather sofas, and matching chairs everywhere. There were framed, signed photos of Roger Staubach, Nolan Ryan and Tom Landry on the walls.

I was told to wait in reception by a very proper-looking young woman in a dark blue pants suit. She sat self-importantly behind a sleek walnut desk under recessed lighting. She looked all of twenty-two or twenty-three years old, fresh from charm school. She acted and spoke as properly as she looked.

'I'll wait, but let Mr Lipton know it's the FBI. It's important that I see him,' I told her.

The receptionist smiled sweetly, as if she'd heard all this before, then she went back to answering the phone calls coming in on her headset. I sat down and waited patiently; I waited for fifteen minutes. Then I got back up again. I strolled over to the reception desk.

'You told Mr Lipton that I'm here?' I asked politely. 'That I'm with the FBI?'

'I did, sir,' she spoke in a syrupy voice that was starting to rub me the wrong way.

'I need to see him right now,' I told the girl and waited until she made another call to Lipton's assistant.

They talked briefly, then she looked back at me. 'Do you have identification, sir?' she asked. She was frowning now.

'I do. They're called creds.'

'May I see it, please? Your creds.' I showed off my new FBI badge and she looked it over like a fast-food counterperson inspecting a fifty-dollar bill.

'Could you please wait over at the seating area?' she asked again, only now she seemed a little nervous, and I wondered what Lawrence Lipton's assistant had told her, what her marching orders were.

'You don't seem to understand, or I'm not making myself clear,' I finally said. 'I'm not here to fool around with you, and I'm not here to wait.'

The receptionist nodded. 'Mr Lipton is in a meeting. That's all I know, sir.'

I nodded back. 'Tell his assistant to pull him out of his meeting right now. Have her tell Mr Lipton that I'm not here to arrest him yet.'

I wandered back to the seating area, but I didn't bother to sit. I stood there and looked out on magnificent, Technicolor green lawns that stretched to the concrete edge of the LBJ Freeway. I was burning inside.

I'd just acted like a D.C. street cop back there. I wondered if Burns would have approved, but it didn't matter. He'd given me some rope, but I also had made a decision that I wasn't going to change because I was an FBI agent now. I was in Dallas to bring down a kidnapper and killer; I was here to find out if Mrs Elizabeth Connelly and others were alive and maybe being held somewhere as slaves. I was back on The Job. I heard a door open behind me and I turned. A heavy-set man with graying hair was standing there and he looked angry.

'I'm Lawrence Lipton,' he said. 'What the hell is this about?'

Chapter Ninety-Six

'**W**hat the hell is this about?' Lipton repeated from the doorway in a loud-mouth, big-shot way. He was speaking to me as if I was a door-to-door brush salesman calling on his company. 'I think you were told that I'm in an important meeting. What does the FBI want with me? And why can't it wait? Why don't you have the courtesy to make an appointment?'

There was something about his attitude that didn't completely track for me. He was trying to be a tough guy, but I didn't think he was. He was just used to beating up on other businessmen. He wore a rumpled blue dress shirt and rep's tie, pinstriped trousers, tasseled loafers, and was at least fifty pounds overweight. What connection could this man have with the Wolf?

I looked at him and said, 'It's about kidnapping, it's about murder. Do you want to talk about this out here in reception? *Sterling.*'

Lawrence Lipton paled, and lost most of his bravado. 'Come inside,' he said and took a step back.

I followed him into an area of cubicles separated by low partitions. Clerical personnel, lots of them. So far this was going just about as I'd expected. But now it would get more interesting. Lipton might be 'softer' than I had expected, but he had powerful connections in Dallas. This office building was in one of the upscale residential/commercial parts of the city.

'I'm Mr Potter,' I said as we walked down a corridor with fabric-covered walls. 'At least I played Mr Potter the last time we talked in the Wolf's Den.'

Lipton didn't turn, didn't respond in any way. We entered a wood-paneled office and he shut the door. The large room had half a dozen windows and a panoramic view. A hat rack near the door held a collection of autographed Dallas Cowboy and Texas Ranger caps.

'I still don't know what this is about, but I'll give you exactly five minutes to explain yourself,' he snapped. 'I don't think you know who you're talking to.'

'Actually, I do. You're Henry Lipton's oldest son. You're married with three children, and a nice house in Highland Park. You're also involved with a kidnapping and murder scheme that we've been tracking closely for several weeks. You're *Sterling*, and I want you to understand something – all your connections, all your father's connections in Dallas, will not help you now. On the other hand, I would like to protect your family as much as possible. That's up to you. I'm not bluffing. I don't ever bluff. This is a federal crime, not a local one.'

'I'm going to call my lawyer,' Lawrence Lipton said and went for the phone.

'You have that right. But I wouldn't if I were you. It won't do any good.'

My tone of voice, something, stopped Lipton from making the call. His flabby hand moved away from the phone on his desk. 'Why?' he asked.

I said, 'I don't care about you. You're involved in murder. But I've seen your kids, your wife. We've been watching you at the house in Highland Park. We've already spoken to your neighbors and friends. When you're arrested, your family will be in danger. We can protect them from the Wolf.'

Suddenly Lipton's face and neck reddened and he erupted with, 'What the hell is wrong with you? Are you crazy? I'm a respected businessman. I never kidnapped or harmed another human being in my life. This is crazy.'

'You gave the orders. The money came to you. Mr Potter sent you a hundred and twenty-five thousand dollars. Or rather, the FBI did.'

'I'm calling my lawyer,' Lipton screamed. 'This is ridiculous and insulting. I don't have to take this from anybody.'

I shrugged. 'Then you're going down in the worst possible way. These offices will be searched immediately. And then your home in Highland Park. Your parents' home in Kessler Park will be searched. Your father's office will be searched. Your wife's offices at the Museum of Art will be searched.'

He picked up his phone. I could see that his hand was

shaking, though. Then he whispered, 'Go fuck yourself.'

I pulled out a two-way and spoke into it. 'Hit the offices and the houses,' I said. I turned back to Lipton. 'You're under arrest. You can call your lawyer now. Tell him you've been taken to the FBI offices.'

Minutes later, a dozen agents stormed into the office with its gorgeous city views and stylish and expensive furnishings.

We arrested *Sterling*.

Chapter Ninety-Seven

Pasha Sorokin was close, and he was watching everyone and everything with great interest. Maybe it was time to show the FBI how these things were done in Moscow, to show them that this wasn't a child's game to be played with rules made up by the police.

He had been there at Sterling's office building in Dallas when the FBI team rushed inside. More than a dozen of them came calling. A strange assemblage to be sure: some dressed in dark business suits, others in dark blue windbreakers with FBI boldly imprinted on the back. Who did they really expect to find here? The Wolf? Others from the Wolf's Den?

They had no concept of what they were getting themselves into. Their dark sedans and vans were parked in plain view on the street. Less than fifteen minutes after they had entered the office building, they came out with Lawrence Lipton in handcuffs, pathetically trying to shield his face. What a scene. They wanted to make a show of this, didn't they? Why do that? he wondered. To prove how tough they were? How smart? But they weren't smart. I will show you how tough and smart you need to be. I will show you how lacking you are in every way.

He instructed his driver to start the car. The wheelman did not look around at his boss in the backseat. He said nothing. He knew not to question orders. The Wolf's ways were strange and unorthodox, but they worked.

'Drive past them,' he ordered. 'I want to say hello.'

The FBI agents were casting nervous looks around the street as they led Lawrence Lipton toward a waiting van. A black man walked beside Sterling. Tall and strangely confident. Pasha Sorokin knew from his informant in the Bureau that this was Alex Cross, and that he was held in high regard.

How was it possible that a black man was given command of the raid? he wondered. In Russia, the American negro was looked down upon. The Wolf had never gotten past his own prejudice; there was no reason to in the US.

'Get me close!' he told the driver. He lowered the rear-passenger side window. The second Cross and Lipton had passed his car Sorokin thrust out an automatic weapon, and aimed it at the back of Sterling's head. Then, an amazing thing – something he hadn't anticipated – happened.

Alex Cross threw Lipton down on to the pavement, and they both rolled behind a parked car. How had Cross known? What had he seen to alert him?

The Wolf fired anyway, but he didn't really have a clear shot. Still, the gunshot rang out loudly. He had delivered a message. Sterling wasn't safe. Sterling was a dead man.

Chapter Ninety-Eight

We transported Lawrence Lipton to the Dallas field office and were holding him there. I threatened to transfer him to Washington if there was any interference from the local police or even the press. I struck a deal with them. I promised Dallas detectives they'd have their turn with Lipton. As soon as I was done.

At eleven o'clock that night I slumped into a windowless interview room. It was sterile and claustrophobic, and I felt as if I'd been there a couple of hundred times before. I nodded to Lawrence Lipton. He didn't respond; he looked just awful. Probably I did too.

'We can help you, your family. We'll keep them safe. Nobody else can help you now,' I said. 'That's the truth.'

Lipton finally spoke to me. 'I don't want to talk to you again. I already told you, I'm not involved in any of the shit you say I am. I'm not going to talk any more. Get my lawyer.' He waved me away.

For the past seven hours he'd been questioned by FBI agents and Dallas detectives. This was my third session, and it wasn't getting easier. His lawyers were in the building, but they'd backed off. They had been informed that he could be formally charged with kidnapping and conspiracy to commit murder and immediately transported to Washington. His father was also in the building but had been denied access to his son. I'd interviewed Henry Lipton, and he'd wept and insisted his son's arrest was a mistake.

I sat down across from him. 'Your father is in the building. Would you like to see him?' I asked.

He laughed. 'Sure. All I have to do is admit that I'm a kidnapper and murderer. Then I can see my father and ask his forgiveness for my sins.'

I ignored the sarcasm. He wasn't very good at it. 'You know we can confiscate the records of your father's company, shut it down? Also, your father is a likely target for the Wolf. We're not here to hurt your family members,' I added. 'Not unless your father is involved in this too.'

He shook his head, kept his eyes lowered. 'My father has never been in trouble.'

'That's what I keep hearing,' I said. 'I've read a lot about you and your family in the past day or so. Gone all the way back to your schooldays at Texas. You were involved in a couple of scrapes in Austin. Two date rapes. Neither case went to trial. Your father saved you then. It won't happen this time.'

Lawrence Lipton didn't respond. His eyes were dead, and he looked as if he hadn't slept in days. His blue dress shirt was as wrinkled as a used Kleenex tissue, soaked with perspiration at the underarms. His hair was wet, dripping little rivers of moisture down to his shirt collar and side-burns. The skin under his eyes sagged and had a purplish tint in the harsh, interrogation-room light.

He finally said, 'I don't want my family hurt. Leave my father out of this. Get him protection.'

I nodded. 'Okay, Lawrence. Where do we start? I'm ready to put your family in protective custody until we catch him.'

'And afterward?' he asked. 'It doesn't stop with them.'

'We'll protect your family.'

Lipton sighed loudly, then said, 'All right, I'm the money-man. I'm Sterling. I might be able to get you to the Wolf. But I need the promises in writing. Lots of promises.'

Chapter Ninety-Nine

I was heading into the deepest darkness again, attracted to it as most people are attracted to sunlight. I kept thinking about Elizabeth Connelly, still missing, and feared dead.

Lipton's father visited a couple of times and the two men wept together. Mrs Lipton was allowed to see her husband. There was a lot of crying among the family members and most of the emotions seemed genuine.

I was in the interrogation room with Sterling until a little past three in the morning. I was prepared to stay later, as long as it took to get the information I needed. Several deals were struck with his lawyers during the night.

At around two, with most of the lawyering done, Lipton and I sat down to talk again. Two senior agents from the Dallas field office were in the room with us. They were only there to take notes and tape-record.

This was my interview to conduct.

'How did you get involved with the Wolf?' I asked Lawrence Lipton after a few minutes in which I emphasized my concern for his family. He seemed more clear-headed and more focused than he'd been a few hours before. I sensed that a weight had been lifted from him. Guilt, betrayal of his family – especially his father? His school records revealed he was a bright, but troubled, student. His problems always centered on an obsession with sex, but he'd never received a day of treatment. Lawrence Lipton was a freak.

'How did I get involved?' he said, seeming to be asking the question of himself. 'I have a thing for young girls, you see. Teens, pre-teens. There's lots of it available these days. The Internet opened new sources.'

'For what? Be as concrete as you can, Lawrence.'

He shrugged. 'For freaks like myself. Suddenly we can get what we want, when we want it. And I know how to search for the nastiest sites. At first I settled for photos and movies. I especially liked real-time films.'

'We found some. In your office at home.'

'One day a man came to see me. He came to the office, just like you did.'

'To blackmail you?' I asked.

Lipton shook his head. 'No, not blackmail. He said he wanted to know what I really wanted. Sexually. And then he would help me get it. I threw him out. He came back the next day. He had records of everything I'd bought on the Internet. "So what do you really want?" he asked again. I wanted young girls. Pretty ones, with no strings attached, no rules. He supplied me two or three a month. Exactly what I fantasized. Color of hair, shape of breasts, shoe size, freckles, anything I desired.'

'What happened to the girls? Did you murder them? You have to tell me.'

'I'm not a killer. I liked to see the girls get off. Some did. We'd party, then they would be released. Always. They didn't know who I was, or where I was from.'

'So you were satisfied with the arrangement?'

Lipton nodded and his eyes lit up. 'Very. I'd been dreaming of this my whole life. The reality was as good as the fantasy. Of course there was a price.'

'A bill had to be paid?'

'Oh yeah. I got to meet the Wolf, at least I think it was him. He had sent an emissary to my office in the early days. But then he came to see me. In person, he was very scary. Red Mafiya, he said. The KGB came up, but I don't know what his connection to them was.'

'What did he want from you?'

'To go into business with him, to be a partner. He needed my company's expertise with computers and the Internet. The sex club was secondary with him, a throw-in. He was heavily into extortion, money laundering, counterfeiting. The club was my thing. Once our deal was struck, I went looking for wealthy freaks who wanted their dreams fulfilled. Freaks who were willing to spend six figures for a slave, male, female, didn't matter. Sometimes a specific target; sometimes a physical type.'

'To murder?' I asked Lipton.

'Whatever they wanted. Let me tell you where I think he was going with the club. He wanted to involve very rich, powerful men. We already had one, a senator from

West Virginia. He had big plans.'

'Is the Wolf here in Dallas?' I finally asked. 'You've got to help me, if you want my help.'

Lipton shook his head. 'He isn't from around here. He's not in Dallas. Not in Texas. He's a mystery man.'

'But you know where he is?'

He hesitated, but finally went on. 'He doesn't know that I know. He's smart, but not about computers. I tracked him once. He was sure his messages were secure, but I had them cracked. I needed to have something on him.'

Then Sterling told me where he thought I could find the Wolf. And also, who he was. If I could believe what he was saying, Sterling knew the name Pasha Sorokin was using in the United States.

It was Ari Manning.

Chapter One Hundred

I sat high in the cockpit of a luxury cabin cruiser in the Intercoastal Waterway near Millionaires Row in Fort Lauderdale, Florida. Were we close to the Wolf now? I needed to believe that we were. Sterling swore to it, and he had no reason to lie to us, did he? He had every reason to tell the truth.

Sightseers came here on motorboat tours, so I figured we wouldn't be noticed right away. Besides, darkness was starting to fall. We drove past mansions that were mostly Mediterranean- or Portuguese-style, but an occasional Georgian Colonial supposedly signaled 'northern money'. We'd been warned to tread lightly, not to ruffle feathers in the wealthy neighborhood, which, frankly, wouldn't be possible. We were going to ruffle a lot of feathers in a few minutes.

On board the cruiser with me was Ned Mahoney, and two of his seven-person assault teams. Mahoney didn't ordinarily go on missions himself. The Director was changing all that. The FBI had to get stronger in the field.

I watched a large waterfront house through binoculars as our boat approached a dock. Several expensive yachts and speedboats bobbed in the water. We had secured a floor plan of the house, and learned it had been purchased for twenty-four million dollars two years ago. Don't ruffle any feathers.

A large party was in progress at the estate, which belonged to Ari Manning. According to Sterling, he was Pasha Sorokin, the Wolf.

'Looks like everybody's having a fine old time,' Mahoney said from the deck. 'Man, I love a good party. Food, music, dancing, bubbly.'

'Yeah, it's jumping. And the surprise guests haven't even shown up,' I said.

Ari Manning was known around Fort Lauderdale and Miami for the parties he hosted, sometimes a couple a week. His extravaganzas were famous for their surprises – surprise guests like the coaches of the Miami Dolphins and Miami Heat; 'hot' musical and comedy acts from Las Vegas; politicians and diplomats and ambassadors, even right up to the White House.

'Guess we're tonight's surprise special guests,' Mahoney said and grinned at me.

'Flown in all the way from Dallas,' I said. 'With our entourage of fourteen.'

The guests, the nature of the glitzy party itself, made the operation tense, which was probably why Mahoney and I felt compelled to make a few jokes. We'd talked about waiting, but HRT wanted to go in now, while we knew the

Wolf was there. The Director agreed, and had actually made the final decision.

A guy in a ridiculous sailor suit was vigorously waving us away from the dock. We kept coming. 'What's this asshole on the dock want?' Mahoney said to me.

'We're full up! You're too late!' the man on the dock shouted to us. His voice carried above the music blasting from speakers in the back part of the mansion.

'Party doesn't start without us,' Ned Mahoney called back. Then he tooted the horn.

'No, no! Don't come in here!' Sailor Suit began to yell. 'Get away!'

Mahoney tooted the horn again.

The cruiser bumped a Bertram speeder and the guy on the dock looked as if he were going to have a stroke. 'Jesus, be careful. This is a private party! You can't just come in here. Are you friends of Mr Manning?'

Mahoney tooted again. 'Absolutely. Here's my invitation.' He pulled out his ID and his gun.

I was already off the boat and running toward the house.

Chapter One Hundred and One

I pushed my way through the crowd of very well-heeled partygoers who were making their way to candlelit tables. Dinner was being served now. Steak and lobsters, lots of champagne, and pricey wine. Everybody seemed to have worn their Dolce and Gabbana, their Versace, their Yves Saint Laurent couture. I had on faded jeans and a blue FBI windbreaker.

Coiffed heads turned and eyes flashed at me as if I were a party crasher. I was, too. The party crasher from hell. These people had no idea.

'FBI,' Mahoney called from behind as he led his heavily armed teams into the crowd.

I knew from Sterling what Pasha Sorokin looked like, and I headed his way. He was right there. The Wolf had on an expensive gray suit, a blue cashmere T-shirt. He was talking to two men near a billowing, blue-and-yellow-striped canopy where the grills were working. Enormous cuts of meat and fish were being prepared by smiley, sweaty chefs, all of them black or Hispanic.

I pulled out my Glock, and Pasha Sorokin stared at me without moving a muscle. He just stared. Didn't make a move, didn't try to run. Then he smiled, as if he'd been expecting me and was glad I'd finally arrived. What was with this guy?

I saw him flash a hand signal to a white-haired man whose arm was draped around a curvy blonde less than half his age. 'Atticus!' he called, and Atticus scurried over faster than kitchen help.

'I'm Atticus Stonestrom, Mr Manning's lawyer,' he said. 'You have absolutely no reason to be here, to barge into Mr Manning's house like this. You're completely out of line and I'm asking you to leave.'

'Not going to happen. Let's move this private party inside. Just the three of us,' I said to Atticus Stonestrom and Pasha. 'Unless you want the arrest to take place in front of all these guests.'

The Wolf looked at his lawyer, then shrugged as if this were no big deal to him. He started to walk toward the house. Then he turned – pretending he'd just remembered something. 'Your little boy's name,' he said. 'It's also Alex, isn't it?'

Chapter One Hundred and Two

She wasn't dead! How good was that? How amazing?

Elizabeth Connelly was lost in her own world again, and it was the best place. She was walking a perfect beach on Oahu's north shore. She was picking up the most amazing seashells, one after the other, comparing the textures.

Then she heard shouts – 'FBI!' She couldn't believe it.

The FBI was here? At the house? Her heart pounded, then nearly stopped, then pounded again, even louder.

Had they finally come to rescue her? Why else would they be here? Oh my good God!

Lizzie began to shake all over. Tears spilled down her cheeks. They had to find her and let her out now. The Wolf's arrogance was about to burn him down!

I'm in here. I'm here! I'm right here!

The party got terribly quiet suddenly. Everyone was whispering, and it was hard to hear. But she definitely heard 'FBI', and that's why they were here. 'Drugs!' Everyone seemed to think so.

But Lizzie prayed this wasn't about drugs. What if they took the Wolf to jail? She would be left here. She couldn't stop shaking.

She had to let the FBI know she was here. But how? She was always bound and gagged. They were so close . . . I'm in the closet! Please look in the closet!

She had imagined dozens of escape plans, but only after the Wolf opened the door and leashed her out to go to the bathroom or walk in the main part of the house. Lizzie knew there was no way to get out of the locked closet. Not tied up the way she was. She didn't know how to signal the FBI.

Then she heard someone making a loud announcement. A male. Deep voice. Calm and in control.

'I'm Agent Mahoney with the FBI. Everyone has to leave the main house immediately. Please assemble on the back lawns. Everyone is to leave the house now! No one leaves the grounds.'

Lizzie heard shoes scraping the hardwood floors – rapid footsteps. People were leaving, weren't they? Then what? She'd be all alone. If they took the Wolf away . . . what would happen to her? There had to be something she could do to let the FBI know she was in here. What?

Someone named Atticus Stonestrom was talking loudly.

Then she heard the Wolf speak, and it chilled her. He was still in the house. Arguing with someone. She couldn't tell who, or exactly what they were saying.

What can I do? Something! Anything!

What, what?

What haven't I thought of before?

And then Lizzie had an idea. Actually, she'd had it before, but always dismissed it.

Because it scared the hell out of her!

Chapter One Hundred and Three

'I'm glad you're here to see this for yourself, Atticus,' the Wolf said to his lawyer. 'This is such bullshit harassment. My businesses are beyond reproach. You know that better than anyone. This is highly insulting.' He looked at me. 'Do you know how many business associates you've insulted at this party?'

I was still restraining myself from his physical threat to my family, to little Alex. I didn't want to take him down; I wanted to take him out.

'Trust me, this isn't harassment,' I told the lawyer. 'We're here to arrest your client for kidnapping and murder.'

Sorokin rolled his eyes. 'Are you people mad? Do you know who I am?' he asked. Jesus, I'd heard almost the same speech the day before in Dallas.

'As a matter of fact, I do,' I said. 'Your real name is Pasha Sorokin, not Ari Manning. Some people say you're the Russian Godfather. You're the Wolf.'

Sorokin heard me out – then he laughed a crazy laugh.

'You are such fools. You, especially.' He pointed at me. 'You just don't get it.'

Suddenly there were shouts coming from one of the other rooms on the first floor. 'Fire!' people were yelling.

'C'mon, Alex!' Mahoney said. He and I left Sorokin with three agents and ran to see what the hell was going on. How could there be a fire? Now?

Guests were rushing out of a large study off the main living room. There was a fire. It seemed to have started in the study. Mahoney and I pushed through the exiting crowd. Apparently, the fire was in a closet. Swirls of smoke came from under the door. A lot of smoke.

I didn't hesitate. I lowered my shoulder and hit the closet door hard. I slammed into it again. The wood cracked this time. I hit it once more and the door collapsed. Thick black smoke billowed out.

I stepped up close and tried to peer inside. Then I saw something move.

Someone was in there. I could see a face.

Elizabeth Connelly was on fire!

Chapter One Hundred and Four

I took a breath then lunged forward into the cloud of smoke and heat. I felt the skin on my face begin to burn. I forced myself inside the walk-in closet. Stooped down. I grabbed Elizabeth Connelly in my arms and stumbled backwards out of the closet with her. My eyes were tearing, my face felt blistered. Elizabeth's eyes were open wide as I removed her gag. Ned Mahoney worked on the rope bindings around her arms.

'Thank you,' she whispered in a voice hoarse with smoke. 'Oh, thank you,' she gasped.

Tears ran from her eyes, smudging the soot on her cheeks. My heart thumped a wild beat as I held her hand and waited for the paramedics to come. I couldn't believe she was alive, but it made everything worthwhile.

I only got to savor the feeling for a few seconds. Shots rang out. I ran from the den, turned the corner, and saw two agents down, but alive.

'Bodyguard came in firing,' the closer agent told me. 'They ran upstairs.'

I hurried up the stairs with Ned Mahoney following close behind. Why would the Wolf go upstairs? It didn't make sense to me. More agents joined us. We searched every room. Nothing! We couldn't find the Wolf, or the bodyguard. Why had they run upstairs?

Mahoney and I did another full walk-through of all the rooms on the second and third floors. Fort Lauderdale police had begun to arrive and helped secure the house.

'I don't see how he got out of here,' Mahoney said. We were huddled together in the second-floor hallway. Puzzled and disgusted.

'Has to be a way out up here somewhere. Let's look again.'

We went back down the hallway when I had a thought. I retraced our steps down the second-floor hallway, checking in several guest bedrooms as I walked. At the far end of the hall was another stairway, probably used by the help. We'd already searched it. Sealed it off at the bottom. Then it suddenly struck me. A small detail that I had overlooked.

I hurried down to the first landing. There was a casement window and a window seat there. It was just as I'd remembered. Two small cushions on the floor. I opened the latched cover of the window seat.

Ned Mahoney groaned out loud. He saw what I'd found. The escape route. The Wolf had gotten out!

'He might still be here. Let's see where this goes,' I said. Then I lowered myself into the opening. There were narrow wooden stairs, a half-dozen of them. Mahoney held a flashlight on me as I climbed down.

'It's here, Ned,' I called back to him. I saw how they'd made it out. A window was open. I could see water a few feet below.

'They went into the Intercoastal,' I called up to Mahoney. 'They're in the water!'

Chapter One Hundred and Five

I joined the frantic search in the waterway and the rest of the neighborhood, but it was already getting dark. Mahoney and I raced up and down estate-lined narrow streets. Then we drove along nearby Las Olas Boulevard, hoping against hope that someone had spotted two men in soaking-wet clothes. But no one had seen the Wolf or his bodyguard.

I wouldn't give up. I went back to the Isla Bahia-estates area. Something was wrong. Why hadn't anyone spotted two men fitting that description? I wondered if they had diving gear in the cellar alcove. How thoroughly had the Wolf planned his escape? What extra precautions had he taken?

Then I let my mind go in a different direction – he's arrogant and fearless. He didn't believe we'd find him and come here to take him down. He didn't have an escape route! So maybe he was still hiding in Isla Bahia.

I passed my ideas on to HRT, but they'd already begun to go door-to-door at the estates. There were dozens of agents and local police combing the exclusive neighborhood in Fort Lauderdale. I wouldn't give up, wouldn't let the others quit. Whatever drove me – stubbornness? perseverance? – had paid off before. But we didn't find the Wolf, or anyone who'd seen him in Isla Bahia.

'There's nothing? No sign? Nobody saw anything?' I asked Mahoney.

'Nothing,' Mahoney said. 'We found a cocker spaniel on the loose. That's it.'

'We know who owns the dog?' I asked.

Mahoney rolled his eyes. I didn't blame him. 'I'll check.' He went away and came back after a couple of minutes.

'It belongs to a Mr and Mrs Steve Davis. The Davises live at the end of the street. We'll bring them their dog. Satisfied?'

I shook my head. 'Not really. Let's the two of us return the dog,' I said. 'I don't know why a dog would be loose this late at night. Is the family home?'

'Doesn't look like it. The lights are off at the house. C'mon, Alex. Jesus. This is hopeless. You're clutching at straws. Pasha Sorokin is gone.'

'Let's go. Get the dog,' I said. 'We're going to the Davis house.'

Chapter One Hundred and Six

We had started toward the Davis house with the brown and white cocker spaniel when a report came over the two-way. 'Two suspicious males. Heading toward Las Olas Boulevard. They've spotted us! We're in pursuit.'

We were only a few blocks from the shopping district and got there in minutes. The cocker spaniel was barking in the back seat. Fort Lauderdale police patrol cars and FBI sedans had already formed a tight ring around a GAP clothing store. More patrol cars were still arriving, their sirens screaming in the night. The street was crowded and the local police were having trouble stopping the pedestrian flow.

Mahoney drove up to the blockade. We left a window cracked for the dog. We jumped out and ran toward GAP. We were wearing flak jackets, carrying handguns.

The store lights were blazing. I could see people inside. But not the Wolf. Not the bodyguard either.

'We think it's him,' an agent told us when we got up close to the store.

'How many gunmen inside?' I asked.

'We count two. Two that we know about. Could be more. There's a lot of confusion.'

'Yeah, no shit,' said Mahoney. 'I get that impression.'

For the next few minutes nothing useful happened – except that more Lauderdale patrol cars arrived on the scene. So did a heavily armed and armored SWAT Unit. A hostage negotiator showed up. Then a pair of news helicopters began to hover over the GAP store and surrounding palm trees.

'Nobody's answering the goddamn phone inside,' the negotiator reported. 'It just rings.'

Mahoney looked questioningly at me and I shrugged. 'We don't even know if it's them inside.'

The negotiator took up an electronic bullhorn. 'This is the Fort Lauderdale police. Come out of the store now. We're not going to negotiate. Come out with your hands up. Whoever's in there, get out now!'

The approach sounded wrong to me. Too confrontational. I walked up to the negotiator. 'I'm FBI, Agent Cross. Do we need to back him into a corner? He's violent. He's extremely dangerous.'

The negotiator was a stocky guy with a thick mustache; he was wearing a flak jacket, but it wasn't secured. 'Get the fuck away from me!' he shouted in my face.

'This is a federal case,' I shouted right back. I grabbed the bullhorn out of his hand. The negotiator went at me with his fists, but Mahoney wrestled him to the ground. The press was watching; to hell with them. We had a job to do here.

'This is the FBI!' I spoke into the bullhorn. 'I want to talk to Pasha Sorokin.'

Then suddenly the strangest thing of the night happened, and it had been a very strange night. I almost couldn't believe it.

Two men emerged from the front door of the GAP.

They held their hands over their heads. They were shielding their faces from the cameras, or maybe from us.

'Get down on the ground!' I shouted at them. They didn't comply.

But then I could see – it was Sorokin and the bodyguard.

'We're not armed,' Sorokin yelled loud enough for everybody to hear. 'We're innocent citizens. We have no guns.'

I didn't know whether to believe him. None of us knew what to make of this. The TV helicopter over our heads was getting too close.

'What's he pulling?' Mahoney asked me.

'Don't know . . . Get down!' I shouted again.

The Wolf and the bodyguard continued to walk toward us. Slowly and carefully. Hands held high.

I moved ahead with Mahoney. We had our guns out. Was this a trick? What could they try with dozens of rifles and handguns aimed at them?

The Wolf smiled when he saw me. Why the hell was he smiling?

'So, you caught us,' he called out. 'Big deal! It doesn't matter, you know. I have a surprise for you, FBI. Ready? My name is Pasha Sorokin. But I'm not the Wolf.'

He laughed. 'I'm just some guy shopping in the GAP store. My clothes got wet. I'm not the Wolf, Mr FBI. Is that funny or what? Does it make your day? It makes mine. And it will make the Wolf's too.'

Chapter One Hundred and Seven

Pasha Sorokin wasn't the Wolf. Was that possible? There was no way to know for sure. Over the next forty-eight hours it was confirmed that the men we had captured in Florida were Pasha Sorokin and Ruslan Federov. They were Red Mafiya, but both claimed never to have met the real Wolf. They said they had played the 'parts' they were given – stand-in roles – according to them. Now they were willing to make the best deals they could.

There was no way for us to know for sure what was going on – but the deal-making went on for two days. The Bureau liked to make deals. I didn't. Contacts were made inside the Mafiya; more doubts were raised about Pasha Sorokin being the Wolf. Finally, the CIA operatives who'd gotten the Wolf out of Russia were found and brought to Pasha's cell. They said he wasn't the man they'd help get out of the Soviet Union.

Then it was Sorokin who gave us a name we wanted – one that blew my mind completely, blew everybody's minds. It was part of his 'deal'.

He gave us Sphinx.

And he told us where we could find him.

The next morning, four teams of FBI agents waited outside Sphinx's house until he left for work. We had agreed not to take him inside the house. I wouldn't let it go down that way. I just couldn't do it.

We all felt that Lizzie Connelly and her daughters had been through more than enough pain already. They didn't need to see Brendan Connelly – Sphinx – arrested at the family house in Buckhead. They didn't need to find out the awful truth about him like that.

I sat in a dark blue sedan parked two blocks up the street, but with a view of the large Georgian-style house. I was feeling numb. I remembered the first time I'd been there. I recalled my talk with the girls; and then with Brendan Connelly in his den. His grief had seemed heartfelt, as genuine as his young daughters'.

Of course, no one else had suspected he had betrayed his wife, sold her to another man. Pasha Sorokin had met Elizabeth at a party in the Connelly house. He'd wanted her; Brendan Connelly didn't. The judge had been having affairs for years. Elizabeth reminded Sorokin of the model Claudia Schiffer, who had appeared on billboards all over Moscow during his gangster days. So the horrifying trade was made. A husband had sold his own wife into captivity; he'd gotten rid of her in the worst way imaginable. How could he have hated Elizabeth so much? And how could she have loved him?

Ned Mahoney was in the car with me, waiting for action:

the takedown of Sphinx. If we couldn't have the Wolf yet, he was our second choice; the consolation prize.

'I wonder if Elizabeth knew about her husband's secret life?' Mahoney muttered.

'Maybe she suspected something. They didn't sleep together regularly. When I visited the house, Connelly showed me his den. There was a bed in there. Unmade.'

'Think he'll go to work today?' Mahoney asked. He was calmly munching an apple. A very cool head to work with.

'He'll know we took down Sorokin and Federov by now. I figure he'll be cautious. He'll probably play it straight. Hard to tell.'

'Maybe we should take him at the house. You think?' He bit into his apple again. 'Alex?'

I shook my head. 'I can't do it, Ned. Not to his family.'

'Okay. Just asking, buddy.'

We waited. A little past nine, Brendan Connelly finally came out the front door of the house. He walked to a silver Porsche Boxster parked in the wraparound driveway. He had on a blue suit, carried a black gym bag. He was whistling.

'Scumbag!' Mahoney whispered. Then he spoke into his two-way. 'This is Alpha One . . . we have Sphinx leaving the house. He's getting into a Porsche. Prepare to converge. Vehicle/license is V6T-81K.'

We heard back immediately. 'This is Braves One . . . we have Sphinx in full sight too. We've got him covered. He's ours.'

Then, 'Braves Three in place at second intersect. We're waiting on him.'

'Should be about ten to fifteen seconds. He's heading down the street. Making a right. It's the route he always takes to work.'

I spoke very calmly to Mahoney. 'I want to take him down, Ned.'

He looked straight ahead through the windshield. Didn't answer me. But he didn't say no.

I watched the Porsche proceed at a normal speed to the next cross street. The Boxster eased into the turn. And then Brendan Connelly ran!

'Oh boy,' said Mahoney and tossed away his apple.

Chapter One Hundred and Eight

'**S**uspect is going southeast. He must have seen us!' A message came over the short wave.

I gunned our car in the direction where the Porsche had disappeared. I managed to get the sedan up to sixty-five on the narrow, winding street lined with gated McMansions. I still couldn't see the silver Porsche up ahead.

'I'm heading east,' I spoke into the two-way. 'I'll take a chance he's trying to get to the highway.' I didn't know what else to do. I passed several cars coming the other way on the quiet street. A couple of drivers sat on their horns. That's what I would have done too. I was going seventy-five miles an hour in a residential area.

'I see him!' Mahoney yelled.

I stepped down hard on the gas. I was finally making up some ground. I spotted a blue sedan approaching the Porsche from the east. It was Braves Two. We had Brendan Connelly from two sides. Now the question was whether or not he'd give up.

Suddenly the Porsche shot right off the road and into a

thicket of bushes that rose higher than the car's roof. The Porsche tilted forward, then disappeared down a steep slope.

I didn't slow down until the last second, then I braked hard and went into a controlled shudder and spin.

'Jesus Christ!' Mahoney shouted from the passenger side.

'Thought you were HRT,' I said.

Mahoney laughed. 'All right then, partner! Let's get the bad guy!'

I steered the sedan through the bushes and found myself on a steep hill dotted with large rocks and trees. When the first branches cleared, I had limited vision because of all the other trees. Then I saw the Porsche smack into a mid-sized oak, and career to one side. The car slid sideways another fifty feet before it finally stopped.

Sphinx was down.

'Let's go get the bad guy!' I shouted.

Chapter One Hundred and Nine

Mahoney and I wanted Sphinx and it was personal with me, maybe with both of us. I let our sedan roll another fifty or sixty yards. Then I braked and the car stopped. Mahoney and I jumped out. We almost slid down the steep hill, which was slippery with mud.

'Crazy son of a bitch!' Ned Mahoney shouted as we stumbled ahead.

'What choice did he have? He had to run.'

'I mean you. You're crazy! What a ride.'

We saw Brendan Connelly lurch out of the damaged Porsche. He held a handgun aimed our way. Connelly fired off two quick shots. He wasn't good with a gun, though. But he was shooting real bullets.

'Son of a bitch!' Mahoney fired a shot and hit the Porsche – just to show Connelly that we could shoot him if we wanted to.

'Put the gun down,' Mahoney shouted. 'Put the gun down!'

Brendan Connelly started to run down the hill but he was

stumbling a lot. Mahoney and I kept gaining on him until we were only thirty yards or so behind.

'Let me,' I said.

Brendan Connelly looked back over his shoulder just then. I could tell he was tired, scared, or both. His legs and arms were pumping in a disjointed rhythm. He might work out in some gym, but he wasn't ready for this.

'Get back! I'll shoot!' he shouted – almost right into my face.

I hit him, and it was like a speeding tractor-trailer back-ending a barely moving compact. Connelly went down, cartwheeling crazily. I stayed upright. Didn't even lose my balance. This was the good part. It almost made up for some of our misses and failures.

Connelly's ignominious roll finally stopped after twenty yards, but then he made his biggest mistake – he got back up.

I was on him in a second. I was all over Sphinx, and it was where I wanted to be. *Mano a mano* with this bastard. He had sold his own wife – the mother of his children.

I threw a hard right-handed shot into the bridge of Connelly's nose. The perfect shot, or close to it. Probably broke it from the crunch I heard. He went down on one knee – but he got up again. Former college jock. Former tough guy. Current asshole.

His nose was hanging to one side. Good deal. I threw an uppercut into the pit of Connelly's stomach and liked the feeling so much I threw another. I crunched another right into his gut, which was softening to the touch. Then a quick, hard hook to his cheek. I was getting stronger.

I jabbed his broken nose and Connelly moaned. I jabbed again. I looped a roundhouse at his chin, connected, bull's-eye. Brendan Connelly's blue eyes rolled back into his forehead. The lights went out and he dropped into the mud, and stayed there, where he belonged.

I heard a voice behind me. 'That how it's done in D.C.?' Mahoney asked from a few yards up the hill.

I stared up at him. 'That's how it's done, Natty Bumpo. Hope you took notes.'

Chapter One Hundred and Ten

The next couple of weeks were quiet, disturbingly, maddeningly so. I found out I was being assigned to headquarters, as Deputy Director of Investigations under Director Burns. 'A big, fat plum,' I was told by everybody. It sounded like a desk job to me, and I didn't want that. I wanted the Wolf. I wanted the street. I wanted action. I hadn't come over to the Bureau to be a desk jockey in the Hoover Building.

I was given a week off and Nana, the kids and I went everywhere together. There was a lot of tension in the house, though. We were waiting to hear what Christine Johnson was going to do.

Every time I looked at Alex my heart ached; every time I held him in my arms, or tucked him in bed at the end of the day, I thought about his leaving the house for good. I couldn't let that happen, but my lawyer had advised me it could.

The Director needed to see me in his office one morning during my week off. It wasn't too much of a problem. I stopped in after I dropped the kids at school. Tony Woods, Burns's assistant, seemed particularly glad to see me.

'You're something of a hero for the moment. Enjoy it,' he said, sounding, as always, like an Ivy League prof. 'Won't last long.'

'Always the optimist, Tony,' I said.

'That's my job description, young man.'

I wondered how much Ron Burns shared with his assistant, and also what the Director had in mind this morning. I wanted to ask Tony about this plum job I was slated for. But I didn't. I figured he wouldn't tell me anyway.

Coffee and sweet rolls were waiting in Burns's office, but the Director wasn't there. It was a little past eight. I wondered if he'd even gotten to work yet. It was hard to imagine that Ron Burns had a life outside the office, though I knew he had a wife and four children, and lived out in Virginia, about an hour from D.C.

Burns finally appeared at the door in a blue dress shirt and tie, with the shirtsleeves rolled up. So now I knew he'd had at least one meeting before this one. Actually, I hoped this meeting wasn't about another case that he wanted me to dive into. Unless it involved the Wolf.

Burns grinned when he saw me sitting there. He read my look instantly. 'Actually, I have a couple of nasty cases for you to work on. But that isn't why I wanted to see you, Alex. Have some coffee. Relax. You're on vacation, right?'

He walked into the room, sat down across from me. 'I want to hear how it's going so far. You miss being a homicide detective? Still want to stay in the Bureau? You can leave if you want to. The Washington P.D. wants you back. Badly.'

'That's good to hear, that I'm wanted. As for the Bureau, what can I say? The resources are amazing. Lot of good people here, great people. I hope you know that.'

'I do. I'm a fan of our personnel, most of them, anyway. And on the dark side?' he asked. 'Problem areas? Things to work on? I want to hear what you think. I need to hear it. Tell me the truth, as you see it.'

'Bureaucracy. It's a way of life. It's almost the FBI's culture. And fear. It's mostly political in nature, and it inhibits agents' imaginations. Did I mention bureaucracy? It's bad, awful, crippling. Just listen to your agents.'

'I'm listening,' Burns said. 'Go on.'

'The agents aren't allowed to be nearly as good as they can be. Of course that's a complaint with most jobs, isn't it?'

'Even your old job with the Washington P.D.?'

'Not as much as here. That's because I sidestepped a lot of red tape and other bullshit that got in the way.'

'Good. Keep sidestepping the bullshit, Alex,' Burns said. 'Even if it's mine.'

I smiled. 'Is that an order?'

Burns nodded soberly. I felt that he had something else on his mind. 'I had a difficult meeting before you got here. Gordon Nooney is leaving the Bureau.'

I shook my head. 'I hope I didn't have anything to do with that. I don't know Nooney well enough to judge him. Seriously. I don't.'

'Sorry, but you did have something to do with it. But it was my decision. The buck passes through here at a hundred miles an hour, and I like it that way. I do know Nooney well enough to judge him. Nooney was the leak to the *Washington Post.* That son of a bitch has been doing it for years. Alex, I thought about putting you in Nooney's job.'

I was shocked to hear it. 'I've never trained people. I didn't finish orientation myself.'

'But you could train our people.'

I wasn't sure about that. 'Maybe I could struggle through. But I like the streets. It's in my blood. I've learned to accept that about myself.'

'I know. I get it, Alex. I want you to work right here in the Hoover Building though. We're going to change things. We're going to win more than we lose. Work the big cases with Stacy Pollack at headquarters. She's one of the best. Tough, smart, she could run this place some day.'

'I can work with Stacy,' I said, and left it at that.

Ron Burns put out his hand and I took it.

'This is going to be good. Exciting stuff,' he said. 'Which reminds me of a promise I made. There's a spot here for Detective John Sampson, and any D.C. street cop you like. Anybody who wants to win. We're going to win, Alex.'

I shook Ron Burns's hand on it. The thing is, I wanted to win, too.

Chapter One Hundred and Eleven

On a Monday morning I was in my new office on the fifth floor at headquarters in D.C. Tony Woods had given me a walking tour earlier that morning, and I was struck by strange, funny details that I couldn't get out of my head. Like . . . the office doors were metal all through the building, except on the executive floor, where they were wood. The odd thing, though, the wood doors looked exactly like the metal ones. Welcome to the FBI.

Anyway, I had a lot of reading to do, and I hoped I'd get used to being in an eleven-by-fifteen-foot office, which was kind of bare. The furniture looked as if it were on loan from the Government Accounting Office; there was a file cabinet with a large dial lock; a coat tree that held my black vest and blue nylon raid jacket. The office also looked down on Pennsylvania Avenue, which was something of a 'perk'.

Just past two that afternoon I got a phone call, actually the first incoming message to my new office. It was Tony Woods. 'All settled in?' he asked. 'Anything you need?'

'I'm getting there, Tony. I'll be fine. Thanks for asking.'

'Good. Alex, you're going out of town in about an hour. There's a lead on the Wolf in Brooklyn. Stacy Pollack will be going with you, so it's a big deal. You fly out of Quantico at fifteen hundred. This thing isn't over.'

I called home, then I gathered some paperwork on the Wolf, grabbed the overnight bag I'd been told to keep in my office, and headed to the parking garage. Stacy Pollack came down a few minutes later.

She drove, and it took us less than half an hour to get to the small private airfield at Quantico. On the way, she told me about the lead in Brooklyn. Supposedly, the real Wolf had been spotted at Brighton Beach. At least we weren't giving up on him.

One of the black Bells was saddled up and waiting for us. Stacy and I got out of the sedan and walked side by side to the helicopter. I remember that the skies were bright blue and streaming with clouds that appeared to be shredding in the distance. A crisp smell of fall was in the air.

'Nice day for a train wreck,' Stacy said and grinned.

A shot rang out from the woods directly behind us. I had thrown back my head, laughing at Stacy's little joke. I saw her get hit and blood spatter. I went down and covered her body.

Agents were running on to the tarmac. One of them fired in the direction of the sniper shot. Two came sprinting toward us, the others ran toward the woods, in the direction of the shots. I lay on Stacy, trying to protect her, hoping she wasn't dead, but wondering if maybe the bullet had been meant for me.

You'll never catch the Wolf, Pasha Sorokin had said in Florida. He will catch you. Now the warning had come true.

The briefing that night at the Hoover Building was the most emotional I had seen at the Bureau so far. Stacy Pollack was alive, but she was in a critical condition at Walter Reed. Most of the agents respected Stacy Pollack tremendously, and they couldn't believe she'd been targeted. I still wondered if the bullet had been meant for me? She and I had been headed to New York to see about the Wolf; he was the chief suspect in the shooting. But did he have help? Was there someone inside the Bureau?

'The other bad news,' Ron Burns told the group that night, 'is that our lead in Brighton Beach turns out to be bogus. The Wolf isn't in New York, apparently he wasn't there recently. The questions that we have to answer are, did he know we were going after him? If he knew, how did he know? Did one of us tell him? I promise that we will spare nothing to get the answers to those questions.'

After the meeting, I was one of the agents invited to a smaller briefing held in the Director's conference room. The mood continued to be somber, serious, and angry. Burns took the floor again, and he seemed more upset by the Stacy Pollack shooting than anyone else.

'When I said that we were going to bring that Russian bastard down, I wasn't using hyperbole for effect. I'm establishing a BAM team to go after him. He said that he would come after us, and he did. Now we're going to come after him, with everything we have, all our resources.'

Heads around the room nodded their approval. I'd heard

of the existence of BAM teams in the FBI, but hadn't known if they were real or not. I knew what the acronym stood for – By Any Means. It was what we needed to hear right now. It was what I needed to hear.

BAM.

Chapter One Hundred and Twelve

Everything felt like it was going much too fast, like it was spinning out of control. Maybe that was right. The case was out of our control – the Wolf was running it.

I got a phone call at home two nights later. It was a quarter past three in the morning. 'This had better be good.'

'It isn't. All hell's broken loose, Alex. It's a war.' The caller was Tony Woods and he sounded groggy.

I massaged my forehead as I spoke. 'What war? Tell me what happened?'

'We got word from Texas a few minutes ago. Lawrence Lipton is dead, murdered. They got to him in his cell.'

I was starting to wake up in a hurry.

'How? He was in our custody, wasn't he?'

'Two agents were killed with Lipton. He predicted it, didn't he?'

I nodded, then I said, 'Yeah.' And so had the Wolf.

'Alex, they got to the Lipton family, too. They're all dead. HRT is on the way to your house, also the Director's, even

Mahoney's. Anybody who worked on the case is considered vulnerable and at risk.'

That got me up out of bed. I took my Glock out of the cabinet beside my bed.

'I'll be waiting for HRT,' I told Woods, then I hurried downstairs with my gun in hand.

Was the Wolf already here? I wondered.

The war came to our house a few minutes later, and even though it was HRT, it couldn't have been much scarier. Nana Mama was up and she greeted the heavily armed FBI agents with angry looks, but also offers of coffee. Then she and I went to wake the children, as gently as we could.

'This isn't right, Alex. Not in our home,' Nana whispered as we went upstairs to get Jannie and Damon. 'The line has to be drawn somewhere, doesn't it? This is bad.'

'I know it is. It's gotten out of control, everything has. The world is that way now.'

'So what are you going to do about it? What are you planning to do?'

'Right now, wake the kids. Hug them, kiss them. Get them out of this house for a while.'

'Are you listening to yourself?' Nana asked as we arrived at the doorway to Damon's bedroom. He was already sitting up in bed.

'Dad?' he said.

Suddenly I was aware of Ned Mahoney coming up behind me. 'Alex, can I have a second?' What was he doing here? What else had happened?

'I'll wake them, get them dressed,' Nana said. 'Talk to your friend.'

I stayed behind with Mahoney. 'What is it, Ned? Can't it wait for a couple of minutes? Jesus.'

'The bastards hit Burns's house. Everybody's all right. We got there in time.'

I stared into Mahoney's eyes. 'Your family?'

'They're out of the house. They're safe for now. We've got to find him, and burn him.'

I nodded. 'Let me go get my kids up.'

Twenty minutes later my family was escorted outside to a waiting van. They climbed inside, like frightened refugees in a war zone. That's what the world was becoming, wasn't it? Every city and town was a potential battlefield. No place was safe.

Just before I climbed in the van, I spotted the photographer posted across the street from our house on Fifth Street. It looked like he was filming the evacuation of our house. How was that?

I'm not sure how I knew who he was, but somehow I knew. He's not from any newspaper, I thought. I felt myself filling with rage and disgust. He works for Christine's lawyers.

Chapter One Hundred and Thirteen

C haos.

The next day, and for two days after that, I found myself in Huntsville, Texas, the site of the federal prison where Lawrence Lipton had been murdered while he was in the custody of the Federal Bureau. No one there had any explanation for how Lipton and two agents had been killed.

It had happened during the night. In his cell. Actually, the small suite where he was kept under guard. None of the video cameras had a record of visitors. None of the interviews or interrogations turned up a suspect. Lipton had most of the bones in his body broken. *Zamochit*. The Wolf's trademark.

The same method had been used on an Italian Mafia figure named Augustino Palumbo this past summer. According to stories, Palumbo's killer had been a Russian mobster, possibly the Wolf. The murder had taken place at the supermax prison in Florence, Colorado.

The following morning I arrived in Colorado. I was there to visit a killer named Kyle Craig, who had once been an

FBI agent, and also a friend of mine. Kyle was responsible for dozens of murders; he was one of the worst psychopathic killers in history. I had captured him. My friend.

We met in an interview room on death row in the Isolation Unit. Kyle looked surprisingly fit. When I'd last seen him he was gaunt, very pale, with deep, dark hollows under his eyes. He appeared to have put on at least thirty pounds, all of it muscle. I wondered why – what had given Kyle hope? Whatever it was scared me a little.

'All roads lead to Florence?' he quipped and grinned as I entered the visiting room. 'Some associates of yours from the Bureau were here just yesterday. Or was it the day before? You know, the last time we met, Alex, you said you didn't care what I think. That hurt.'

I corrected him, which I knew would annoy Kyle. 'Not exactly what I said. You accused me of being condescending, and told me that you didn't like it. I said, "Who cares what you like anymore?" I do care about what you think. That's why I'm here.'

Kyle laughed again, and the braying sound he made, the baring of his teeth, chilled me. 'You always were my favorite,' he said.

'You were expecting me?' I asked.

'Hmm. Hard to say. Not really. Maybe at some time in the future.'

'You look like you have big plans. You're all buffed.'

'What plans could I possibly have?'

'The usual. Grand delusions, homicidal fantasies, rape, the slaughter of innocents.'

'I do hate it when you play psychologist, Alex. You didn't make it in that world for a good reason.'

I shrugged. 'I know that, Kyle. None of my patients in Southeast had money to pay me. I needed to start a practice in Georgetown. Maybe I will someday.'

He laughed again. 'Talk about delusions. So why are you here? No, I'll tell you why. There's been a terrible miscarriage of justice and I'm being released. You're the messenger of glad tidings.'

'The only miscarriage is that you haven't been executed, Kyle.'

Kyle's eyes sparkled. I was one of his favorites. 'All right, now that you've charmed me, what is it that you want?'

'You know what I want, Kyle,' I said. 'You know exactly why I'm here.'

He clapped his hands loudly, '*Zamochit!* The mad Russian!'

For the next half an hour I told Kyle everything I knew about the Wolf, well nearly everything. Then I gave him the kicker. 'He met with you on the night he came here to kill "Little Gus" Palumbo. Did you set up the kill for him? Somebody did.'

Kyle leaned back and seemed to be considering his options, but I knew he'd already decided what he meant to do. He was always a step or two ahead.

Finally he leaned forward, and beckoned me closer. I wasn't afraid of Kyle, at least not physically, not even with his extra pounds of muscle. I almost hoped he'd make a move.

'I do this out of love and respect for you,' Kyle said. 'I did meet with the Russian last summer. Ruthless chap, no conscience. I liked him. We played chess. I know who he is, my friend. I might be able to help you.'

Chapter One Hundred and Fourteen

It took me another day at Florence, but I finally negotiated a name out of Kyle. Now could we believe him? The name was checked and rechecked in Washington, but the Bureau was becoming confident that he had given us the Red Mafiya leader. I had doubts – because it came from Kyle. But we had no other leads.

Maybe Kyle wanted to use it to try and blow me up, or embarrass the Bureau. Or maybe he wanted to demonstrate how smart he was, how well-connected, how superior to us all. The name, the person's position, made the arrest controversial and risky. If we went after this man, and we were wrong, the embarrassment would stick to the Bureau.

So we waited for nearly a week. We checked all of our information again and did several interviews in the field. The suspect was put on surveillance.

When we had completed the due diligence, I met with Ron Burns and the Director of the CIA in Burns's office. Ron got to the point. 'We believe he's the Wolf, Alex. Craig is probably telling the truth.'

Thomas Weir from the CIA nodded my way. 'We've been watching this suspect in New York for some time. We thought he'd been KGB back in Russia, but there wasn't conclusive evidence. We never suspected Red Mafiya, never the Wolf. Not this man. Not given his position with the Russian Government.'

Weir's look was intense. 'We increased the levels of audio surveillance to include the apartment where the suspect lives in Manhattan. He's making arrangements to go after Director Burns again.'

Burns looked at me. 'He doesn't forgive and forget, Alex. Neither do I.'

'Is that it? We go to New York and arrest him?'

Burns and Weir nodded solemnly. 'This should be the end of it,' said Burns. 'Go and take down the Wolf. Bring me his head.'

Chapter One Hundred and Fifteen

This should be the end of it. From Director Burns's mouth to God's ear.

The Century is a famous art deco apartment building on Central Park West, north of Columbus Circle, in New York City. For decades it has been a residence of choice for the well-to-do and famous actors, artists, and business-people, but especially for those who are humble enough to share space with working-class families who've passed down their apartments for decades.

We arrived at the building around four in the morning. HRT immediately took over the three main entrances on Central Park, Sixty-Second' and Sixth-Third Streets. This was the largest bust I had been a part of, definitely the most complicated: the New York City Police, FBI, CIA and Secret Service were all involved in the operation. We were about to take down an important Russian. The head of the trade delegation to New York. A businessman himself, supposedly above suspicion. The repercussions would be severe if we were wrong. But how could we be wrong? Not this time.

I was at the Century, along with my partner for the past week or so. Ned Mahoney was hardworking, honest, and tough in the clutch. The head of HRT had been to my house, and even passed Nana's inspection, mostly because he'd grown up on the streets of D.C.

Ned and I and a dozen others were climbing the stairs to two penthouse floors, since the suspect's apartment was on twenty-five and twenty-six. He was powerful and wealthy. He had a good reputation with Wall Street and the banks. So was he the Wolf? If so, why hadn't his name ever come up before? Because the Wolf was so good, so careful?

'Be glad when this is over with,' Mahoney said without a huff or puff as he mounted the stairs.

'How did it get out of hand like this?' I asked. 'There are too many people here.'

'Always too much politics. Better get used to it. World we live in. Too many suits, not enough workers.'

We finally reached twenty-five. Ned, me, and four other agents stopped there. The rest of the team continued to twenty-six. We waited for them to get into position. This was it. I hoped this was it. Was the real Wolf on one of these two floors?

I heard an urgent voice in my earpiece. 'Suspect coming out of a window! Man in his underwear jumped from the tower! Jesus Christ! He's down on the landing between the towers. He's on the roof. Running.'

Mahoney and I understood what had happened. We rushed down to the twentieth floor. The Century had two towers that rose up from twenty. A large expanse of roof connected them.

We burst out on to the roof and could just about make out a barefoot man in his underwear. Even in the darkness, the figure gave the impression of being burly, balding and bearded. He turned and fired at us with a pistol. The Wolf? Balding? Burly? Could this be him?

He hit Mahoney!

He hit me!

We went down hard. Chest shots! Hurt like hell! Took my breath away. Fortunately, we were wearing Kevlar vests.

The man in his underwear wasn't.

Mahoney's return fire took out a kneecap; my first shot struck his thickset stomach. He went down spurting blood and howling.

We ran to the side of Andrei Prokopev. Mahoney kicked away his gun. 'You're under arrest!' Ned yelled into the face of the wounded Russian. 'We know who you are.'

A helicopter appeared between the Century's dueling towers. A woman was screaming from one of the windows several stories above us. Suddenly, the helicopter was landing! What the hell was this?

A man came out of a window in the tower and dropped to the roof.

Then another man. Professional gunmen, it looked like. Bodyguards?

They were quick on the draw and began shooting the instant they hit the roof. HRT returned fire. Several shots were exchanged. Both gunmen were hit and went down.

Neither got up again. HRT was that good.

The helicopter was setting down on the roof. It wasn't media or police. It was there to get the Wolf and whisk him away, wasn't it? There were shots from the helicopter. Mahoney and I fired into the cockpit. There was a rapid exchange of gunfire. Then the shooting stopped inside.

For several seconds the only sound on the roof was the loud, eerie whir of the helicopter's rotor blades. 'Clear!' one of our agents finally yelled. 'They're down in the copter!'

'You're under arrest!' Mahoney screamed at the Russian in his underwear. 'You're the Wolf. You tried to attack my house, my family!'

I had something else in mind, another kind of message. I leaned in close and said, 'Kyle Craig did this to you.' I wanted him to know, and maybe pay Kyle back some day.

Maybe with *zamochit*.

Chapter One Hundred and Sixteen

I hoped to God it was over now. We all did. Ned Mahoney flew back to Quantico that morning, but I spent the rest of the day at FBI headquarters in lower Manhattan. The Russian Government had filed protests everywhere they could, but Andrei Prokopev was still in custody and State Department people were all over the FBI offices. Even a few Wall Street firms had questioned the arrest.

So far, I hadn't been allowed to talk to the Russian again. He was scheduled for surgery, but his life wasn't in danger. He was being grilled by someone, just not by me.

Burns finally reached me at around four o'clock in the office I was using in FBI-New York. 'Alex, I want you to head back to Washington,' he said. 'Flight arrangements have been made. We'll be waiting for you here.' That was all that he told me.

Burns signed off so I didn't get the chance to ask any questions. It was obvious that he didn't want me to. Around seven-thirty I arrived at the Hoover Building and was told to go to the SIOC conference area on six. They were waiting for me there. Not exactly waiting, since a shirt-sleeves meeting was already in progress. Ron Burns was at the table, which wasn't a good sign. Everybody looked tense and exhausted.

'Let me bring Alex up to date,' he said when I entered the room. 'Have a rest, kick back. There's been a new wrinkle. None of us are very happy about it. You won't be either.'

I shook my head and felt a little sick as I sat down. I didn't need new wrinkles, I had more than enough already.

'The Russians are actually cooperating for a change,' Burns said. 'It seems that they're not denying that Andrei Prokopev has Red Mafiya connections. He does. They've been monitoring him for some time themselves. They hoped to use him to penetrate the huge black market still coming out of Moscow.'

I cleared my throat. 'But.'

Burns nodded. 'Right. The Russians tell us – now – that Prokopev is not the man we're looking for. They're certain of it.'

I felt completely drained. 'Because?'

It was Burns's turn to shake his head. 'They know what the Wolf looks like. He was KGB after all. The real Wolf set us up to believe he was Prokopev. Andrei Prokopev was one of his rivals in the Red Mafiya.'

'To be the Russian Godfather?'

'To be the Godfather – Russian or otherwise.'

I pursed my lips, took a breath. 'Do the Russians know who the Wolf really is?'

Burns's eyes narrowed. 'If they do, they won't tell us. Not yet anyway. Maybe they're afraid of him too.'

Chapter One Hundred and Seventeen

L ate that night I took the decision to return to my home. I sat at the piano on the sun porch with one of Billy Collins's poems running around my head. It was called 'The Blues' and was about the band giving sympathy to a lonely musician who had lost his lover. Which was what I was thinking about as I sat at the piano and made up a melody to go with the poem. We had lost. It happened a lot in police work, though nobody wants to admit it. Lives had been saved, though. Elizabeth Connelly and a couple of others had been found; Brendan Connelly was in jail. Andrei Prokopev had been caught. But we seemed to have lost the big one – for now anyway. The Wolf was still out there. The Godfather was free to do what he did, and that wasn't good for anybody.

The next morning, I arrived early to meet Jamilla Hughes's flight into Reagan National. I had the usual butterflies before her plane got in. But mostly I couldn't wait to see Jam. Nana and the kids had insisted on coming to the airport. A little show of support – for Jamilla. And for me. For all of us, actually.

The airport was crowded, but relatively quiet and peaceful, probably on account of the high ceilings. My family and I stood at an exit from Terminal A near the security check. I saw Jam, then so did the kids, who started poking me all over. She was wearing black from head to toe; she looked better than ever, and Jamilla always looked good to me.

'She's beautiful, and so cool,' Jannie said and lightly touched the back of my hand. 'You know that, don't you, Daddy?'

'She is, isn't she?' I agreed, looking at Jannie now, rather than at Jamilla. 'She's also smart. Except about men, it would seem.'

'We really like her,' Jannie continued. 'Can you tell?'

'I can. I like her too.'

'But do you love her?' Jannie asked in her usual no-nonsense, get-to-the-heart-of-the-matter-way. 'Do you?'

I didn't say anything. That part was between Jam and me.

'Well – do you?' Nana joined in.

I didn't answer Nana either, so she shook her head, rolled her eyes.

'What do the boys think?' I turned to Damon and little Alex. The Big Boy was clapping his hands and grinning, so I knew where he stood.

'She's definitely all that,' said Damon, and he started to grin. He always got a little goofy around Jamilla.

I moved toward her and they let me go alone. I snuck a glance, and they were grinning like a Cheshire cat family. I had a lump in my throat. Don't know why. I felt a little spacey and my knees were weak. Don't know why either.

'I can't believe everybody came,' Jamilla said as she slid into my arms. 'That makes me happy. I can't tell you how much, Alex. Wow. I think I'm going to cry. Even though I'm a tough-as-nails homicide detective. You all right? You aren't all right. I can tell.'

'Oh, I'm fine now.' I held her tight, then I actually picked Jam up, set her back down.

We were quiet for a moment. 'We're going to fight for little Alex,' she said.

'Of course,' I told her. Then I said something that I'd never told Jamilla before, though it had been on the tip of my tongue many times. 'I love you,' I whispered.

'I love you too,' she said. 'More than you can imagine. More than even I can imagine.'

A single tear ran down Jamilla's cheek. I kissed it away.

Then I saw the photographer taking pictures of us.

The same one who was at the house the day we were evacuated for personal safety.

The one hired by Christine's lawyer.

Had he gotten Jamilla's tear on film?

Chapter One Hundred and Eighteen

They came to the house on Fifth Street; they came about a week after Jamilla went back to California.

Them again.

One of the saddest days of my life.

Indescribable.

Unthinkable.

Christine was there with her lawyer and Alex Junior's law guardian, and a case manager from Children's Protective Services. The case manager wore a plastic ID around her neck, and it was probably her presence that bothered me the most. My children have been raised with so much love and attention, never with abuse or neglect. There was no need for Children's Services. Gilda Haranzo had gone to court and been granted a declaration of order giving Christine temporary guardianship of little Alex. She had won custody based on the claim that I was 'a lightning rod for danger', putting the child in harm's way.

The irony of what was happening was so deep that I almost couldn't stand it. I was trying to be the kind of policeman that most people wanted, and this was what I got? A lightning rod for danger? Is that what I was now?

And yet – I knew exactly how I had to act this morning on Fifth Street. For little Alex's sake. I would abandon all my anger – and focus on what was best for him. I would be supportive during the handover. If it was possible, I wouldn't let anything frighten the Boy, or upset him. I even had a long printed list of Alex's likes and dislikes ready for Christine.

Unfortunately, Alex wasn't buying any of this. He ran behind my legs and hid from Christine and the lawyer; I reached around and gently stroked his head. He was shaking all over, quivering with rage.

Gilda Haranzo said, 'Maybe you should help Christine take little Alex to the car. Would you please do that?'

I turned and tenderly wrapped my arms around the Big Boy. Then Nana, followed by Damon and Jannie, knelt beside him for a group hug. 'We love you, Alex. We'll visit you, Alex. You'll come see us, Alex. Don't be scared.'

Nana handed Alex his favorite book, which was *Whistle for Willie*. Jannie gave him his love-worn plush cow 'Moo'. Damon hugged his brother and tears started down his cheeks.

'I'll be talking to you tonight. You and Moo,' I whispered and kissed my son's darling little face. I could feel his heart going fast. 'Every night. Forever and a day, my sweet boy. Forever and a day.'

And little Alex said, 'Forever, Daddy.'

Then they took my son away.

EPILOGUE

WOLVES

Chapter One Hundred and Nineteen

Pasha Sorokin was due at the courthouse in Miami at nine o'clock on Monday morning. The van he rode in was escorted from the federal prison by half a dozen cars; the route wasn't known by any of the drivers until the last possible moment before departure.

The attack took place at a stoplight just before the cars would have gotten on the Florida Turnpike. They hit with automatic weapons, but also rocket launchers, which took out most of the escort cars in under a minute. Suddenly, there were bodies and smoking metal everywhere.

The black van that Pasha Sorokin was riding in was quickly surrounded by six men in dark clothes, no masks. The car doors were yanked opened and the police guards were beaten and then shot dead.

A tall, powerful-looking man strode up to the open door and peered inside. He smiled playfully, as if a small child was in the prison van.

'Pasha,' the Wolf spoke, 'I understand that you were going to turn me in. That's what my sources say, my very good sources, my incredibly well-paid sources. Talk to me about this.'

'It's not true,' said Pasha, who meanwhile was cowering in the middle seat of the van. He wore an orange jumpsuit and his wrists and ankles were bound by chains. He no longer had his Florida tan.

'Maybe, maybe not,' said the Wolf.

Then he fired one of the rocket-launchers point blank at Pasha. He didn't miss.

'*Zamochit*,' he said and laughed. 'One can't be too careful these days.'

Turn the page for a preview of
the next compelling thriller featuring
Alex Cross . . .

JAMES PATTERSON

LONDON BRIDGES

headline

THE WEASEL RETURNS, AND WHAT A NICE SURPRISE

Chapter One

Colonel Geoffrey Shafer loved his new life in Salvador, Brazil's third-largest city and, some would say, its most intriguing. It was definitely the most fun.

He had rented a plush six-bedroom villa directly across from Guarajuba Beach, where he spent his days drinking sweet caipirinhas and ice-cold Brahma beers, or sometimes playing tennis at the club. At night, Colonel Shafer – the psychopathic killer known as the Weasel – was up to his old tricks, hunting on the narrow, winding streets of the 'Old City'. He had lost count of his kills in Brazil, and nobody in Salvador seemed to care, or to keep count either. There hadn't been a single newspaper story about the disappearances of any young prostitutes. Not one. Maybe it was true what they said of the people here – *when they weren't actually partying, they were already rehearsing for the next one.*

At a few ticks past two in the morning, Shafer returned to the villa with a young and beautiful street-walker who called herself Maria. What a gorgeous face the girl had, and a stunning brown body, especially for someone so young. Maria said she was only thirteen.

The Weasel picked a fat banana from one of several plants in his front garden. At this time of year he had his choice of coconut, guava, mango and pinka, which was sugar apple. As he plucked the fresh fruit, he had the thought that there was always something ripe for the taking in Salvador, which he believed was paradise. *Or maybe it's hell and I'm the devil,* Shafer thought and chuckled to himself.

'For you, Maria,' he said, handing her the banana. 'We'll put it to good use.'

The girl smiled knowingly and the Weasel noticed her eyes – what perfect brown eyes. *And all mine now – eyes, lips, breasts.*

Just then, he spotted a small Brazilian monkey called a mico trying to work its way through a screened window and into his house. 'Get out of here, you thieving little bastard!' he yelled. 'G'wan! Beat it!'

There came a quick movement from out of the bushes, then three men jumped him. *The police,* he was certain, *probably Americans. Alex Cross?*

The cops were all over him, powerful arms and legs everywhere. He was struck down by a bat, or a lead pipe, yanked back up by his full head of hair, then beaten unconscious.

'We caught him. We caught the Weasel first try. That wasn't very hard,' said one of the men. 'Bring him inside.'

Then he looked at the beautiful young girl, who was clearly afraid, rightly so. 'You did a good job, Maria. You brought him to us.' He turned to one of his men. *'Kill her.'*

A single gunshot ruptured the silence. No one seemed to notice or care in Salvador.

Chapter Two

The Weasel just wanted to die now. He was hanging upside down from the ceiling of his own master bedroom. The room had mirrors everywhere and he could see himself in several of the reflections.

He looked like death. He was naked, bruised and bleeding all over. His hands were tightly cuffed behind his back, his ankles bound together, cutting off the circulation. Blood was rushing to his head.

Hanging beside him was the young girl, Maria, but she had been dead for several hours, maybe as much as a day, judging by the terrible smell. Her brown eyes were turned his way, but they stared right through him.

The leader of his captors, bearded, always squeezing a black ball in one hand, squatted down so that he was only a foot or so from Shafer's face. He spoke softly, a whisper.

'What we did with some prisoners when I was active – we would sit them down, rather politely, peacefully – and then nail their fucking tongues to a table. That's absolutely true, my weasely friend. You know what else? Simply plucking hairs . . . from the *nostrils* . . . the *chest* . . . *stomach* . . . *genitals* . . . it's more than a little bothersome, no? *Ouch,*' he said, as he plucked hairs from Shafer's naked body.

'But I'll tell you the worst torture, in my opinion anyway. Worse than what you would have done to poor Maria. You grab the prisoner by both shoulders and shake violently until he *convulses*. You literally rattle his brain, the sensitive organ itself. It feels as if the head will fly off. The body is on fire. I'm not exaggerating.

'Here, let me show you what I mean.'

The terrible, unimaginable violent shaking – while Geoffrey Shafer hung upside down – went on for nearly an hour.

Finally, he was cut down. 'Who are you? What do you want from me?' he screamed.

The head captor shrugged. 'You're a tough bastard, but always remember, *I found you*. And I'll find you again if I need to. Do you understand?'

Geoffrey Shafer could barely focus his eyes, but he looked up to where he thought the captor's voice came from. Finally, he whispered, 'What – *do you – want? Please?*'

The bearded man's face bent close to his. He almost seemed to smile. 'I have a job, a most incredible job for you. Believe me, *you were born for this.*'

'Who are you?' the Weasel whispered again through badly chapped and bleeding lips. It was a question he'd asked a hundred times during the torture.

'I am the Wolf,' said the bearded man. 'Perhaps you've heard of me.'

Mary, Mary

James Patterson

Somebody is murdering Hollywood's A-list.

A well-known actress has been shot outside her Beverly Hills home. Shortly afterwards, the *Los Angeles Times* receives an email describing the murder in vivid detail. It is signed Mary Smith.

More killings and emails follow – the victims are all major Hollywood players. Is it the work of an obsessed fan or a spurned actor, or is it part of something far more terrifying? As the case grows to blockbuster proportions, FBI agent Alex Cross and the LAPD scramble to find a pattern before Mary can send another chilling update.

Filled with the ruthless and shocking twists that make his fans hunger for more, MARY, MARY is James Patterson's most sophisticated thriller yet.

'Pacy, sexy high-octane stuff' *Guardian*

'Packed with white-knuckle twists' *Daily Mail*

'This author knows precisely how to manipulate his readers' *Independent*

978 0 7553 4939 5

headline

Cross

James Patterson

Alex Cross was a rising star in the Washington, DC, Police Department when an unknown shooter killed his wife, Maria, in front of him.

Years later, having left the FBI and returned to practising psychology in Washington DC, Alex finally feels his life is in order ... Until his former partner, John Sampson, calls in a favour. John's tracking a serial rapist in Georgetown and he needs Alex to help find this brutal predator.

When the case triggers a connection to Maria's death, could Alex have a chance to catch his wife's murderer? Will this be justice at long last? Or the endgame in his own deadly obsession?

CROSS is the ultimate, high-velocity, high-emotion thriller, and the one Alex Cross's fans waited years to read.

'This story has elements of Hitchcock's *Vertigo*, and its page-turning quality is in a class of its own' *Independent*

'A fast-paced, electric story that is utterly believable' *Booklist*

'Unputdownable. It will sell millions' *The Times*

978 0 7553 4940 1

headline

Double Cross

James Patterson

Just when Alex Cross's life is calming down, he's drawn back into the game to confront the Audience Killer – a psychotic genius who stages his killings as public spectacles in Washington, DC, and broadcasts them live on the net.

In Colorado, another murdering mastermind is planning a triumphant return. From his maximum-security prison cell, Kyle Craig has spent years plotting his escape and revenge. Craig prefers to work alone, but if joining forces with DC's Audience Killer helps him to get the man who put him away then so be it.

Both are after the same detective – Alex Cross.

From the man the *Sunday Telegraph* called 'the master of the suspense genre', DOUBLE CROSS has the pulse-racing momentum and electrifying thrills that have made James Patterson a No. 1 bestselling storyteller all over the world.

'James Patterson does everything but stick our finger in a light socket to give us a buzz' *New York Times*

'A novel which makes for sleepless nights' *Daily Express*

'Pacy, sexy, high-octane stuff' *Guardian*

978 0 7553 4941 8

headline

Cat and Mouse

James Patterson

First came the stunning bestseller, ALONG CAME A SPIDER, which introduced its memorable hero, Washington, DC, detective and psychiatrist Alex Cross. Then the explosive novels KISS THE GIRLS and JACK AND JILL proved that no one can write a more compelling thriller than James Patterson – the master of the non-stop nightmare. Now he brings us CAT AND MOUSE.

Psychopath Gary Soneji is back – filled with hatred and obsessed with gaining revenge on detective Alex Cross. Soneji seems determined to go down in a blaze of glory and he wants Alex Cross to be there. Will this be the final showdown?

CAT AND MOUSE is a powerful and exciting thriller with the electrifying page-turning quality that is the hallmark of megaselling author James Patterson.

'A fast-moving thriller . . . a good time is had by all' *Daily Telegraph*

'Patterson does everything but stick our finger in a light socket to give us a buzz' *New York Times*

'Keeps the pedal down on the action and suspense' *Washington Times*

978 0 7553 4932 6

headline

The Beach House

James Patterson and Peter de Jonge

The blockbuster of the summer is an unforgettable story of wealth, betrayal, sex and murder.

The second that Columbia law student Jack Mullen steps down from the train at East Hampton, he knows that something is very wrong. As he greets his family, his kid brother Peter lies stretched out on a steel gurney, battered, bruised – dead. The police are calling the drowning an accident. Jack knows that's wrong. Someone wanted his brother dead.

But the establishment says otherwise. Jack tries to uncover what really happened on the beach that night, only to confront a wall of silence; a barricade of shadowy people who protect the privileges of the multi-billionaire summer residents. And when he discovers that his brother had nearly $200,000 in his bank account, Jack realises Peter wasn't just parking cars to make a living . . .

The Beach House is a breathtaking drama of revenge and sexual intrigue – with a plot so absorbing and a finale so shocking it could only have come from the unique mind of James Patterson, writing with his co-author of *Miracle on the 17th Green*, Peter de Jonge.

Praise for James Patterson

'I can't believe how good Patterson is. I have never begun a Patterson book and been able to put it down' Larry King, *USA Today*

'A master of the suspense genre' *Sunday Telegraph*

'James Patterson does everything but stick our finger in a light socket to give us a buzz' *New York Times*

978 0 7553 0017 4

headline